PASSION PATROL SERIES
GUILT

Hot cops. Hot crime. Hot romance.

Emma Calin

ISBN:
ISBN-13: 978-1-9164411-9-4

DEDICATION

This book is dedicated to 'Diesel', a Belgian Malinois police dog, who died in action fighting terrorists in Saint-Denis, Paris, France, 18th November 2015.

CONTENTS

CHAPTER 1

Three a.m.

Exclusive house.

Intruder disturbed.

Violence.

Emergency call to Scotland Yard.

Officer responding CO185 dog unit.

Floor the pedal, blue lights on.

Routine.

First unit on scene. Assess situation. Big guy, superficial head wound bleeding, pointing toward open country.

Update Control. Assistance. Ambulance.

Vehicle doors, running feet on gravel, adrenalin wiping fifteen years off her thirty-five. A newly trodden track ran through grass and the scent was fresh. PC Helen Marx tried to keep pace with her German shepherd as he bounded ahead on the long leash. They were in open green field land, where London kept uneasy truce with nature. The first light of mid-summer dawn snapped blurred monochrome photos as she ran.

A figure broke cover two hundred yards ahead. Breathless call.

"Stop or I release the dog."

A blur of feral hunting speed as eight-year-old Lanza stepped up once again to his duty. A flash of fire. A crack, a cry.

She slammed her fist into the suspect's face, as Lanza held on with his last strength. There was a plea in his eye. Still he kept his jaw locked on the arm as the guy writhed and kicked. She drew her cuffs and running on instinct snapped the metal onto his wrists. He tried a vicious head-butt. She drove her foot hard into his groin. Game over.

Lanza slumped down into the long damp grass. She assessed his condition. Bright foamy blood and a sucking chest wound. In minutes he would bleed to death. Looking back toward the house she could see running figures and the blue roof lamps of other police units. She spotted the firearm and covered it with her foot. Lanza was dying and she could do nothing.

The big man from the house knelt down alongside the dog.

"Do your police stuff with that idiot—looks like a bullet straight through the lung. I'll do what I can."

She watched as he turned the limp animal over, placed his fingers into the sucking wound and felt the neck for a pulse. He pulled out a cell phone and spoke quickly with a slight accent.

"It's a dog. He needs fluids or he'll bleed out. Just get here. Drive straight across the down in a four-by-four."

Lanza was dying. She could think of nothing else. The suspect was kneeling. The bastard deserved to die for what he'd done. She was a cop, not a killer. She'd already thrown a punch in anger, but she could and would deny that.

"You're under arrest. You don't have to say anything...."

Other officers were everywhere. A scenes of crime guy was bagging up the gun. A detective was talking to the suspect. Lanza was dying. She knelt at his head and stroked back his ear. He flicked open an eye.

"He's fighting," said the big man. "Those guys heading for us will be a top team I assure you."

She watched the bouncing headlights of an approaching Landrover.

"Vets, doctors, or what?"

"Vets, of course. The best ever. They're neighbors."

A man and a woman sprang from the vehicle. Within seconds they had an IV drip running.

"I've alerted the surgery. We'll stabilize for a few minutes, then go for it. Can you guys do a high-speed escort?" said the man, pulling on surgical gloves.

Helen fought back her nausea and desperation.

"Sure, I guess—has he got a chance?"

"He's still alive and he wants to live. I can say no more than that."

She looked back to the big guy who was holding out his hand

to pull her up. He spoke gently.

"What's his name?"

"Lanza."

He smiled slowly with a slight shake of his head.

"That's incredible. Now, can you fix a police escort to the RSPCA animal hospital in Putney and we don't want any speeding tickets."

She looked around, realizing that half the top brass of the Metropolitan Police was surrounding her. How much time had passed? Her sole focus had been Lanza. The man and woman were lifting him into the Landrover. A uniformed inspector finished talking into his radio.

"Helen, jump in the back of Oscar Lima Four. They're the blue light escort so go for it. By the way—well done. Everyone's praying for him."

She'd never prayed but she'd take any prayer in any faith. *He could not die.* She would not let him die. She'd held him as a pup. He was due to retire and she'd been considering going back to regular duty rather than train a new dog. Generally, dog handlers were family guys and she was no longer in that mold. She stayed quiet during the ride. She knew the crew didn't want to talk about Lanza, like she was already some kind of police widow at the Christmas party alone. No one thought he was going to make it. How the hell had that big guy known who to call? Why were so many big hats at the scene of a burglary?

As they arrived at the animal hospital two further medicos in scrubs rushed out to join the team. Within seconds Lanza was gone and she was left alone in a waiting area. Was this it now? She'd not been there when her man had hit a roadside bomb in Afghanistan and she'd kept it together. She'd been puppy walking Lanza then and Captain James Marx was coming home with hopes of joining her in the Job. She'd held it all together then.

But now she could not. She slumped in helpless sobs like a pathetic girlie civilian. This was not the show she wanted the world to see. *Cut it out, Helen. No one wants some woman bawling over an old dead dog. That's not what they pay cops for.* She took deep breaths and walked outside. The dawn had given way to morning as the city shook off its night, littered as always with the debris scattered by pitiless time. The traffic on the South Circular Road created an ocean roar of sound. And nobody cared if an old dog died. London would take it all on its shoulders and never even shrug.

"You must be exhausted."

It was his voice—the big guy from that house. A wound on his forehead had been closed with steri-strips. In any other place, on any other day, she'd smile and bathe for as long as she could in the soul of this man. "Please...."

She sniffed and wiped away tears. His arms were open to her—for no reason.

"Please," he repeated.

And he was holding her.

"I'm sorry. Not many folks want crying cops."

She had to stay cool, drag out some gallows humor from the police manual of cynical self-denial.

"There was me thinking you were a woman."

His body was powerful, his manner confident and assured of how his presence would play with others. To rest here like this against him was unprofessional but just so liberating. She could cry a lifetime onto this nameless man.

CHAPTER TWO

He brought her a coffee from the machine. He hadn't asked. She realized she hadn't even looked at him. She didn't want to think of anything other than Lanza. Anything else would somehow be unfaithful. It had been over an hour. She stared at the blue swing door through which she knew the yes or no would come.

"You always know if a jury will say guilty or not guilty," she said.

"You do?"

"Sure. If they look the prisoner in the eye then he's out of jail. If they keep their eyes down, he's in trouble."

"I believe he'll pull through," he said.

A jolt of anger shook her. What did he know? What right did he have to give her false hope just to cheer her up in some pathetic way. Like she needed some feel-good crutch.

"Believe?"

She could tell he'd picked up her resentment.

"I'm sorry. I just said what was in my heart, my gut. I wasn't thinking about how you might see my intrusion."

He'd caught her signal, tuned in to her at once. She flicked her eyes to his and found them on her face. Large dark eyes with strength and sorrow speaking to her. This man was deep or had the shallow tricks of the actor. She sighed.

"I didn't—"

"You didn't need some idiot to mess with your own hopes."

Voices approaching the swing doors. He took her hand. He didn't ask.

A bespectacled man in green scrubs pushed through with his shoulder, cleaning his hands with practiced professionalism. Another day, the usual routine. He looked up and smiled. And held

5

her eyes.

"Hi, I'm Simon Leonard. He's with us, but weak. He's breathing on two lungs. These next few hours are critical."

"Can I see him?" she asked.

"Not for a while. The last thing we want is infection." He turned to the intimate stranger at her side who was still squeezing her hand. "Marco, what the hell happened?"

"A burglar I suppose. We struggled and he ran onto the downland. I phoned police. I saw what happened with the dog and called the best vet in the world."

"Ha! The best vet living next door. You were lucky I'd just come home from an emergency. If I'd been in bed...."

As the two men talked she was alone to take in the news. Chains inside her snapped.

"Thank you, thank you, thank you." Words and tears tumbled from her helter-skelter.

"You need to rest yourself. I imagine you've worked all night," said the vet in a kind voice.

"What time is it?"

"It's nine-thirty on a sunny summer day in London town."

She'd lost track of everything. There would be arrest reports and the usual paper chase of official forms. She'd abandoned her police vehicle at the scene. And this guy was still holding her hand. No, she was squeezing *his* hand. She'd lost the plot. She stepped away and finally took the time to study him. He was about six feet, big-chested and strong. His hair was dark, wavy, and long onto his collar. At a guess he was forty-three years old. There was an olive tint to his skin and a passionate sensuality to his wide mouth and expressive lips. Then there were those eyes, those dark eyes staring back with brazen self-confidence. He knew what they could do to a woman. A woman like Helen Marx. Now this was a novel feeling. Metropolitan Police Constable CO 185 was someone else and that was a role she knew how to play.

"I've let everything slide. I've got to be somewhere doing something. I've just got to focus. I've had no other thoughts but Lanza."

He kept his kind gaze on her as he spoke in his rich voice.

"Someone somewhere must be thinking about you and where you are?"

6

She nodded slowly as she thought. A man like this couldn't be interested in her so her response wouldn't matter. All the same he was knocking at a tender door and if ever she were to open it to man like this....

"Yeah, sure but they're used to it."

"You guys are something else. I can't imagine how much I'd worry if my partner were a cop."

"It's just a job."

"Lanza took a bullet that could just as easily have been for you."

He was right. His words took her mind back to what had happened.

"Or you for that matter. The detectives must be needing to get a witness statement from you."

"I told them I'd be there once I'd checked up on you and Lanza."

"Did anyone want you sooner—like immediately? Like they've got an armed criminal locked up and they need to crack on. Maybe you shouldn't be wasting time with me?"

"People only argue if you give them choices. I told them you and your dog were my priorities."

She smiled. This was the kind of man who just assumed he would do what he thought best and no one would stop him. What the hell was he in the world? She was curious but didn't want to show it. As a professional it concerned her that he would be holding up the show on her account.

"So now you're free to help the police get that piece of shit locked up for a few years. But, thanks for—"

"Caring," he interrupted.

What was he on? Caring and all that stuff was for civilians.

"Caring is good stuff," she said.

He raised an eyebrow. He'd picked up on her flatness. He was an emotional weathervane.

"Yes, caring is good to give but not always so easy to take. I chose caring because I do."

She wanted him to go. Hard-working officers would be needing his statement and she had to admit, she didn't want to get used to having him on her case. What sort of man was this? He'd been so calm in giving first aid to Lanza, as if blood and trauma was no surprise.

"Thanks for the what you did at the scene. Had you seen that sort of stuff before?"

"Only once in the back streets of Naples, but then it was men."

His expression was so open and kind, but this wasn't the time to go deeper.

"I don't really know your name—Marco, I think. Please, I'm good, and I want you to help the police and the population of London rather than care about me."

"Yes, Helen, it's Marco Ambastilias. I'll do what you want and you're right. I'll be following up on Lanza." He turned to walk away then spun back. "And you."

She waited. How odd she must have looked with her disheveled hair and crumpled uniform. Her sergeant had come and she'd done her reports. He'd offered some leave and she'd taken it, after all what's the use of a dog cop without a dog? She'd started to doze.

"You can come through for a few minutes."

She looked up into the kind face of a veterinary nurse who was gently pressing her shoulder. She followed through the swing doors, into a world of antiseptic smells and machines like in any hospital. Lanza was in an oxygen tent.

"He'll stay sedated for a while yet. His respiration levels are a bit low but climbing. We can't risk him struggling with oxygen by tube because his sternum is severely damaged and will require further surgery and plating."

"Further surgery?"

"Once he's a bit stronger. Mr. Leonard is a top specialist and he's confident."

She watched the rise and fall of Lanza's chest. His eyes were closed and his body so still.

Helen bent down and got as close as she could to his head.

"Good boy," she whispered.

A paw twitched, a tail gave one thump on the white-sheeted table.

"He knows you're here," said the nurse.

And there she stayed. A few cops came and went, a few

sandwiches and coffees kept her body alive. A press guy from Scotland Yard took shots of Lanza for the next morning's papers. And there she stayed.

"Helen, Lanza's coming round and we have to fix his chest. He won't be able to function as he is. His oxygen is up and we've controlled the bleeding. Now it's time to turn him bionic." She watched the face of the vet. It was 4 a.m. Already they were wheeling him away. "You need to look after yourself. You've done everything you can here. We'll call you."

CHAPTER THREE

The doc was right. She needed to get away, go home. She took a deep breath of the dawn air as she stepped out. A white Alfa Romeo Giulietta, on Italian plates, pulled up alongside her.

"Good job I called by if you're ready to leave."

"Marco? Is it polite for me to ask what the fuck?"

"Very polite. I spent half the day with Inspector Scarpia at Croydon police station. After I have business to do and then I called by only to see how Lanza was doing because you didn't want me to care about you."

"It's dawn, 4:15 in the morning."

"So, we miss the traffic."

"How long have you been out here?"

"I'm beginning to see that cops keep asking questions."

She was so tired but even so it warmed her to think that he was there. So tired, so tired, and yet her brain turned over a word he'd used. She slumped down in what should have been the driver's seat of the car. OK—Italian car, left-hand drive.

"Scarpia—chief of police—Tosca, Puccini."

He slapped his hand on the steering wheel.

"Yes, you call your dog Lanza. You just had to like opera."

"It's a long story Marco, please, please."

She was exhausted and right now she couldn't talk about Lanza or how he got his name.

"So, Helen, your address?"

"Donnybrook Road, Streatham SW16. You don't have to do this."

"If I *had* to do it, I'd refuse on principle."

The car was pulling away. She must be stinking and haggard. This was the most attractive man she'd ever met. She was letting this domineering person take her over and just carry her along. The first red London buses dotted the streets like poppies in the cornfields of her childhood. She wanted to tell him that, so he would know her a little more, glimpse some petticoat of her soul. The words stuck and tangled as familiar streets turned foreign to her exhausted mind. She remembered him opening the front door of her house with her keys. She remembered falling into bed. She remembered a drawing of curtains, a hand on her back, a long drink of iced water. Then darkness.

Lanza! She'd been lying awake and her mind had been empty. Her cell phone was ringing.

"Yeah?"

"Helen, it's Simon Leonard. I didn't call before because I guessed you'd need to sleep."

"Yeah, yeah. What's the news?"

"He's good and stable. He's got some titanium where he once had bone. His days of backflips are over. We'll be reducing his sedation over the next three days. Once he's supporting his own weight we'll see where we need to go from there. I'm hoping he'll be fixed up for his retirement and some casual walks on the common."

"Thank you so much. I've not even thought about payment."

"Anything the police don't cover Marco has promised to pay without limit."

"What?"

"Helen, we're talking about Marco Ambastilias. He has worries enough, but money isn't one of them."

Oh my God. Oh, my crazy God. Marco Ambastilias—the name on half the music in Captain James Marx's collection. Music she'd not touched since the day she'd learned he would never come home to take a precious vinyl or a CD from the shelf himself. Marco Ambastilias, tenor star of Covent Garden, La Scala, and the New York Metropolitan. Since that crack of gunfire, she'd thought of nothing else but her dog, a pup her man had named after tragic opera legend, Mario Lanza, a few days before he'd gone off on his final tour of duty.

She needed a drink. She needed a friend. The first part was

easy, too easy. The second part was difficult, too difficult. She realized she'd slept in her uniform. She took a long shower and kept things simple. She poured a long whisky and water but rationed the water for the sake of the environment. It wasn't even a weak joke if she couldn't share it. Since the day she'd brought Lanza home as a pup, she'd never been alone in the house. Now she really was a solitary drinker. The scotch hit her brain with an empty stomach hammer. Had Marco put her to bed? Had she embarrassed herself or him? She'd spoken to him as if he were just any man. He'd talked to her as an equal, had almost seemed to court her approval. She didn't have his cell phone number but she would never dare call him. All the same, if she had his number she could thank him. She took another drink. If a cop couldn't get a phone number who could? Then, if he called she would know his number and maybe answer, maybe not.

"Hi, it's Helen Marx," she told the veterinary receptionist.

"Everything's going well. I'll just see if I can track down Mr. Leonard—"

"No, don't trouble him. Marco—Mr. Ambastilias—gave me a lift home and I left my bag in his car. I don't suppose you've got his cell number there?"

"Well, I shouldn't really."

"I'm a cop, not a stalker."

"Sure, it's 00397565239279. Don't tell him I told you."

"Fancy Italian number, eh? Thanks."

She took another drink and studied the number she'd tapped onto her screen. She would never press that call button. She never would, but a cat can look at a king. She hit the button.

"Marco?"

"Si."

"Helen."

"I was worried you didn't find my number."

"I didn't, so I pulled a cop stunt. Why didn't you sing outside my window? Did I blow my one chance?"

"I'm glad you called. I wanted. I needed—needed to ask you a couple of police things."

"I hope you pay your taxes. We check up before we give out free answers to international superstars."

"I can hear you've come back to life."

"I've watered my roots with water and a dash of scotch. My courage is tartan today."

"I've seen your courage, Helen."

His voice was slow and actually beautiful.

"So, you need police advice? I need something too."

"What?"

"Something you should never ask for. Right now, I need a friend and if you weren't some famous big shot I'd be asking you to get your shoulders round here for me to sob on."

"Look, forget the hype. I'm that opera guy's body double and that's our secret. Did you eat yet?"

"Not quite."

"Then we eat Italiano alla casa mia– see you in venti minuti."

"Ciao."

Bloody hell. She'd done it now.

CHAPTER FOUR

Look, he wanted legal advice for free. It was as simple as that. He wasn't going to be interested in a thirty-five-year-old brown-haired woman who defined average in her own mind. As she dressed, she spotted a slip of paper by her bed. It was Marco's number with the words "anything any time." She threw on some black jeans, a yellow T-shirt and some white pumps. It was the evening of a midsummer day and the air was warm. She pulled her hair into a ponytail as she picked up a blue denim jacket and of course her police warrant card ID. She took a deep breath and tried to quell her racing heart as the Alfa Romeo pulled up outside. He'd scrubbed up into a breathtaking hunk in a light blue Italian suit.

She hated driving with civilians, and Marco was an Italian civilian with the steering wheel on the wrong side of the car. His one-handed vehicle control technique swung between the exotic and the passionate. With his free hand he emphasized his conversation.

"How do these big tough cops work, when beautiful girls like this distract them?"

"Did I miss something?"

"Yes, you miss that uniform."

"I guess your work clothes get pretty exotic."

He swerved around a truck, blaring his horn, but didn't answer.

"You need some police advice?"

He turned to study her face.

"Marco—watch the road," she half yelled.

"You see, the police worry if you look at a cell phone, but how can a man not look at a beautiful woman?"

"How can a man not smash into a bus?"

He laughed and shook his head.

"OK, I won't look at you again. Yes, I need advice. I need to talk something through because I don't know what to do."

"You must have access to top cops. I'm a foot soldier who scraped through the law modules at Hendon police school."

"You know good from bad and you know about people. We're nearly at my house and we can talk with maybe a glass of wine."

His mood had become more serious, almost sad. He troubled her with his change of temperament. She was sure he could act out any part and maybe a simple cop who'd never walked the stage could be taken in.

They stopped on the drive. An electric blue Aston Martin Vanquish S was already parked.

"Wow! That's a lot of car," she said.

"It's too much bloody car." Marco had already sprung out and was striding to the front door. His body language displayed almost rage. "You fucking shit. Get out of my home."

Some cop-instinct had her quickly catching him up as he stood shouting in the center of the grand hallway. This wasn't acting. She heard a door slam on the upper floor. A young man in grungy teen-type clothes appeared on the wide stairs and started to slouch toward them.

Marco's face was set and white. His fists were clenched. If he pulled his trigger that young man was going to hospital and Marco was going to jail even if she had to lock him up herself. The boy wasn't picking up on the danger and by the look of his eyes his perceptions were blurred by artificial substances. She guessed he was nineteen and surely the Aston Martin couldn't be his.

"I was invited. Cressida called me."

His posh, accented voice was a little slow. Fuck! This wasn't weed. This had the look of heroin. Marco took a step forward. She stepped in front of him staring into his face.

"No—no way are you touching him. He's a kid and he needs help."

His eyes fixed on hers. Every second she could hold his attention on her would calm the fire. His eyes snapped back to the boy.

"Look at you, Peter. A fucking junkie."

"I'm cool. I'm going."

"Marco, stay where you are and remember we're the adults here." She watched his fists unclench and his head sag onto his chest. The fate of this young lad was a police job.

"Peter, that's never your car?"

"Yeah, why not?"

"His pocket money could run the Metropolitan Police and look what he does with it," said Marco.

The kid started to walk on out to the car. Helen grabbed his arm.

"That's far enough if you're thinking of driving."

"You can't stop me."

She pulled her police warrant card and held up to his face.

"I've stopped you."

He tried to pull away.

"If you want a pain hold I can put you in one. If you act up I'll arrest you and search that car."

He nodded. She could see he had no aggression.

"Heroin, right?"

He nodded and stared at the floor.

"Give me the keys or you'll be doing cold turkey in a police cell tonight."

As he threw them down she tried to clear her mind. Arresting kids for simple possession solved nothing, but that was her duty. She quickly drew a picture in her mind of a group of spoilt rich brats using whatever they could get to take the edge off their pampered boredom.

"Who's supplying you?"

No answer came and she'd not expected one. To take this further would lead her well out of her depth. If she knew he had drugs and let him go she'd be in deep shit with the police.

"Looks to me like you've had one too many beers, Peter. In fact, you smell like a brewery. Mr. Ambastilias is going to call you an Uber cab. Get yourself home and drink plenty of water. Get your folks to collect the car and tell them to bring proof of ownership. Give me your name and date of birth."

"Peter Ivan Lodovitch. Twenty-first May two thousand."

"You got a police record yet?"

"Not much...."

Behind her Marco snorted his derision.

"He's just out of rehab. I'll call him an Uber."

Helen pulled out her cell phone and took a portrait picture.

"It's just for my personal album," she said.

Within a couple of minutes, a cab pulled up. The lad gave an address in Chelsea which she noted as she watched the car drive away. Both he and Marco had had a lucky escape.

"Helen, thank you. God, in that moment I felt capable of killing him."

"I'm not sure I did the right thing."

"You were perfect and we do need to talk."

Something was sparking in her mind and she needed to know the truth.

"That incident last night was part of all this, wasn't it?"

"Yes, but right now I'm not sure exactly how. That guy last night was a serious armed criminal. Helen, maybe today I didn't tell the police everything. My daughter, Cressida, is involved with these people. I have to protect her."

"You lied to the police about the burglary?"

"Not lied. I did some damage-limitation for the sake of my family."

She shook her head. For a moment she busied herself opening the hood of the Aston Martin.

"What are you doing?" he asked.

"Protecting our collateral. I'm separating the electrical plug on the fuel injection system. There'll be another set of keys and whoever comes for the car may not want to talk. This way they get to ring the doorbell. I'd like to see who shows up and maybe get a photo."

"You're a pro."

"I'm a dog cop without a dog. We know who shot Lanza and you're going to tell me why he was here or at least be honest about what you know. Beyond that there's bigger fish to fry and the oil is heating up."

"I invited you for a meal."

"And I'm holding you to that Marco. When do I get to meet Cressida?"

17

CHAPTER FIVE

His hands were a blur as he chopped garlic, onions, and fresh tomatoes. He harvested basil and oregano from an herb garden outside the kitchen door. From the window was the view over Kenley Aerodrome which had once been a Battle of Britain Spitfire base. The house was big but not palatial or dripping with the feel of money even though with London prices it would cost several million pounds.

"So, what does the world's greatest Italian opera singer cook for guests?"

"Well, I'm sure you know I'm an ex-opera singer and never the greatest but I'm doing *gnocchi con pollo e funghi*."

He spoke so quickly and she had no idea what it was. She decided to stick to business

"Will Cressida be eating with us?"

"That's something I never know. She's eighteen."

"And an adult. I wonder how many times I said that half a lifetime ago."

"Did anyone listen?"

"No one listens to soldiers in the British army. You're not there to express your rights."

"You were a soldier at eighteen. Why was that?"

"Cos they wouldn't take me at sixteen. I'm a groundsheet girl in a spreadsheet world."

"You're sensational."

"You should see me with a glass of full deep red wine."

Marco slapped the palm of his hand on his forehead.

"*Dio mio*! I'm so bad a host. That punk distracted me. We both need that drink."

She'd stopped worrying about getting home and she'd rather

not think about Marco's driving. He selected a bottle of Barolo from a rack and poured two glasses which more or less emptied the bottle. She couldn't believe this man was serving her wine when he had mixed with the elites of the world for half his life. He had sung at royal weddings and requiems for heads of state. Here he was chopping onion and talking to her about *her* life. *You could almost start to feel a little urge for this man. No, forget it. Helen, just don't go there.* But how could she feel so relaxed with him?

"Salute," he said, touching glasses and holding, holding, holding her eyes. She took a deep drink that shook hands with the scotch she'd had at home. Sod it. She could have died a couple of days ago and never rejoiced in the joy of wine again. She took another swig and noticed he did the same.

"I'll feel braver with a little wine to do my talking," he said.

"Then perhaps I'll feel brave enough to listen."

"Look, Helen, I asked you to eat with me but you know, I wouldn't ask a woman just like that if she had someone—a husband or someone—"

"Maybe I have."

"Maybe you don't."

His face was serious and thoughtful. Was he acting out a part? He was touching nerves inside her and she didn't mind the feeling at all.

"So, do I?"

"I know your story. I know it like I saw a newspaper headline. I've been around your detectives and they tell me without me asking. I knew enough to believe I could ask you here."

"Because you wanted my police advice?"

"I want that too."

She smiled back at him, this big guy in his apron, dipping a finger in the sauce. She wasn't trying to back him up, but that was how she coped with men. That was how she had coped with men up until now. She couldn't forget that at the animal hospital he'd opened his arms to her and he'd held her.

A sound caught her ear. A car engine was cranking. Someone wanted their quarter of a million pounds of car back. She went to the front window, taking a video on her cell of two men on the drive. A flashy custom black American Chevrolet van, with smoked windows, had also shown up. One guy was white, the other mixed race. She filmed long enough to be sure of an ID.

"Marco, how deep is your girl in with this trash?"

"I wish I knew."

"It's about time to find out. Simple question, OK. Bust these guys and risk them telling their story about her, or let it run until we know what the fuck we're doing? Bottom line—is she in deep enough to get busted?"

"Helen, let it run. Please keep her out of this."

His tone was almost a plea.

They stepped outside.

"Gentlemen, looks like you need a tow truck. We've got one coming up from the central police pound I think."

"Police?"

The white guy jumped out of the driving seat and stared at her. Some instinct told her it was best to keep her police ID in her pocket.

"Some punk tried to break in and abandoned his car. Is he a friend?"

They didn't need to think twice. The other hood pulled an old-style 38 revolver and covered her as they ran to the van. Within seconds they had gone.

Helen went to the car. Now they had both sets of keys. Pulling the hood release and reconnecting the fuel injectors she slid into the seat and started the engine.

"Time for a little drive," she said.

Marco was speechless.

"I'm not going far. Just up the road."

She drove the sleek machine to a quiet stretch of road two blocks away, stopping across the entrance of a house with a Neighborhood Watch sticker on the gate. She stepped out, left the door open, the radio blaring, and the headlights on. It would only be ten minutes maximum before a concerned citizen called the police. The vehicle was lousy with drugs and maybe more. The reek of skunk-weed and the pique of crystal was overwhelming. She had turned the corner and no eyes were on her even if someone had seen her get out. A path led onto the down-land and reached Marco's house from the back garden. She strolled into the kitchen. A beautiful dark-haired girl was seated at the table stroking a black Labrador dog. Her cheeks were wet with tears.

Helen spoke before she'd really thought it through. This bawling brat must be Cressida.

"This game's getting real, young lady. You'd better be worth it."

The dog looked up, sad eyed and catching her anger. She stroked his head and suddenly felt a surge of emotion.

"Hey, no one's blaming you, boy." The dog's tail thumped. His snout butted up and his tongue wrapped around her hand.

"Helen, this is Cressida and Sam."

Marco performed almost a theatrical entrance into the kitchen, arms wide and eyes to heaven.

"Just what does a woman have to do to get fed in this house?"

In a surreal moment, the girl laughed. Helen spoke realizing she'd already drunk too much and would have busted the driving breath-test machine.

"If you like my pathetic jokes I hope you're going to be joining us. Sam has already agreed."

Cressida nodded. It sure beat an evening at home in front of the TV.

The food was beyond delicious. When had she last eaten a proper meal? She could feel the tension in Marco and the fear in his daughter. Several times she caught Marco's eye and gave him a nod of reassurance. If she was going to get the story here it would be alone with the girl. Christ, what was she but a frightened kid?

"You know about my dog, Lanza?"

"Yeah. Papa says he's going to pull through."

"I'll be going to see him first thing."

Cressida gave a weak smile. She might have smoked a bit of weed, but the kid looked clean. Helen had had no time to learn anything about these people. The girl must have, or have had, a mother. Her life just could not have been normal with a superstar father and all the showbiz hangers-on. She watched the girl from the corner of her eye. She was pale, cheekbones prominent, skin too white for her dark hair, shunting food around her plate without taking a mouthful. An eating disorder could be an issue. She searched for some portal into this unknown young woman's life. She decided to try family relationships.

"My father cooked a piece of toast once. I microwaved the

baked beans. We were a great team."

Cressida fired her a quizzical look.

"A team?"

"You know, two hopeless chefs joining up to create a classic English cuisine."

"I've never cooked with Papa. He's always perfect with everything."

"Everything? Did you ever tell him the English drive on the left?"

She shot a glance at Marco not to intervene in defense of himself.

Cressida laughed. "Sure, I've told him but he says that the English always want to be different. He believes he's educating them."

"Girls, what is this? Hashtag 'Me too' against Marco who feeds you perfect food, who never crashes a car?"

Helen turned her eyes to him and flashed him a thank you. He'd spotted the ball play and trusted her with the pass. That Barolo wine must be magic. This girl loved and respected him, was in awe of him, perhaps. Helen quickly considered her next tactic but Cressida jumped in.

"You're famous aren't you. You're on YouTube—just everywhere."

"Me?"

"Well, you know, not *you yourself*. Like, your dog."

"I had no idea."

"The police called in the Press—hero dog and all that sickly public relations stuff."

Helen lashed out a reflex response. "Lanza *is* a hero. No PR, no sophisticated sneering at humble people's love for animals, as if it's just a way to create the right image. Pin your ears back and listen. A dog like Lanza would die for you or me in the service of law and order whatever you think of that. Maybe that's shit to you. No wages, no medals just an unbreakable bond of trust and loyalty. He didn't take that bullet for trashy fame or applause. He took it for me."

She pulled back. God, she'd lost it and sounded off. She'd been so rude as a guest in Marco's home. She looked down, ashamed. She heard a chair push back and footsteps as Cressida left the table. She buried her face in her hands.

"Marco, I'm so sorry. She was only making small talk. She's a kid and I've just off-loaded a lifetime of frustration on her."

She felt his hands on her shoulders, stroking away her anger and regret.

"Helen, you opened your heart and that is never wrong. Cressida likes to be cool and intellectual. The police aren't always…."

"Kind, liberal, or modern. God, Marco, I know that. The fragile blooms of young ideas are so weightless that the bullets and knives of criminals just pass straight through like trying to clear morning mist with a sword."

"There's some poetry in you, Helen. It is something beautiful."

"There's a nasty bitch in me that's just overreacted to a casual inexperienced remark."

She heard another sound behind her.

"Papa. Sam needs a walk."

Helen knew she'd drunk too much. Deep breath time.

"I'm coming. I mean, may I? Look I miss my dog, so please…."

"So, you leave Marco Ambastilias to sing alone over an audience of dirty dishes," he said with a wide smile.

"Cressida, that's an offer you can't refuse."

"Great. Let's get out," said the girl.

CHAPTER SIX

Helen drew in great lungfuls of the warm, summer dusk air. Sam pulled on his leash as Cressida headed for the road.

"I'm so sorry about jumping down your throat. You don't know me. I don't know you. I don't know Marco. You call him Papa, I notice."

"I don't know you either, but just now he spoke of singing over dishes. He's never spoken of singing or music in the house for two years."

"Why?"

"You don't know?"

"It started with my mother. She left him—left us. Ten years ago. It was in all the papers and gossip magazines. These days she lives in Moscow with Alexander Nurevski, the ballet producer. Then I came back into his life and finished him off."

"Cressida, I'm a cop, and cops kind of miss the news and celebrity updates. Who is your mother?"

"Zelda Mitchell. Come on, don't tell me...?"

"Yeah, look of course I know her. Well, know her from the cinema and the Cannes film festival and the Oscars."

"Yeah, then there's me, like podgy girl who wants to be ... well, what does it matter what I want to be?"

"Honey, when I told my parents I wanted to be a soldier my father asked me if I was a lesbian."

"Hey, that's gross. What did you say?"

"He used to play soccer. I asked him if he wanted to hang out with boys because he wanted to see penises. He was the proudest guy there when I marched off to war as a second lieutenant. So, shock me with your ambitions."

"Not movie star. Not diva. Science. Don't laugh, but I really do want to do something. Not with my face or my carefully upraised tits, not with hitting the high notes, but with ideas."

"I love it. What ideas?"

"It wouldn't matter. When you're a celeb kid no one's going to cut you any slack. You're a celeb brat trading on your second-hand fame and contacts. You can't escape."

"This is the point where I'm supposed to argue and say you can overcome all that. But fundamentally, I think you're right."

Cressida looked at her wide eyed.

"Fuck, yeah, do you really get this?"

"Not completely, but that's only because I'm twice your age and I'm not you. Is this a good time to talk about crime, drugs, and Aston Martin cars?"

"You're a cop. Has Papa brought you in to save me?"

"You're thinking my thoughts for me. I bet there's a boyfriend somewhere in this."

"Boyfriend? A fat monster like me?"

In this moment this wasn't where Helen wanted to go. Eating disorders and self-image dysfunction couldn't be cured with a couple of timely clichés.

"Hey, what does that make me? Looks like neither of us has a boyfriend then. Mind you, guys can put a lot of crap in your life."

They'd strolled onto the down-land. Cressida bent to let Sam off the leash and then kept her head down. Helen knew she was softly crying but trying not to let on. This kid was a mess and she needed to share.

"Cressida, if you're worried or afraid, we can work with that. Obviously, your papa has told you I'm a cop and you know about Lanza. No one is looking to drag you off."

"I wanted friends and now—"

"You know I shouldn't have moved that car. I did it to protect you because your papa asked me. Maybe you wouldn't like to answer questions about it. I've interfered with evidence already so we're in this together."

"You could be in trouble?"

"If we don't stick together. If you told the cops what happened, that those guys had a gun and that I haven't reported it, yes Cressida, I'm in massive trouble."

As she explained, Helen herself began to see that the emotion of what had happened to Lanza, added to her own confused feelings about Marco's arrival in her life, had led her to some poor decisions. Poor decisions as a cop. For now, she'd not judge the woman.

"I mess up everything and everyone," sobbed the girl.

Helen was no mother figure in her own mind, yet some instinct had her reach for Cressida and hold her. She had no right to promise something it would probably be beyond her power to deliver. And yet—

"Honey, let's work through this together, OK? The good guys are on your side and I'll stay with you. That's my promise. Now we need to open Pandora's box and see what we're looking at. Do you agree?"

"I can't."

"Then I might as well own up to what I did, walk away from all this and take my punishment on the chin."

Helen winced a little at her manipulation but she had to use what small leverage she had. She was sure she was dealing with a soft innocent girl who'd gotten into something, well, who knows? But something with money, drugs, and guns. "So, first tell me what trouble you yourself could be in."

Cressida was returning her warm hug, but not responding. Time for some experienced cop guesswork.

"You smoked some weed, snorted some coke. You're not saying no and you're not saying yes so there's nothing for me to tell your papa is there? You're eighteen and I've no right to tell him."

The girl searched into Helen's face for trust.

"Yes, the crowd, the group all do."

"Have you ever supplied drugs to others or carried out deliveries and stuff like collecting cash?"

"Not things like that."

Helen knew she was hiding something, so did a double back to let her relax.

"So, how did it start?"

"A girl told me that speed could help me lose weight. I got to know some guys who had that stuff."

"Where was this?"

26

"At Val du Globe, my boarding school in Switzerland."

"I don't suppose there's any point in me telling you that you don't need to lose weight."

"There were popular girls who weighed seventy pounds and you couldn't be a friend if you were fat. It was a club."

"A clique of stupid lying cows I'd say. Did you ever see them on the scales? Did they hold a weigh-in like boxers at morning assembly?"

Cressida laughed. It didn't look like she was used to irreverence toward the *populars* of this world.

"So how did you end up living in London?"

"I finished school and I didn't get my exams and Papa brought me here to work with a couple of tutors. When I got my baccalaureate, I went to an English university because my friends are here."

"Friends who do drugs?"

"Some."

"Like that boy with the car and the heroin issue?"

"His father is *the* Sergei Lodovitch who owns the football clubs and the racing car team."

"And he's a junkie, Cressida. He's injecting poison into his blood and killing himself."

"I know and sometimes he knows."

It was now full dark night and Sam had returned from his joyful orgy of tail wagging, tracks, and scents. Helen didn't want this first blind stab at friendship to become an interrogation. They began to walk back to the house.

"Thanks for trusting me, Cressida. That's valuable to me."

"Really?"

"Yeah, sure. Cops don't often get to function like regular humans. Before we get back and it's just you and me, is there anything in your life or at the house that we need to consider?"

As Helen was speaking she knew that if the response was delayed or was a question in return it would be a ploy to play for time.

"Like what?"

"Like I know that's an evasion. Like a wooden crate marked top quality cocaine wraps; buy one get one free."

"Peter left a parcel. Last night, Papa wasn't going to be at home—"

Helen let out a long sigh. Since she'd arrived at the house with Lanza all she had thought about was what had happened. She'd not talked to Marco about the details of the burglary. It sure was time to start thinking like a cop again.

"So, someone showed up to collect their goods and got an unexpected opera singer instead?"

Cressida was nodding.

"And whatever it was, is still at the house and men with guns want it back?"

"It's in my room now. That night, I left the French doors open and the box on the table, just to one side. When all the noise started, I ran down and rescued the box."

"Why the hell did you agree to any of this?"

"They said they'd tell Papa I was on drugs and that's why I'd failed my exams. I didn't want to keep it, but Peter is in really deep with them and he begged me...."

"Why did he want to leave it with you?"

He just said he couldn't risk keeping it. His suppliers thought he might have been spotted and told him to leave it somewhere secure. I don't know who they are."

"It's OK, we'll find out and we will look after you. We need a long conversation and all this is going well above my pay grade. You can't deal with this any more on your own and neither can I. For now, let's just sleep on it all."

Helen took her hand and walked calmly as Cressida dealt with Sam. She fought to stay clear in her own mind, which was awakening and firing in cold police mode. Two points filled her thoughts. First mistake. She'd driven that car away and hadn't worn gloves. Her fingerprints would flash up if Scotland Yard dusted the car and ran an elimination program. Second mistake, she'd left Marco alone at the house and there was something there that guys with guns wanted. As they walked to the back gate, she would know soon enough if they'd called by. She needed to think.

CHAPTER SEVEN

A man was singing. Not just any man, not just any song. She knew it, had cried to it with James although he pretended not to. The aria *E lucevan le stelle* was the highlight from Puccini's Tosca.

Cressida stopped her.

"Papa is singing. He gave up when I broke his heart and failed him."

"I bet he never said that."

"No, but I said it to myself and it's true. If he's coming back to life, I'll die if I break him again."

Helen choked back a street-hardened cop's desire to mock any form of drama-queening. These folks were from a different thread of life which in kindness she would say was artistic, and in anger would say was self-indulgent exaggeration.

"My gut feeling is that it's too hot with cops around here for your associates to show up overnight. I'll be talking to your papa but what we've discussed is between you and me. Don't leave the house and don't call anyone or communicate in any way until we talk again. Do you understand that?"

"Yes," said Cressida.

Helen gave her a hard stare and a nod of appraisal.

"If you let me down, forget any idea of me helping you ever," she added.

They waited for a couple of minutes while Marco completed his performance. Helen called to him as they entered. "Bravo Maestro. Encore."

Cressida kissed him on both cheeks and then turned to Helen and did the same.

"See you all in the morning," she said.

Marco dried his hands and led her through to the book-lined grand lounge. He poured two brandies from a decanter and motioned for her to sit on the sofa. He took a chair facing her and caught her eyes in his inescapable hold.

"So, how good or bad are things?"

"I imagine you mean with Cressida. I didn't pump her for information to report back to rampaging Papa."

"That's good, but these people with drugs and guns aren't going to evaporate, are they?"

"Unlikely, Marco. Look, I've made a couple of mistakes and bitten off more than I can chew. I'm not even a lowly detective. I'm a kennel maid with a siren and blue lights."

"Tell me what I can do with her. I'm guessing she's involved with drugs. I'm guessing she's maybe anorexic. She came back from university last week and it shocked me to see her. All I, all we thought about, was our own careers—you know, me and Zelda. She had the best, but she had no one."

"And now you don't perform or travel. You stay at home to care for her and to make her eat pasta. All she eats is guilt. What is her relationship with her mother?"

"They're in touch, but some bond isn't there. Never was, I think."

"She's an adult in the eyes of the law and you can't make her eat or keep the right company when she's at uni."

"So where do I go with this? There's armies of shrinks and counsellors, but I don't want to pass her on to strangers. She's my child."

"I'm going to think about all that if I ever get to know more. In the meantime, some fog has cleared in my brain. A while ago you told me you hadn't given the detectives the whole story about your supposed burglary. There's no forced point of entry is there?"

"No, the police told me that."

"And what did you say?"

"I said I'd come in late from a meeting and had a report to read. I was sitting here when I heard a sound. I went through to the French windows and there was a young guy in the room. He pulled a gun, I charged him and he brought it down on my head. He ran out onto the open land and I called police. A few minutes later you screamed in. I pointed to where he had gone and the bastard shot your dog."

"So, you told the police all you know."

"There was one thing. I think I'd seen him before. He was in that Aston Martin with Peter Lodovitch once, when they came here around New Year time. It seemed odd. He's a lot older, maybe thirty."

"Well, we've got him locked up. Why didn't you tell the police that?"

"I know Peter is close friends with Cressida and her circle. I didn't want to hint that my daughter was in any way connected."

"Like asking her about drugs and if she knew this man?"

"Yes, exactly."

"In your opinion how did this man get into your house?"

"The French doors were open."

"Careless or what?" she said with a deliberate cynical tone to her voice.

"Yes, careless."

"You don't need to be a cop to ask a few simple questions, do you?"

He looked down into his brandy glass.

"What can I say? How can I see my little girl in this way? She doesn't know that I recognized him and I know, if I go there, it will lead to a conflict. She's an adult and can just go from me, to do whatever. Or maybe die."

Whether it was art or subterfuge he was reaching into her heart. He'd cared enough to come for her. She watched him stand and open his arms to her. For God's sake she didn't have to move or respond to him. These folks were not her problem. And yet— there was a need in her, a desire in her for this man from a different continent of consciousness, to hold her. A man who had sung before thousands in total confidence and who was now as lost as any simple guy with a kid off the rails. His arms were around her and she knew that no such other place would ever exist for her again. She felt his kiss on her hairline and hugged him back in response. That brought his hand to the back of her head to stroke and feel her hair. She needed not just to surrender.

"If you're waiting for a duet, it's a long wait."

"Singing is a story about life, not the real thing. No theatre is big enough for your grasp on life."

31

"You mean I'm an armor-plated cop and you guys are delicate flowers."

"I mean perhaps you're a snail and I'm a slug."

"Marco, that's the most romantic thing any man has ever said to me."

He was laughing and so was she. He held her away a little as automatically her lips rose to meet the kiss that was in both their hearts. *That's screwed it, Helen, you stupid cow.* She could pretend, but that lurch in her belly and the warmth in her panties couldn't lie.

She sat down, breathless.

"Marco, let's keep this simple."

He nodded agreement.

"At least for now."

"Now, works for me. I'm going to stay right here tonight and so should you. Like you say, these creatures are not going evaporate. In the morning I'm going to see Lanza and then I'm going to go and see the cavalry.

"And Cressida?"

"Nothing I know puts her in any police file so far. I get the sofa, you get the chair. Leave a couple of lights on to deter any curious bad guys. Sweet dreams.

CHAPTER EIGHT

Her body clock was still running the night shift mode. Everything was quiet except for the odd twitch and murmur from Sam and the occasional passing car. Marco had fallen into a profound slumber. The WIFI router box caught her eye. The local network lamp had started to flicker. Maybe a computer was updating or maybe Cressida was streaming a movie. Maybe she was messaging. Helen had asked her not to communicate. She came to full alert. It was 4:45 a.m. when she heard a movement on the stairs. Outside a car pulled up, a dark BMW X5. She held back, feigning sleep to make sure she learned as much of the story as possible. She could see Cressida in the hallway, carrying a small backpack. Time to intervene. She moved swiftly toward the girl's back and in one movement blocked her legs and put her in a neck hold.

"Looks like you can't be trusted."

Cressida tried to pull away but her meagre body had little strength.

"Is that car waiting for you or just what's in that bag?"

"Just the bag."

"Did you mention to your friends there was a cop in the house?"

"I didn't know you'd stayed."

"And you didn't check. It's not the time to tell you but you just aren't cut out for crime."

Marco had woken up and joined them in the hall.

"What the hell?"

"Good question. For now, I want the registration of that car and a shot of the driver and any other occupants. Marco, get out the back and come around to the end of the street. Don't stand out or close on them. Get a few shots with your mobile. I'll give you three minutes."

He left at once while Helen checked her watch. "You, young lady, are going to phone them to say you've discovered a cop in the house because the local police are watching out for burglars. No arguments, no nothing. Get the number up and be ready." Helen didn't release the girl. She half suspected she'd bolt for the door. The time ticked by. "Now, do it. Do it."

Cressida pushed the button. The answer was instant.

"Get out, get away. There's cops here. Yes, the burglary spooked them. There's a cop right downstairs. Go."

At once the BMW moved away.

"I'm going to let you go, but don't even think about getting away."

She could hear Marco coming back into the kitchen.

"Helen, Cressida, tell me what's happening."

"Did you get some shots?"

"Yes."

"Send them to me, I'll check them out. Now it's time to talk."

Already Cressida was crying. She looked ill and terrified.

"The only way from here is up, honey. You and all of us have to get ourselves out of this mess. Direct question. What's in that bag?"

"I don't know. Peter said not to ask and not to touch anything."

"He gave you whatever it is?"

"Yes. He does their deliveries. He picks stuff up."

"Why would anyone leave something, anything with you? It's got to be drugs, right?"

Marco stepped forward and threw an arm around Cressida's shoulder.

"I'm not angry. Three times now we've had serious criminals at our home. Twice I've seen firearms myself and I bet these guys had guns. What the hell are we into here?"

They moved to the lounge. Helen emptied the rucksack onto the floor. There was one box, about a foot square. It was surprisingly heavy and lavishly wound with heavy-duty plastic tape. Underneath was a sealed plastic layer. Her estimation was that it was intended to be airtight.

"I'm not going to touch this let alone open it. Every fiber and every layer will be evidence. Those guys really, really, want this don't they? Where did you get it Cressida?"

"Peter brought it three days ago. He said he would collect it later. He had tried to deliver it to someone, but things went wrong and they wanted him to store it somewhere safe, not near him in case he'd been spotted."

Marco stood up and paced the room.

"And you agreed, you stupid child. Christ how fucking dim are you?"

Helen shot him a glance.

"Your papa is frustrated, Cressida. You must understand that."

Helen was thinking hard. Her next task would be to hand over everything she knew to the brains at Scotland Yard. Maybe she could cut some sort of deal for herself. As far as she could tell the bad guys didn't know she had their photos and car registrations.

"Cressida, how many of your circle of friends deal with Peter? You know what I mean?"

"Maybe between twenty and thirty."

"He supplies them with drugs?"

"Yes, people call him."

"And where does he get the supplies?"

"From some people in the business?"

"And who are these individuals?"

She didn't answer. Helen studied her face, staring her down with controlled aggression.

"Peter used a strange word once but said I must never repeat it."

"That was before people started waving guns at your papa and me. I don't have to mention what they did to Lanza, do I?"

"The word was something like SOV. It didn't make any sense to me."

Oh my God. Helen's heart did an extra beat. Before she spoke she needed to think.

Marco jumped in impatiently.

"Do you know them, Helen? They must be some sort of drug gang."

For sure she'd heard of SOHV, but for now she couldn't share her knowledge. All units had received a highly secret briefing from

Metropolitan Police Special Branch that this bunch of hard-core extremists were on the loose and active. SOHV stood for Scimitar of Holy Vengeance. There was nothing about them in the public arena. She knew the CIA and FBI were screaming warnings at the Brits based on their own intelligence. For now, she had to play it down with these guys. They were all just so lucky still to be alive. Well above her head, police bosses would have the big picture and they wouldn't be sharing it with her. She just had to play dumb.

"Doesn't ring any bells with me. There's hundreds of drug gangs but I'll sure be putting that name up to the experts."

It was 7:30 a.m. Marco made tea as if it were a regular morning. Helen set out her agenda and did *not* expect dissent.

"I'm going to check on Lanza. Then I'm going to contact my superiors and tell them everything I know and everything you know. From now on we stay together and we all tell the truth. We'll all be interviewed separately and detectives will check all our stories against the others. The truth, the whole truth and nothing but the truth."

"It's the only way," said Marco seriously. "And you Cressida?"

She scowled. Her mood seemed edgy leading Helen to suspect she might have a speed or coke habit. Very likely she would have exchanged her secret package for some very adult sweeties. She decided to take no chances.

"Give me your phone."

The girl didn't move and kept her eyes down. This could get ugly but the result would be the same.

"Give me your phone." Helen held out her open palm and let her toss it at her with a show of petulance. "This will be evidence. You think I'm a rotten bitch but remember you're still alive to dislike me. If you don't do exactly what I say from this moment on I will arrest you."

Within a few minutes they'd left the house, Marco at the wheel, heading for the Animal hospital. In a plastic shopping bag Helen carried the package and she wasn't about to let it out of her sight.

A nurse led them through to a small private room. Lanza was lying on a sterile sheeted mattress.

"He's still sedated," whispered the nurse.

"Good boy," said Helen as she stooped down.

At once his tail pounded the mattress. He was trying to stand as she stroked his head. Again, and again he tried to get up. Even in his heartbreaking state he was trying to reach her bag. He was what the police called a general-purpose dog but he had a secondary training on explosive detection and bomb disposal. The package—Lanza was trying to warn her. Helen knew what he was saying. She needed to keep this calm or there could be panic.

"Good boy, good boy, I've got it covered." She turned her attention to the nurse. "How's he doing?"

"He's gaining strength and we're hopeful. He's still critical. This time tomorrow we'll know."

Lanza had calmed now he knew she'd understood him. Helen looked back to Marco and Cressida. She was sobbing as her father held her. In the hands of Scimitar of Holy Vengeance, she would last for less than a second. Now was the moment to face up to the harsh truth of life. She'd been a soldier of the crown, she was still a cop. Regardless of her stupid entanglement with these innocents, there was a clear job to do. She took a deep breath and stepped out into the corridor. A serious but beautiful woman with half a dozen guys in suits were blocking the exit.

"Helen, I'm Deputy Assistant Commissioner Anna La Salle of Scotland Yard. These gentlemen are my colleagues. We called at your home address but you weren't there. Lanza is in everyone's heart—and I mean everyone in this city and beyond. We need to have a de-brief—urgently."

As Helen looked into the face of this woman she was aware that other officers were leading Marco and Cressida away. Helen felt ridiculous holding her shopping bag.

"Ma'am, this was my next job. I've got a lot to explain."

"We can start with your prints in an Aston Martin found abandoned in Kenley."

"That's easy to explain but first I think someone needs to look at this package. Lanza has just told me it's explosives."

"How? He's only barely alive. That would be incredible," said this elegant dark-haired woman of a little over forty years.

"Not for my little boy."

CHAPTER NINE

They all reached the car park. Helen knew she would be separated from Marco and Cressida. Maybe she would never see him again? Maybe there was no possibility of anything between them in any case.

"I want just to say goodbye to Marco if I may?"

The older woman gave her a sideways glance.

"You're not under arrest, Helen. If Lanza is right it might be best to put that package in the car."

She stashed the bag and looked across to Marco, finding his gaze fixed on her. It would be ridiculous and unprofessional to hug him, probably for the last time. When things had been at their worst for Lanza and she was alone, he'd been there for her. She would never be able to put that aside. Seeing her move toward him he opened his arms and stepped forward to hold her.

"I asked things of you that were wrong, I think now."

"You're a father and a good man and I wanted to help you. This thing's too big for us to control. I thought she'd merely fallen in with the wrong kids, but there's a far bigger picture."

"I know. I'll call you as soon as I can. These gentlemen wish to talk to us."

"You want to call me?"

"As long as you want to take the call."

"Call me," she said.

As she moved back, he reached his hand to her cheek and looked into her.

"I'll be thinking of you, Helen."

Even in her state of turmoil and worry, she smiled back.

"I'll be holding that thought."

Time re-started and he went to one of the unmarked police cars. She walked back to Deputy Assistant Commissioner Anna La Salle.

"Ma'am, thank you. I know that might have seemed inappropriate."

To Helen's astonishment Anna La Salle laughed.

"One day, when all this is over I'll tell you my own story. For now, let's get to Scotland Yard."

The two women slid into the rear seat of the black Jaguar XF Sportbrake, the shopping bag sitting between them. A driver was already in place as they moved off into the morning London traffic. Around them a flow of international citizens lived their lives without thought of attack or terror. And yet both women knew this deathly threat stalked its innocent prey both day and night.

"Ma'am, I know I screwed up. I moved that car to keep any heat off Cressida Ambastilias. I had no idea what she was into. The guys who came for it pulled a gun but I got pictures of them and their vehicle."

"You did? Did you think you were going to fight off a bunch of armed thugs on your own?"

"I don't think I was thinking."

"That package on the seat. We need to get it assessed and we don't need to take it into Scotland Yard. We also don't need to splash the fact that we've got it at all. If your boy Lanza is right, I'll be surprised if it's not C4 or Semtex plastic explosive. I'm sitting here calmly because I don't think there's any form of detonator in that package."

Anna La Salle made a call on her cell phone.

"Guys, may have a project for you. Pick us up on the tracker and I'll call you with a rendezvous."

Evidently, she was a big cog in a major machine. She turned to Helen with a friendly smile.

"I'm a dumb cop like you if we forget all the fancy titles. The guy who shot Lanza was a regular small-time crook. Some bigger fish had given him that gun and paid him to do the pickup. He didn't know it but when he'd handed over the package, he was very probably going to be wasted. Getting locked up saved his life. We're going to know a lot more when we've de-briefed you. And we can drop the ma'am, we're just cops, OK?"

"What—do I just call you Anna?"

"You got it."

"Anna—that package may well be connected to Scimitar of Holy Vengeance."

Anna La Salle didn't move at first. Then she snapped her grey eyes to Helen's face."

"Are you serious?"

"Yeah, that young guy Peter Lodovitch used a word sounding like SOV. Cressida had never heard of them and thought it was just a gang name."

"That might explain why he's dead. That's why I needed to speak to you. They found him on a park bench at 2:00 this morning, apparently a heroin overdose. The blood toxicity was so high that you have to suspect someone helped him."

Anna leaned forward and gave a couple of directions to the driver. The vehicle turned right over Lambeth Bridge, did a circuit of the roundabout and then headed back over the bridge—a classic anti-surveillance tactic. Anna was talking on her cell phone.

"Dean Bradley Street in two minutes," she said with clipped authority in her voice. The Jaguar took the Horseferry Road and then a right, pulling in to a disabled parking bay. Within a minute a plain Ford Ranger pulled up alongside. Helen looked at the two guys on board, recognizing at once the style and imprint of soldiers. Anna handed over the bag.

"Give me everything, speed of light will do unless you can be faster. Code Sirius."

The Ranger sped away. Helen was intrigued.

"I don't suppose you're going to tell me who they are?"

"They're military bomb guys. We'll know what it is, where it's from and who's touched it."

They cruised sedately on past the Palace of Westminster and around Parliament Square. Within five minutes they'd swung off Victoria Embankment into New Scotland Yard.

They took a lift from the underground car park to the top floor. Anna La Salle ordered a pot of coffee from a uniformed officer and went to the window overlooking the River Thames and the slowly turning London Eye.

"Helen, if you're a terrorist there's eight million residents and maybe two million tourists presenting one of the biggest static

40

targets in the world every minute of the day, every day of the year."

Helen took in the enormity of this woman's responsibility. Any attack or outrage by religious lunatics would be held up to her as her personal failure.

"An amateur like me must piss you off," she said.

"You did, but a woman with a big heart and courage makes me even more proud. Do you have feelings for the great Marco Ambastilias?"

"Of course not. We're from very different places. He asked me to keep his daughter out of the shit, like a father would. I tried to help, but it wasn't that simple."

"Right. Helen, tell me the story of the world's greatest tenor and a hero cop while we relax with some coffee. Everything in this office is recorded just so you know. In the meantime, we'll need your cell phone for those photos.

Helen handed over both her own device and the one she'd taken from Cressida. A plainclothes officer took them away. She took a deep breath and emptied the entire sack of her experience since she had arrived at Marco's house with Lanza. She'd reached the conclusion when Deputy Assistant Commissioner Anna La Salle took a call. The older woman leaned back in her seat and looked up at the ceiling or maybe to heaven.

"Guys, thanks for that. Tell me, could we swap it for something else? How much of that stuff was held in Libya?"

Helen could hear nothing of the other end of the call, but she gathered it was the military bomb guys reporting in on her package. She studied the currents in Anna's face as she clicked off.

"Helen, you don't have the security clearance to know about much of this but I'm going to tell you. Your little Cressida was holding thirty odd pounds of advanced plastic explosive. From what you say it belongs to this terrorist group called Scimitar of Holy Vengeance. We believe the thief who shot Lanza received his instructions from a guy the CIA tracked from Iraq to Tripoli, but had lost somewhere in the Mediterranean Sea. This man is a vicious terrorist called Badu al Bagwandi. He was one of the guys in the BMW X5 who turned up at dawn at Marco's house this morning. The other man was Harum Jaba Mushti, a gun-for-hire mercenary from Somalia. Marco got some great shots of them."

"Are they part of this Scimitar of Holy Vengeance group?"

"It looks that way, but we didn't know they were in London. The great thing—the most fantastic thing—is they don't know we're onto them. Their method is to use regular crooks for errands while they stay in the shadows. For sure they were desperate to retrieve that package and had to take some risks. They showed out and you had the presence of mind to get pictures."

"But they know police seized that kid Peter's Aston Martin and arrested the guy who shot Lanza."

"Well, the Peter problem has been filed in the morgue. The other guy has identified his contact from photos and the bad guys don't know that."

Helen tried to focus her mind on the current situation. An obvious question was drilling its way out of her head.

"These terrorists obviously want this explosive. Where do they think it is now and where do we take it from here?"

Anna La Salle stroked her chin.

"It's that sort of question that sits on my desk. For sure they don't know the cops have got their parcel. They may have more explosives and we know they can make their own. The Manchester bomb at the Ariana Grande concert was homemade TATP."

Helen sighed. All of this was well above her experience and knowledge. God, what had she gotten into? And what the hell had Cressida gotten into?

"Anna, that kid, Cressida. These killers will come after her for their parcel...."

"Exactly and we have to play that with precision. What did you make of her?"

"Bit of a brat. She lied to me about a couple of things. At heart she's a good kid. Her parents divorced and she was pushed out into exclusive schools while they lived megastar lives. My feeling is that she's got a speed habit which started with slimming drugs."

Anna paused before she spoke, walked to the window and once again looked out over the River Thames. She kept her back to Helen as she began.

"I'm just thinking out loud now. Before anything happens, I'll need to speak with folks way above my head and with guys like the CIA and FBI. You told me you had no feelings about Marco Ambastilias, but I noticed his body language toward you. If it had been dark I'd have seen the spark."

Helen almost blushed. Anna was so high above her in the rank structure that she couldn't believe she was still a human, let alone a woman like her.

"He just cared about Lanza. He's a sweet guy who saw that I needed a hug that's all."

"Like a hug with his eyes on yours. Helen, maybe you don't know too much about man hugs."

"I guess not. Look I had a husband and he was my only guy and then—"

"I know your story. I pulled your file and your personal life is none of my business. Let's just say you may feel nothing about Marco, but my detective juices kind of don't believe you. I don't have to ask him because he's a larger than life guy who wears his heart like a suit."

"Ma'am—Anna, he's a handsome cosmic star. I'm a plain-Jane nobody and why am I ever going to see him again?"

"It was just a crazy idea running through my head. I'd be asking you to put your head in the lion's mouth. You see, those terrorists know that there's a woman at Marco's house, probably a girlfriend. His daughter's got their parcel and someone's going to knock on her door. Just one big happy Ambastilias family maybe?"

"Anna, I'd do whatever police duty the job requires. Anything else is fantasy."

Anna gave an amused snort.

"Honey, there's nothing better than a hot fantasy. Look, get something to eat in the canteen. Marco and Cressida have gone to Paddington Green for interview by my officers. I'll be frank. I'm going to see the prime minister and the home secretary. I want to nail these bastards by the balls but the politicos may not let it run."

"Let it run?" asked Helen.

"Sure. There's a group of up to twenty of them. I got involved when a mega-powerful Russian oligarch's son dies and the Kremlin phones Downing Street in the middle of the night. Your bit of intelligence completes a picture. MI5 and the CIA are all over this SOHV, but the bosses may want the cops to just scoop the ones we know. That would leave the rest to bring all their nightmares of murder to the world. I want them dead or in prison for life. This Scimitar of Holy Vengeance group are the distilled hard core of all the killers from Afghanistan, Iraq, Somalia, Libya and on and on. They're here on a mission and it's not a shopping trip. Leaving them at liberty in order to identify their network and all their operatives is one hell of a risk."

"But one you're prepared to take?"

"Yeah, but maybe I won't be sleeping too well for a while. Like I say, there's folks above me who might have a different view. Enjoy some lunch, Helen, but stay there. We've got your cell phone so pick up a pager from my assistant. Be within fifteen minutes of this building. *Bon Appetit.*"

CHAPTER TEN

She ate without tasting. For the past eight years, her life had been built around Lanza. On non-working days he still had to be fed and exercised. Suddenly her life had no focus. Even as she tried to think of her dog, Marco hijacked her mind. Had she really felt that hot surge in her sex when he had held her? She didn't like to admit it but when they'd kissed at his house she had wanted more, wanted to press herself against him, wanted him inside her in a way that she had never ever desperately wanted any man. She let the fantasy wash over her, his seed jetting into her belly as they kissed. The picture in her mind was turning her on, dear God, was making her want to come, squeeze her legs together, hold her clitoris tight and feel the seam of her jeans against her groove. If she were alone now she'd do it, push inside herself to be his hot bursting cock and say his name. Something had re-awakened in her, something delicious and oddly sinful. She would never tell a living soul, but she had never felt that heat and urgency for her husband when he was alive. How the hell did a married woman cope if that desire came into her life? She had loved James as an equal. She had a strong sexual drive, but she had never wanted to be helpless and abandoned to him. With Marco she'd wanted to open her body and feel his ecstasy letting go in her fertile juice. A deep lust from the jungle of time had come to the surface in her soul and there was no way she was ever going to be the same woman again. Maybe it would be with some lesser guy, someone who was kind, who liked the same music, films, and pizzas. Who could tell her he loved her. Perhaps that would be enough? But it would never fill the fantasy she'd built and would always run on a loop when she had her secret little buzzy man in her hand to touch

45

the spots to set her free to dream.

She wanted to get out into the air. It was June, and London was wearing its sleeveless summer frock. She strolled up to the Houses of Parliament and watched the to-and-fro of traffic on Westminster Bridge, a place where a lone amateur terrorist Khalid Masood had run down and killed five people before stabbing an unarmed cop to death. Only a little over a year had passed. Tourists and Londoners formed a scar tissue over the wound but some families would never heal. Now there were twenty or more hardened fanatics from Scimitar of Holy Vengeance in London. Against them were the forces of Scotland Yard and for sure, everything the Americans could provide with their own intelligence and agents on the ground. The woman with whom she'd been chatting like a big sister had the exposed heart of this city beating in her hands. Anna La Salle was a force of nature whereas Helen Marx was a dog handler without a dog.

Her old-fashioned pager was bleeping. The message read *1700 hours, conference room 7th floor. Anna LS.*

Helen's heart pounded. Suddenly it all seemed real. She'd be the least significant person in the room. Perhaps that made it easier. After all, what could she do? She made her way to the location and slipped in through the open door. There was a grand table with a few officers in uniform and others in plain clothes dotted around. She caught a few foreign languages and a fair bit of American. She took a seat and hoped to look inconspicuous. She sensed a shadow and looked to the side. A tall grey-haired man in the uniform of a British Army general was addressing her in a loud military voice. She stood and saluted out of reflex habit.

"Well, I'm damned. Captain Marx isn't it?"

"Sir, yes."

"Last time we met was at Basra when you were leading the bomb dog training for Iraqis."

"Yes, sir"

"Good show. Glad to see you here. Bloody sorry to hear about your husband. Top man he was. You're a civilian now I suppose?"

"Yes, sir."

"Can't be helped, but I know you'll be putting up a firm fight all the same. Well done."

"Thank you, sir."

The general strode away as Helen re-took her seat. She had absolutely no idea who he was but he clearly knew her and about her husband. For a man near the top of the army, that was impressive. A female uniformed chief inspector took a seat next to her.

"Blimey, you must be important. Old 'both-barrels' has never diverted his cavalry charge to speak to me."

The new arrival was darker skinned and frankly stunning to look at. "I'm Shannon and if you don't know the big picture, we're in the same boat."

Her accent was pure Peckham, her smile warm and generous. Her air was mischievous.

"Constable Helen Marx...."

"Christ you're Lanza's mum, ain't ya? Privileged to meet you, Helen. How is he?"

"I'm not his mum exactly, but thanks. He's stable. I saw him this morning, but I don't know when I'll be able to get back."

"If you don't get a better offer I'll give you a ride, if you'll let me see him too. Not often I get to meet A-list celebrities."

A serious looking guy in a dark suit took the head of the table. Helen saw Anna La Salle at a top seat. The man spoke in a deep, educated voice.

"Thanks for coming, everyone. If you don't know me I'm Dickon Maltravers from up the road, so that's the formal stuff. What we've got here is maybe the biggest single coordinated and trained terrorist group ever to be in one place and, without doubt, in a capital city. We know two identities and more or less where they are. Intelligence suggests there are another twenty or so we don't know. They don't meet up, they don't use accessible cell phones or the internet. We know they infiltrated a group of well-connected teenagers, apparently with the intention of hooking them on drugs and then supplying them. A young man, Peter Lodovitch, worked as their courier, but had found out who they were, we think, because Russian agents told his father. Needless to say, he's dead. This group has no fear of death. You know just from the press that Sergei Lodovitch, the boy's father, is a close friend of President Pinupskin. We know that he has dispatched agents with access to chemical nerve poisons to find the killers. They will die, but die very publicly, to leave a message on the wall. Ladies and gentlemen, the death penalty has never meant much to suicide bombers. Public humiliation such as being defeated by women is worse than death to them. Pinupskin knows that and he is cold-war KGB through and through. If the Russians get these guys, their warrior women will shit on them and put their shame on YouTube. And that's before the Svetlanas castrate them for the camera and feed them their own dicks."

The man allowed himself a small smile and paused while something of a cheer went up in the room.

"So, we don't have that freedom. We don't know why they're here. We do *not* know what horror they intend to bring upon innocent people in the name of Holy Vengeance. Each of you will be briefed by your own team leaders. Probably none of you will ever know the whole picture. We have the terrorists, we have the Russians who will be operating independently, solely to humiliate and destroy them, and we have the rest of us protecting our citizens and bringing these bastards to legitimate justice. Thirty pounds of plastic explosive is part of the scenario, if only we knew what, or if there is any more. Before you go to it, guys, I'm just going to give a nod to Helen Marx who is the handler of Lanza, the superstar police dog. She's in this room today. Their courage and fast response in facing an armed criminal alone started this ball rolling so if you need any extra motivation—do it for Lanza."

People were standing up. A guy with an FBI badge hanging from his breast pocket called out.

"Fuck, yeah. Do it for Lanza"

"Do it for Lanza" echoed the meeting.

Helen felt embarrassed but also proud. Few things could unite a world, but her little boy had achieved it. Now he just had to live. He had to live. Now she had to be with him. Another speaker was detailing teams. To Helen, everyone was part of a huge machine except her. She was so relieved to hear Anna's friendly voice.

"OK. We're a team, but I'm going to be distant. Shannon will be your leader if you accept your assignment, Helen."

"Ma'am—Anna, I'll do what a cop has to do."

Anna La Salle smiled slowly, but carried an air of gravity.

"OK. You'll be the live-in partner of Marco Ambastilias. You'll be stepmother and jailer of his daughter, Cressida. You'll deal with the handover of the missing package to our would-be mass murderers. You will confront them and convince them you are acting as a concerned mother. When they come, they will talk to you and our guys will be ready."

"Me?"

"One of them saw you at the house and you spoke on the drive when they came for that car. You aren't going to change their mental picture of their situation. To them you're Marco's wife or partner. Anyone new would spook them. We have to hope that Peter Lodovitch died before he said anything about you. I have to say that if they do know who you are, you'll be facing utter peril alone."

"Are the authorities going to give them back their package?"

"Oh yeah, wrapped just the same, with the same weight texture and smell. The only difference is that our stuff will be missing a little chemical tweak. A suicide bomber could still blister his balls but that's as bad as it could get."

"So, they won't know it's been switched?"

"We're gambling that these guys focus on murder and don't trouble too much with volatile chemistry. Their shit has been prepared in Libya by Bin Laden's students so we're riding our luck that they won't double check the mix or do any tests."

"They must be looking for Cressida now."

"Yeah, you bet they are. This is the story. When you get home from all day shopping with Marco and Cressida she's going to answer their calls at last because you took her cell. Then she slags off her stepmother for forcing her to fix up her wardrobe for the Ascot races and for Wimbledon tennis. Of course, she's still got the stuff but her wicked stepmother won't let her out. Then she rings off because the new witch in her life is coming up the stairs."

"You should have been a movie director."

"Police work is an acting job, as if you didn't know, Helen. So, the wicked stepmother has overheard the call and finds the package. She phones them and tells them she's the vile witch in Marco's life. All she wants is for them to leave the girl alone. She knows there's drugs in the parcel and she *will not* tolerate them in the house or for Marco to know about it. She wants them out of their life forever or she'll call the cops. The only reason she's not calling them now is because he's a superstar singer and the press would be all over them. She makes a rendezvous away from the

49

house the next day. She demands secrecy because the only way she got Cressida to cooperate was by telling her that Marco would never know about her issues with drugs. Helen, they've seen you at the house, so you look kosher, civilian stepmother. The story fits. For them, what's not to like?"

"Anna, you've sold the deal. Of course, I'll do it. Is there any chance I could see Lanza tonight?"

"Chief Inspector Knightsmith will drive you to the animal hospital. I ought to tell you that when you meet these guys you won't have body armor. You won't have a radio or be wired up. You're a dumb civilian woman and we can't risk a gun."

"Lanza went in with less than that every day of his working life," said Helen.

"Best ever answer," replied Anna La Salle.

Helen walked quickly with her new boss DCI Shannon Knightsmith who had reappeared dressed in a Nike track suit.

"Can't risk anyone seeing you with a uniformed cop. The only good thing about being in a uniformed role is that you never have to choose what to wear for work."

"I'd never seen it that way."

"I'll be in plain clothes for the rest of this project. Before we separate this evening, I'll give you a clean cell phone. It has no set numbers and no memory capacity, you know, just in case."

"In case I don't make it and they search me."

Shannon nodded and shot her an appraising glance.

"You OK with that? Don't answer. I can see you've got the balls. Now, we analyzed Cressida's phone and we've gotten into her Facebook, Instagram and What's App files. There's teams looking at everything so you don't need to play detective on that. All the same you can nag her for details as if you didn't know. To be straight up with you Helen, I don't trust her, from what I've seen."

"She knows what I am and could blow me out. People with addictions would sell their mothers."

"You're right and she's a bloody weak link. She's more worried about her speed and weed than she is about London's crime statistics. We need to keep her around to maintain normal contact with her group and maybe liaise with the guys she knows. So far, she's only in touch with one of them and that's this Badu al

Bagwandi. He's known as a suicide bomb gang-master. Up until now, he's kept himself out of the starring role. Cressida simply thinks they're drug dealers."

"So, what are these people planning to do?"

"That, my dear Watson, is a job for the cops. Locking up Bagwandi or his mate Mushti wouldn't help. They wouldn't talk and these guys operate as lone wolves. They probably access a dark web page for instructions and coordination. MI5 are watching twenty thousand individuals who live here as residents."

"The guy who did the briefing said he was from 'up the road.' What did that mean?"

"Along the Thames Embankment. That was M from the James Bond films. He's head of MI6."

CHAPTER ELEVEN

They walked from the building into the evening sunshine on Victoria Embankment. A deep gray BMW 740i pulled up. The two women slid into the back seat.

"Helen, our driver is Kaitlyn Thorn. She's a class-one pursuit driver and she'll be on this team."

"Nice to meet you," chirped Kaitlyn. "Don't suppose you're going to let me pat your dog."

"I'll see what shape he's in. He loves to meet people."

"Kaitlyn might be driving you, particularly if you have to be somewhere fast."

Their driver was younger than Helen, maybe thirty. Her hair was blonde but cut harshly into spikes. She wore ripped jeans and a tight-fitting T-shirt, revealing a tattoo of a sort of naked mystic goddess figure on her arm. At a glance this girl was a bit of a character and not the regular cop design. Instinctively, Helen liked her already.

They all walked together into the reception area of the animal hospital. The nurse looked up.

"Better get ready for a bit of a shock. Come on through," she said in a flat tired tone.

Helen's heart lurched. This sort of life-and-death stuff would be routine to these people. She followed, leaving Shannon and Kaitlyn at the desk. This had to be bad news. She covered her face with her hands as if to hide from the brutality of existence. She heard the sound of a dog's paws on the floor tiles. Looking down she saw Lanza walking slowly toward her with his crooked grin and his wagging tail swaying his whole body from side to side. She knelt down and cradled his head as Lanza licked tears from her cheeks.

"Will he live?"

"He's doing well. When he came off the anesthetic he was able to stand and now he's walking. He has a lot of pain but that should reduce."

She stroked down his side. His chest and belly had been shaved. Large surgical staples held together a long incision.

"Poor boy. My poor boy."

He sat down on his haunches and placed a paw on her thigh as if to comfort her.

She heard Shannon and Kaitlyn behind her. Lanza stood to greet them with tail wags and licks of their hands.

"He's a tough pro. It's incredible that he detected those explosives. He's going to make it."

A thought filled Helen's mind which she had to express.

"What will happen to him if I don't make it?"

She knew that without a handler to look after him in retirement the bosses could have him put to sleep.

"He'll be cared for, I'd see to it," said Shannon.

"And if that failed, I'd go to the papers and the TV and sod the trouble," said Kaitlyn.

Now this girl was feisty. Helen would like to know more of her career to date. She couldn't imagine she had a regular CV or discipline record.

They parted at Marco's front door. Shannon handed her a personal cell phone and another loaded with Cressida's number.

"There's armed cops everywhere, but you won't spot one. You're a civilian stepmother. I've taken the decision not to put a marksman in the house because I need Cressida to feel at home and relaxed with you just as a family. We haven't told the girl that we've swapped the package. She believes it's drugs. You mustn't give any hint of terrorist involvement. Luckily Lanza couldn't talk when he warned you. Neither Marco nor Cressida are any the wiser and we want to keep it that way. The package looks identical and they've got it in the house already. *Capisce?*"

For sure, Helen could see the logic.

"Yeah, I got it."

"Cressida makes the contact at 9 p.m. A world of spies and geeks will be tuned in. You snatch the phone and tell them you don't want drugs in the house. You don't want cops because of media scandals. You'll hand the stuff over on the promise they'll never come near the house again. To some extent you're going to have to cooperate with them. You're Marco's girlfriend, not a streetwise cop and for sure, not an ex-army captain."

Helen gave a nervous laugh. "I've only ever been a kennel maid."

"We've not written you a script because these guys are cute and could pick that up. It's got to feel real so just freestyle it. You're a total star and I have total confidence in you. A detective is at the house with them and will leave when you're inside. Good luck."

Helen found the door opening as she approached. A burly looking guy came out and nodded as he passed her on the way to the car. She heard the wheels on the gravel and she was alone with her mission. A deep breath and she was ready. Marco almost ran to her as she entered.

"Helen, I was so happy when they said you'd be coming back."

"So was I."

"Were you really? That's beautiful."

She studied his expressive face, his open arms, his ease and confidence in expressing passion and emotion. Of course, he was a performer and she was a calculating soldier at heart. In Iraq she'd learned to stay shut down and watchful and never to show what she was thinking.

"Beautiful is a colorful word, Marco."

"Yes, like the sea is gray until the sun gives it a thousand colors."

"You really should be on the stage."

He chuckled. With everything that was happening how could her focus have wandered off into a lilting kind of conversation with him? In the lounge she could see Cressida. They had a few minutes before she had to make the call—that call which could, potentially, rewrite the future history books of London and maybe beyond.

"Marco, you know we need to hand over the drugs. They tell me you've been briefed on what's going to happen?"

54

"Yes, and I don't want you to meet these criminals."

"Every time cops go out they're looking for criminals. It's a bad day if you don't find one. I think we can agree that I'm a better meeter-and-greeter than Cressida."

"And your colleagues will track the drugs and put them all in jail."

"That's it—end of story and we all go back to cutting the grass, walking the dog, or performing opera. Simple."

"You're amazing. A woman—"

"I hope there's not a patronizing patriarch in there somewhere."

"No, there's a guy who was born to chivalry and honor. A male with a beating heart for a beautiful female he admires. Nature. Simple."

His eyes were hard on hers in a tiny flash of irritation. As she looked back he softened. Dear lord, he could sweep her up and admire her and she'd submit to nature without a second thought. Once this little bit of business was over.

She went through to the lounge where Cressida was seated, staring into space.

"We've just got to stick together, get these bloody drugs out of the house and then we can get on with our lives. I'm on your side all the way," said Helen.

The girl looked thin, tired and exhausted. She spoke quietly without expression.

"They told me Peter died of an overdose. He was my friend."

"That's terrible isn't it, I'm so sorry. Let's get all this behind us and get all our problems sorted. I trust you and you trust me. We're a team, OK?"

Cressida nodded. It was time to call her contact. Helen sat down on the sofa next to her, ready to make her move. She'd been in tighter spots but her mouth was dry. The cell was on speaker.

"It's me, Cressy."

"Where the fuck did you go? You got that parcel?"

The voice was gruff with a South London accent. She guessed a white guy, mid-twenties.

"Yeah, can you get me some crystal?"

"You stupid little cow. Where are you?"

"I'm at home with Papa and his new girlfriend. She's like a

bitch playing mother and bigging herself up. Tam—please Tam—can you get me something?

"I want that parcel, like now."

"You can't come now. They've got extra cops in the area after that dog got shot. I'll try to get out and meet you."

Helen gave the girl a nod and snatched the phone.

"Whoever you are and I don't care, this is like the bitch playing mother who's just found your drugs."

"Who the fuck?"

"I told you who I am. Listen, I'll bring you that parcel myself tomorrow morning—well away from here. Then I don't ever want any drugs in this house again. Do you understand me? You leave Cressida alone and that's the end of the matter. You don't want cops in your business and neither do we."

"You're that cocky slut who showed up when we came for the car. We should have pulled the fucking trigger."

"Well, you didn't, did you. I'll give you your stuff and that's an end to it. I know you've got guns and I haven't. What's not for you to like?"

"You could be setting us up."

"Like I want the girl involved with the cops and the press all over Marco. I just want you lot to fuck off and run your drug business without involving this family. No burglars, no thugs on the doorstep."

"I'll call you back."

The connection ended. Helen let out a sigh and without thinking hugged Cressida.

"You were fantastic."

"You're a cool liar, I guess that's what cops do. You're not my mother," she answered.

Helen swallowed her anger and an urge to smack the brat's face. This kid couldn't be trusted. Helen tried to fix her eyes, but she looked down.

"Mummy knows best, my dear. Mummy's going to meet the nice men with guns, who killed your friend Peter and who shot Mummy's dog. Mummy's been trying to keep you alive and out of prison."

She felt a surge of guilt. This poor kid was an adult in law, but a baby bird fallen from its nest before time. Her drug habit was robbing her of rational judgement. She knew love by its absence and as an ache she couldn't place or soothe.

"I know," Cressida answered, taking her hand.

An unfamiliar cell phone was ringing. It was the one Shannon had given her.

"Top job guys, we've fixed his location in Tooting. This Tam is the white man who came for the Aston Martin. He's a small-time crook running errands for Badu al Bagwandi. He believes that package is drugs. Just wait for his call and cooperate. We'll know who he's contacted for advice."

Shannon's voice was calm but Helen's own heart was racing. She only had time to take a deep breath before Cressida's cell phone rang.

"Yeah?"

"You know who this is. Take the Thames Clipper water bus from the London Eye. Be there at eleven o'clock. Get to the Emirates cable car at Royal Docks. Carry the cell phone you're on now. Keep the parcel in the rucksack. Any nonsense and we'll be taking it out on your little family at home. We'll be watching."

"Fine. How will I know who to give it to?"

"You'll be told."

The connection ended. She walked out of earshot and phoned Shannon.

"I guess you got that."

"Yeah, they're cute enough. They can see who's on that boat and follow you to the cable car. Anyone with you would show out. Some of the passengers getting on and off will be our guys watching them watching you. Don't look for anyone or try to check anyone out like you were a cop. We'll be staked out. We can't rule out a snatch, maybe a motorcycle ride-by or a straightforward knife point street robbery. The way they've set it up I think they want to check out surveillance. They're planning something spectacular and they need to be sure they're not in the cross-hairs. Good job, Helen. Get some sleep."

Sleep? How the hell was she going to sleep? Cressida was on her feet. She looked terrible with dark circles around her eyes. She needed help which no cliché or amateur could provide.

"You did great and that's you out of this. Once I've delivered the parcel maybe we can hang out a bit. Did you ever think about a career in the army or police once you've got your degree?"

"You are joking, aren't you?"

"Hey, I like you even more. Most people say I'm too serious."

"I'm going to bed. When can I get my phone and iPad back?"

"Tomorrow, once I've done the handover."

Cressida pulled a weary face and walked slowly to the stairs.

"Don't try anything," said Marco. "There's cops everywhere out there. I love you."

CHAPTER TWELVE

"Some wine, some human time please and maybe you'll tell me what you have to do tomorrow?" he said, holding his strong arms open to her. She surrendered into his embrace, but fudged details of her mission.

"Tomorrow's a quick handover at Vauxhall. Marco, you'll make me want this more."

"That's a shame because I wanted you to say more and more and more and more. Helen, all my life I was performing an exaggerated passion, a selfish passion. A performer's life is as big as his imagination, but too small for his real-life child. Now I see that, and now I'm holding a woman rich with genuine heart. I thank the stars that I met you."

"Marco, I'm a simple woman. I'm that horrible term, a widow. I've not met someone like you. You skate on desires and make voids into dreams and leave us applauding illusions but—"

"But still in the same place. Yes, I understand that and that is why the high note at the end of the aria is also a cliff edge fall back into yourself. That is why I longed to sing. Believe me Helen, I understand addiction."

"You're amazing, but you should carry a health warning. I want stuff, and you *long* for it. I want pleasure, and you *crave* ecstasy. I feel sadness, while you feel *heartbreak.* You're a whirlwind, and I'm not tied down, so I'm afraid."

"No one has ever understood this like you. You've seen men die in the army. You've faced your own dangers and the risk of death. I have risked a flat note or the boos of the crowd. I hit the top note and the world loves me. You stop a bullet and the world shrugs."

She looked up into his face. The truth was that his art and passion were also the lessons of lust betrayal and death which cops swallowed for breakfast. Maybe the distance between them was a nearly closed orbit of the human soul? Tomorrow she knew too well she'd be in danger. Her feelings and reflexes were at a peak and this night she wanted her body to know this man. This time she pulled him into her, kissing him deeply, reveling in the animal juice of him.

"Come and eat a little with, of course, a fine Chianti. I did a wonderful Neapolitan pizza."

She seated herself at the old-fashioned farmhouse type table.

"You made real pizza?"

"Yes, I made a trip to the supermarket, but I drove fast in an Alfa Romeo so the whole show is almost the real thing."

She laughed. She hadn't considered he might have a sense of humor, let alone self-mockery.

"Why don't you sing any more, Marco?"

He slid the pizza from the oven onto a wooden board and cut segments with a wheel, as if he hadn't heard the question.

"Because I lost belief. I lost pride in myself. You've seen my child and how a selfish father does so much harm by doing nothing."

His voice was almost broken and his eyes carried an awful sadness. Could she, should she offer an opinion or advice?

"I can see your sense of guilt and understand that. Do you know how guilty Cressida feels about you *not* singing?"

"That's not the sort of thing she says to me."

"She told me. You know, you could both be getting into a vicious circle here."

"I'm so happy she spoke to you on this level. Her mother never really acknowledged her. All she did was pose in bikinis so all the world would say she was perfect after her baby. Believe me, the studios work hard on those images."

"She's an adult so she can make her own choices in life. To me, she needs urgent help."

"You're right of course, but first she has to see it. It breaks my heart to be helpless."

"None of us are helpless in any way in this life. Maybe we don't know the way to go, but you love her and she loves you.

Love is like a paddle on the floor of the boat if you don't express it. Love will row the boat to shore, but only if you use it."

He had looked up into her eyes. The contact between them was unwavering, hypnotic. It was beautiful to look at him, into him. Could it be he was feeling the same as his gaze brushed her skin?

"Helen, I believe in you so much. You're real and speak wisdom from hard lessons."

"You mean I'm not dramatic, artistic, and beautiful."

He put down the cutting wheel and suddenly knelt before her on the floor, taking both her hands.

"You are beautiful. You have a face I just want to look at. And there is so much more."

Could it be that he was genuine? This was the great Marco Ambastilias who had sung with supreme divas. How did she know when he was acting? Did *he* know if he was acting?

"I guess you haven't met too many soldier girl-cops who spend their time with dogs. If I tried to sing it would be like a wolf on a moonlit night."

He tightened his grip on her hands and drew her towards him.

"You won't admit to yourself what you are under all that. You're afraid I'll find it and then I'll have you like a secret picture in my pocket."

He was irresistible and very possibly right about her. He let go of one hand and ran it through her hair to the back of her neck. Then he eased her lips to his with the softness of two clouds meeting and joining in a perfect sky. Now, there was nothing else in this universe but this connection. She felt the warmth of his breath on her cheek, felt his hand trace down her shoulder and across her breast. Maybe he hadn't meant that touch but the jolt shot to her sex and released a groan of pleasure. She kept her eyes closed so as not to send a brazen signal even though her body had already betrayed her. This time his hand slipped between her arm and her body, sending an ooze of longing to her nipple and down through her belly. When he spoke, his voice was thick and husky.

"Maybe I am wrong to touch you, but I want to so much."

"Don't touch what you don't want to keep."

He gave a deep sigh as his hand moved again to cover her breast and stroke her hardening nipple. Each movement pulsed down to her sex and throbbed in her clit. Had she really said that to him? The kiss had left her breathless, unaware of how much she was responding to him, placing his hand on her thigh, longing for him to release her. It had been so long since a man had been close to her. Her panties were drenching as she felt the first waves of orgasm building in her whole belly. She eased herself back and opened her eyes. She wanted to come but not fully clothed at his table. She took a deep breath. She had just caught the wave in time even though delicious ripples of pleasure flicked through her thighs and sex. She had never got this close with a kiss and never sat with a man, looking into his eyes as pings of orgasm thrilled her body.

"Marco, please." What was she wanting to say to him? "Please don't make me feel this way if you're going to shut me out when it's over." The question pin-balled around her mind.

"Helen, please."

She smiled as he chuckled. He was standing, grinning, moving back to his pizza board.

"The body must eat and the mind must think. If I stop dreaming will you be gone?" he said.

"You can never remember dreams. I'm going to eat a slice with a glass of wine and then see if I can remember you."

He leaned toward her and kissed her hairline.

"If you think you won't remember me, I won't give you any wine to damage your memory."

She reached for a glass and held it out. He filled it to the brim.

"After tomorrow, what will the police bosses do with you?"

"Good question. Lanza was about to retire so I was due to start walking a pup to replace him."

"You want that?"

"Not sure. Maybe try to be a detective? Maybe not be a cop? First I'll get through tomorrow."

As soon as she had said the words she knew she'd set the wrong tone. Marco had no knowledge of Scimitar of Holy Vengeance or the dangers she faced. To him she was handing over a package of drugs to a crook. She knew that if they decided to test the goods she was in trouble. Possibly they would just kill her anyway. She could see concern in his face.

"Why can't I come with you?"

"Because this is a police operation and I don't want you there like you wouldn't want me wandering onto the stage at the New York Met Opera, asking you what I should be doing."

He smiled and nodded while refilling her glass.

"You have an annoying female habit of being right too often."

His words and tone reached into her on some new human pathway. She searched for his eyes wanting to send him a wordless message. A message that she was falling in love with him and couldn't stop. Maybe no one could ever stop when this process began, but maybe she'd have a chance if she'd ever felt this way before. For a second, a dark cloud of guilt chilled her. She'd loved James but had never fallen in love with him. They had arrived on the firm ground of love without the fall. Without the risk and pain.

"Tomorrow's a routine day, Marco. I've finished my wine and you're still here."

He showed her a marble-tiled bathroom but made no reference as to where she would sleep. She showered and realized she had no change of clothes. Everything had been a whirl of cops, guns, and desire. For now, she let the powerful water jets wash away her cares. Still she throbbed from his contact and made sure no urgent current finished her climb to her climax. She'd never been so turned on and ready to yell out her lust. She finished and wrapped herself in a thick luxurious bath towel. She peered out onto a landing and saw an open door along the way. She entered a plush bedroom with an ensuite walk-in shower room. There was a sound of running water and a very special humming from a male voice. She closed the door and reposed on her front resting her chin on her elbow. She kind of accidentally let the fabric fold to press a little on her clitoris as she waited. She wanted to come, needed so much to come. She smiled as he appeared, his long dark wavy hair swept back touching his shoulders. His body was powerful and firm with dark chest hair arrowing down to his half erect thick cock. She pressed secretly into the towel before letting her absolute animal need roll her over to show him her open sex. She was shameless, brazen, so turned on it hurt. If he didn't come to her now she would have to touch herself. As she closed her eyes she saw his cock rock hard in his need for her. Lips were at her belly, strong hands lifted buttock cheeks to let his kiss find her pulsing

63

clitoris. His tongue swirled small circles taking her above the point of her normal crashing wave. His finger had probed inside her. A collision of joys was pushing up like a beautiful straining song, building and building. It was going so high she just couldn't hold on. His lips were kissing into her juice and flesh and now was the release. Now, now, now! She let out a cry of utter abandon. She pulled his head tight to her to ride out the rip and pull of her spasm. Wave after wave rocked her, drenching, groaning, and spilling out a woman's passion for a man. She subsided a little, conscious more of him. Now she wanted him, that thick cock hot in her belly, spreading her and holding her open. He was at her side, kissing her own juice and lust against her lips. She loved that taste of wet sex. His hand soothed her soaking pussy lips against her clitoris as his tongue found hers. She came again sobbing out her helpless pulses of joy into his kiss. She wanted that hot cock deep, deep inside her. She gripped him, wanting to come and come squeezing her tube against his relentless shaft. He moved above her taking his weight on his powerful arms. As his tip teased at her entrance she looked up at his broad shoulders and his smiling dark eyes, lost in the ecstasy she was offering him.

"Go inside me, Marco, do it in me," she growled.

His hard cock filled her, pushing at the limit and stroking her sweet cummy spot. The thrill of him pulsing inside her wiped out her restraints. She wanted to come. She reached down for her sex and touched her clit. She wanted to come just as he let go, so that his seed would shoot as she was coming too. His motion was strong and untiring. She could come just with the pleasure of his cock. He began to tense, was groaning, was beginning that climb.

"I want to come. I want you to come in my pussy."

He let out a grunt as she felt his hot cum spurt inside her. A touch of her clit zapped her to the same point.

"Fuck, do it, do it in me."

Her words jolted out with each pulse of his jetting seed. She heard his deep lust thick voice.

"Sweet woman, my lover."

She held his barrel of a chest as the shocks of his orgasm flowed into the river of her hot juice. She had his trace inside her. This gorgeous man had felt joy inside her. She had set herself free of all restraint, thrown away all modesty. Still her own aftershocks buzzed through her. Never ever had she even imagined such feelings. Simply, she hadn't known that such desire and release were possible. Were there people who already knew, maybe people she worked with or passed her in the street? He was lying on his back and brought his arm around her to rest her head on his chest. Even now the pressure of his flesh on her sex sent shudders through her. When he spoke, she could feel the vibration of his voice against her cheek. She was a female and this was a male.

"I wanted you so much."

"Past tense?"

"It's over. It was a beginning. Already I want you more."

CHAPTER THIRTEEN

How could it be that he filled her again at dawn and still she
wanted more of him? How could that be, with everything of the
coming day ahead? The wine and the passion had pushed
everything out of her mind.

"Marco, I've got no clean clothes here."

It was 7 a.m. as he slept spooned into her. He mumbled
against her skin.

"Yes, you have. The cop who was here left a couple of bags.
They're in the wardrobe."

"Which wardrobe?"

"My wardrobe."

"Huh! So, you knew I'd be sleeping here with you."

"It's a well-known fact that a beautiful woman can always
smell new clothes and you'd home in. All I knew for sure was that
you're beautiful."

She sprang out, very physically conscious that she'd spent a
night of animal passion. She showered in the ensuite wet room,
still feeling the pulse of wicked pleasure in her sex. It had been so
long, and her release made sense of the word longing. She wanted
him so much. Dare she say what she'd wanted even to herself?
She'd wanted that hot seed to root in her belly and to hell with
anything else sensible in her life. Oh, to cradle a child, a being
sprung from his talent and passion. She wanted to hold that fluid
inside her. And how the hell could she be dreaming nonsense when
this very day she'd be facing God knows what of danger? She
pulled two large paper carrier bags from his wardrobe, aware that
he was watching her. Maybe he often watched a naked woman in
his room. He was rich, famous and handsome. One bag was

underwear from Marks and Spencer.

"Choose a color," she said holding up one black and one white pair of panties?"

"I'll take the white if you wear them until you go. That way I still have a thrill of you."

"Marco! That's—well, that's sexy, but kind of very direct."

"It's honest. Should I ever lie to you about the jungle beast inside a man? All the great operas and symphonies take these refined cultured people back to smell and taste. If they don't they're the popcorn, not the show."

"OK, Tosca's panties for her Cavaradossi. Just remember she was a jealous woman." She laughed and carried on. The other bag was from Top Shop in Oxford Street. She did *not* want a dress. She chose beige linen trousers and matching jacket. There were some flat grey shoes and a useful bag of cosmetics. Some kind of soul-sister had done her shopping. She took in her look in the wardrobe mirror. She liked it. She liked the slight pout of her lips, the slight forward angle of her pelvis, the slight insolence in her eyes. How she had shriveled, been happy in her nothingness. It had rained and the desert had flowered. And a poor dead husband left to blow away in the dust. How could she have done this?

She had no appetite for breakfast. Tonight, she would feast—if she were still alive. For now, she had to put her own life aside and focus on her duty. There was a text message from Detective Chief Inspector Shannon Knightsmith.

Get a ride to Brixton tube. Get to Vauxhall and walk to the Thames Clipper pier. Take the boat to North Greenwich and walk to the cable car. Someone will be with you all the way. Make no eye contacts. Keep the rucksack on your back. You're a sightless soundless mule. When the final contact is made you just want peace and these drugs out of your life. You have no armor, no weapon, and no angle. De-brief over lunch on me. Shannon x.

How simple it all sounded. Marco was watching her with those warm eyes.

"Can you give me a lift to Brixton?"

"Hey, now you want an Italian to drive you."

"I want an opera singer to drive me. You know, follow the score, follow the conductor."

"OK, you get that metronome guy, tick-tock, tick-tock, four to the bar."

"We need to keep Cressida with us. I need to be sure she doesn't kind of tip off a guy with a gun."

Behind her there was a yell. Helen spun round to see the girl's angry face.

"You fuck, you bitch, is that what you think of me?"

"Honey, my life is built on suspicion not trust. It's not personal, it's survival."

"Well, fuck you. You can't keep me here."

Helen swallowed any spite in her response.

"I'm meeting people we know have guns and are prepared to kill. You think they're your friends because they give you enough shit to kill you too. If keeping me alive means putting you in cuffs, I'll fucking do it and walk away without a look over my shoulder."

Cressida looked down, sobbing.

"I wouldn't sell you out. I was angry because you saw me like that."

Once again, her tough cop reflexes had jumped down her throat. She wanted trust and acceptance more than anything.

"I want to trust you."

"I know I tried to get away, and called them when I promised not to—"

"Honey, addiction is not a personality, it's not a soul, it's a body in prison. You've got a dependency habit and in a few hours' time we're going to start getting you out of jail. You want trust and believe me I want trust from you more than you know. Now let's go."

Helen knew she had to move, sweep the girl up in the necessity of the moment. "Come here."

She held her frail thin body close to her own. "Friends, OK? And friends say what's on their mind. I've got a job to do and then we'll really start to bug each other."

"I want you to come back. I do."

"Then I'll be coming back for both of us."

"And me," added Marco.

If she hadn't known better she would have said his eyes were a little moist with a tear.

He drove sedately like an English gentleman and set her down

68

outside the tube station. Like a knight, he stepped out to open her door. She whispered in his ear.

"I left you something under the covers. Think of me."

Then she was off and away. A cop on a mission. Sure, she'd worn the panties and sure there'd be her own trace mixed with his. Just the thought of her naughtiness thrilled her. She mustn't look at strangers, so she'd stay wrapped up in her dreams.

The tube train was hot and stuffy, maybe no one, maybe everyone was watching her. She was pleased to surface at Vauxhall and walk past the MI5 homeland security headquarters on the south bank of the Thames. It was a lovely day to stroll the embankment, taking in the view of the river and the Houses of Parliament to her left on the far side. It was eerie knowing that she was being followed, probably tracked, by CIA satellites. Maybe her final destination was a bluff, maybe there'd be a snatch at any minute. Don't look round. Just don't look round. For sure the cops had built in this walk along the river bank for a purpose, almost certainly to spot followers. She had to hope that the terrorists believed she was just a civilian and just expected her to show up at the cable car. If anything spooked them she was sure she'd be dead in an instant.

She queued with tourists for the water bus at Waterloo pier as the London Eye towered above. Even her fear and tension couldn't block her thoughts of Marco and the passion they'd shared. When this job was over what the hell could her future be? She could dream but it could never be with him, things like that just never happened. But what did he want from her and what about Cressida? She wasn't a mother and she wasn't a counsellor, but she felt the beginning of a connection with the poor lost kid.

The powerful boat zipped along the water, roaring under Tower Bridge and sliding through the shadows of the Canary Wharf skyscrapers. The thought of what terrorists could do in such a place was terrifying. And the world had already seen what these people could do. The vessel nudged in to North Greenwich Pier. There were maybe fifty passengers, all of whom she had studiously ignored. There was every race and shape of mankind on board and as far as she could tell, no one had given her a glance. A party of schoolchildren with teachers followed her from the pier. Christ, what the hell could they be going to witness? She just kept walking, waiting to buy her ticket. A curt male voice spoke from behind her.

"Don't look round. Get a return."

She used her Oyster card London travel pass. A man was right behind her, now with his hand on the strap of her rucksack. He moved alongside her as they entered the lift to go up to the platform. He put his arm around her shoulder possessively. Now she looked into the profile of his face. It was the mixed-race guy who'd pulled the gun on her when they'd come for the Aston Martin.

"You're even better looking than I remember. You're lucky I'm not asking you to pay for my car."

Her heart was pounding. She was a civilian. She was supposed to be scared and out of her depth. Play the part, Helen.

The party of school kids were all around them, excited. For sure they wouldn't all fit in one car. They arrived at the platform where the cars passed slowly by. A uniformed guard scanned them with a metal detector. He held back the kids and ushered them into the gondola—just her and this guy. He nodded at the guard.

"Thanks, mate. Any time I can help you," he said.

They started to climb the steep slope out of the station. "He's a good man. I told him I wanted to propose to you in mid-air. I even got a ring on the Brick Lane market to show him. Anyway, it wasn't a lie was it? Here's my proposition. I take the bag, you stay on the car and go straight back. If you've set us up there'll be a nice surprise when you get off. I'm just going to make sure you haven't got a cell phone."

"Fuck off. My phone cost good money."

"Yeah, and my Aston Martin was half a million quid."

She had to bite her tongue. She knew the car wasn't his but as a civilian she wouldn't have that information. This guy was a regular East End crook, playing the big man.

"I wanted that car off the drive. I wanted these fucking drugs out of the house and out of our lives. That's all I want. Why set you up? I could have just called the cops."

The guy nodded and gave her an interested once over.

"That opera bloke got himself a nice bit of bitch meat I'd say."

"You touch me and I'll scratch you up so bad you'll have to hide your face for a month."

"Hah! Bit of London girl spirit in you, gal. Chuck the bag down and I'm going to pat you over for a phone or whatever else."

They were hanging 160 feet above the River Thames. A barge beneath them looked like a toy. These gentlemen had thought this out. There was no escape and if she played the cop card she'd certainly be dead and the terrorists would be alerted.

"Raise your arms. I'm going to enjoy this," he said.

"Don't forget your face and I can fucking bite."

She let him pull the phone from her jacket pocket. Thank God it was a cheap supermarket special with no stored numbers.

"Ain't much of a thing for a woman like you is it?" he said examining the cell.

"Not much of a prize for muggers then is it?"

He smiled broadly.

"You're a wise girl. I could really like you."

Just maybe here she could use some wiles and go an extra mile.

"I'm not against you, mate. I'm not out of the top drawer of society myself. Getting rich, getting ahead in this life is tough. I just don't want them drugs near me or the girl. Tell me, did you really buy a ring to con that guard?"

"Yeah, sure I did."

"You're smart, I'll give you that. Can I have it?"

"You're a cheeky cow."

"Yeah, so can I have it or not?"

"Just for your fucking front, I'll give it to you."

He reached into his pocket and pulled out a ring box and opened it. At a glance it was a solitaire diamond.

"Nice bit of brass and glass," she said smiling and taking hold of it. "What was I worth? A fiver?"

"A tenner sweetheart. I ain't no cheapskate."

She laughed. She'd spent a decade on the streets with this flavor of criminal and she was a woman reeling in a puffed-up Mr. Big who liked the ladies.

"So, who's the boss out of you two? I guess it's the white man."

"Fuck off. I manage stuff for some international guys. I'm on the way up."

The gondola was descending into the station on the north side of the river. The guy was standing, holding the rucksack. He stepped off.

"She's staying on," he told the guard.

He walked toward the stairs. The car did a swing round and several passengers joined her for the return trip. A middle-aged woman winked, yes perceptibly winked. She clutched the elbow of an older man, maybe her father who walked hunched with a stick. The stairs away from the platform were still visible. Briefly she saw the white guy who'd tried to start the Aston Martin. Two hooded men were holding him. Then there was a flurry of a struggle and several figures in ski masks flashing knives in a frenzy. She saw the blood gush from the throat of the man who'd taken the bag. As the gondola climbed steeply up to the first pylon all she could see were two men bleeding out on the floor. Could it be a figure was standing over them with a cell phone filming the horror? A couple of the passengers yelled and a pale guy seemed to be panicking. She had no idea what to do. Could she stop the acting? Was there anyone good or bad among the other passengers? She risked a glance at the woman who had winked. She nodded in return with an untroubled expression, turning to look out of the window as if she'd seen nothing."

"We're safe now, son. It's that gang stuff. Bloody knife gangs everywhere now," said an elderly man in a frail voice, touching the pale guy's shoulder. "Wasn't like that years ago. We solved it all with a knuckle sandwich in them days."

The panicky guy calmed. Helen smiled at the old man. For sure he wasn't an agent. She told herself she hadn't noticed anything and looked at the view from the window. The O2 Arena reflected the summer sun with its white roof like a giant albino turtle on the edge of the river bank. The world was turning on and she was a civilian now, free of her package. Someone would tell her when she could stop acting but for now she was just a face in the crowd. She stepped from the gondola and opted for the stairs. The elderly man and his helper kept up with her.

"Black London taxi on the corner over there. Why don't we all share a ride and save some cash," he said.

Was this a trick? How was life possible if you could trust no one? The old guy was walking quickly as his supposed daughter gave a flick with her head towards the cab."

"Look at that cab number. CO185 I think," she said quietly.

Helen jolted. That was her police service number. They knew who she was and instinctively she trusted the woman. The old guy opened the door and spoke to the driver.

"Go, just fucking floor it, but don't show out."

Helen took a jockey seat facing the odd couple. The old man was peeling off a moustache and discarding his thick spectacles.

"Jesus, that was close. Helen, totally brilliant. I'm Henry Boleyn-Percival—you know, from up the road."

Helen had learned that "up the road" meant James Bond territory.

"And I'm PC Paula Middleton. They chose me cos I'm a size sixteen going on eighteen and I look too mumsy for adventure. My old man Max knows these East End thugs and so I'm kind of family. Christ that turned into a bloodbath."

"Who got topped and who did it?"

"Your charmer fiancé was Roly Haskins, a con man, pimp and armed robber on brave days. The other boy was Tam Dashwood. He was a high value car thief and amateur drug dealer. There's going to be some big gangster funerals next week."

"Fiancé? How do you know about that?"

"The cable car was bugged, Helen. You did a great job," said the geriatric special agent. "The ski mask set were true SOHV terrorists. They showed up at the last minute, did the business, and got the video."

"Why the hell do they want a video?"

Henry Boleyn-Percival took a deep weary breath indicating a slight impatience with a dumb cop.

"Terror is the executive arm of a political party called Fear. The Fear party have their agents and tentacles in every area of our lives. Major world leaders are led around by the Fear party. Now and again these guerrilla politicians need to show their power. When the time is right those knife killings will be on YouTube. The message to free people is clear. Vote Fear or we kill you."

Helen listened with a sense of chilling horror. A mob of these terrorists had arrived in London and anyone could be a victim. She had a sudden thought. They were in a public black London cab. She jerked her thumb at the driver who was female and wearing a flat peaked cap. PC Paula Middleton smiled.

73

"I'd thought you'd met Kaitlyn. This is a Job cab—you know, one of ours."

Christ this was a long way from running after dogs. She'd stumbled into a movie set with actors making a story about world politics and mayhem. She wanted her own simple life, her dog Lanza, her home, and maybe just one thing new. Marco, she wanted Marco.

CHAPTER FOURTEEN

Of course, they weren't going to let her slip away and go home. The cab dropped them in Whitehall and they walked separately to New Scotland Yard by different routes. How normal life seemed, even though the English summer had turned to rain. The Horse Guards, Nelson's column in the distance swarming with tourists and regular Londoners, improvised an umbrella ballet. All was calm as a caterpillar of Facebook-selfies gave birth to a butterfly of happy memories. So far.

It seemed that the police world had forgotten her. Helen took the lift to the seventh floor where she'd first met Deputy Assistant Commissioner Anna La Salle. A hand tapped her shoulder.

"Helen, you're a pro. Had eyeballs on you all the way," said Chief Inspector Shannon Knightsmith.

"All the way? Did you catch my engagement in mid-air and the knife orgy after-party?"

"We always thought that the terrorists would waste our local boys. We could have jumped in but we need to follow the trail. Those killings will just go down as routine London knife murders. It's an inside page story for a slow news day."

"So, who's got the package now?"

"Scimitar of Holy Vengeance, in the shape of Badu al Bagwandi. He's scurried away to his little hidey-hole in Newham. Now we need to see who turns up."

"Who did the killings?"

"The leader was Harum Jaba Mushti. He's a veteran of Iraq, Nigeria, and Somalia. The others were clean-skin home grown talent trying to impress. One works in a fried chicken joint and the other drives a delivery van. One's married with a baby, the other's engaged to a girl in Pakistan. You know, just regular boys you'd sit with on the bus. These hard-core terrorists get inside these kids like a virus that takes over their minds. We've got the chance here to cut the head off the snake."

In the conference room a dozen or so operatives of different agencies were already seated. Anna La Salle was talking seriously to a large deep-voiced American who had an air of calm authority. A handsome woman of about fifty in a wheelchair was seated with them and clearly very involved. Anna looked up and acknowledged Helen's arrival with a gesture of her hand, signaling both her and Shannon to go to her office. A few minutes later the big American guy, the woman in the wheelchair, Anna La Salle, and a pretty much film star male in his early thirties joined them. Shannon exchanged air kisses and handshakes. Evidently this was some sort of inside club. She felt very small and out of place. Anna spoke.

"Helen, that was so cool today. Look, I know that you were a cop with a dog just a few days ago. We had to send you on that handover unarmed because those crooks had seen you at the house and they needed to believe the story and pass it on to their bosses. Believe me, none of us slept well knowing what we were asking you to do today. And by the way, here's your cell phone."

"I had a great night," said Helen, dismissing the realization that the phone must have been recovered from the dead body.

Shannon Knightsmith took up the thread.

"We drew your file. Your military record is exemplary with a decoration for gallantry. Your police record has nothing but praise for you. You're in this room because we're sure we can rely on you. These folks are going to tell you who they are."

"Helen, it's an honor to know you and I ask that you give my best wishes to Lanza," began the American. "I'm Michael Harrison, director of the W.I.F, that's the World Intelligence Forum. My lady colleague is Stella Boursellino, CEO of Sackman-Platinum Bank and the young apprentice is Mr. Randolph Quinn. For now, I'll just say it's great to have you on board. Let's just agree we're here working with your government and all other agencies. Our story is too long to tell now, but please understand that whatever you have to do will be with our authority. And I mean, whatever is necessary to beat these murderers."

Helen realized that she was staring open-mouthed at him.

"Honey, he means if you have to waste a few of these bastards, just suck it up and enjoy your work," said Stella in a smoky American voice.

"What? Authority from a bank?"

Helen's mind couldn't absorb this crazy dump of information.

"Everything will become clear. For now, just keep your mouth shut and understand that there's a world of good guys backing you up. In fact, I'm such a good guy that I'm going to order us all some coffee," said the young hunk she remembered as Randolph.

"I'd love a cup of Yorkshire Gold tea," said Shannon laughing, "but it's a bit too luxurious for Scotland Yard."

"I'll have a tea," said Helen, unable to stop a smile at the surreal comedy of it all.

Randolph spread his hands and looked to the ceiling.

"Why do girls always want what's not on offer?"

He really was quite a dish. Helen watched his slow perfect smile as his eyes fell on her. But the effect was nothing like Marco. His smile was like the warmth of the sun and everything else was a cold distant star. She was alive and maybe they could be together at least one more time.

Anna touched her arm.

"We want you to stay close to Cressida Ambastilias. Her dead friend, Peter Lodovitch, was the link between all of her circle of friends. We believe they targeted him because of his drug addiction and for sure they've tried to hook as many of these kids as possible. But why? But *why*? Needless to say, we want you to find out by getting in amongst them. Are you OK with that?"

"Do they know I'm a cop?"

"Not yet but we can't ever be sure that someone won't find out. Cressida knows it could endanger your life and the team who interviewed her feels she's just about OK to trust. We do know she's our weakest link. Remember, this is all about drugs. Any leak about terrorists could send this city into a mass panic with citizens attacking anyone who looked different or had a different faith. Scimitar of Holy Vengeance want to provoke that kind of stupid shit."

"Of course, I'll do it. I'd like to be able to be with Lanza, too, and has anyone asked Marco if he wants me around his house or life?"

Helen was certain that Anna flicked a look at Shannon with a knowing expression in her eye.

"A woman kind of feels stuff like that for herself, doesn't she? Besides, he's a father and a citizen wanting to help make a better world."

Helen nodded agreement. Anna La Salle was no fool and for sure she knew or had guessed Marco's sentiments.

Randolph came back with coffees and two teas.

"A cup of the old Rosie Leigh for a couple of English roses," he said in a smooth mid-Atlantic tone. Helen liked his cheeky-boy London style. He was gorgeous and knew it. If he had a special girlfriend she'd be unwise to let him stray too far unsupervised.

"Let's start the main meeting. Helen, welcome to the team. Remember, no one but us ever talks about this group."

Dickon Maltravers from "up the road" chaired the conference.

"You know who I am. I know most of you, so let's go. Bit of a mess out there on the pavement, but no worries. So, where are we now? Bagwandi has the explosives. We don't know if there are more and we have no idea what they're going to do. So far, no other SOHV personnel have appeared. We know who the knife-men are and we're letting them run. If they use them again it will most likely be as suicide bombers. Our FBI friends are telling us that they're intercepting internet traffic indicating up to twenty active terrorists are in London. OK, now for the big news."

He paused, drank a sip of water, and pointed to a picture coming up on a screen behind his head. "This man needs no introduction. I'm showing you a picture to prove I'm a master of digital technology in case you think I'm some old duffer."

Helen and most others in the room chuckled. He had a sense of humor even though he was as important as a man could be.

"Yes, it's our old mate Kashi ben Quaffir, lunatic fanatic leader of Scimitar of Holy Vengeance. He's the high priest of murder and holds no religious faith except his own twisted theology of power. Ladies and gentlemen, kneel down because he is amongst us. Somewhere, and boy would we like to know where. We know he took off in a private plane from Tripoli and flew under the radar into Spain. Sources tell us that he entered Britain in the back of a truck loaded with oranges, which delivered to a supermarket depot on the edge of London. CIA satellites have located a GPS positioning trace of a cell phone linked to him. He's here, and if he's here he wants to pose on top of whatever pile they're planning. Finally, let's not overlook the Russians. Forget regular politics served up to the masses. They're here to kill these lunatics and they're not too bothered about collateral damage. We want to identify the whole network and if the Russians kill them on UK soil, that would of course be a breach of diplomatic protocols. I also don't give a shit. They've got some tough agents and believe me, I'm not trying to fall out with them. Let's just say that we have the same targets and don't be surprised if we end up working together. I've been assured by their government, and *we all know that's just one guy*, that his operatives will not cross swords with ours. You've just got to trust brothers and sisters—until someone shits on your doorstep. Go to it."

Helen found herself looking blankly into space. What the hell was going to happen? At any minute citizens could be attacked by terrorists. Even though one pack of explosive had been neutralized, there could be more and they had a dozen ways to carry out their holy vengeance. To play her own part she had to get to grips with Cressida and she had no idea where to start.

"Kaitlyn's outside if you want a ride," said Shannon.

She could get used to this life of luxury vehicles and professional drivers. She flopped into the front seat of a black Jaguar XF and let out a long sigh. How normal the world looked.

"Bit of a day?" asked Kaitlyn, easing the car around Parliament Square.

"Just too much really. In the army and as a dog handler they give you a job and there's some sort of job description. This is just freestyle."

Kaitlyn gave a warm laugh.

"Helen, I know exactly how you feel. There was a day before I met Randolph and then a crazy ride into a world out of control."

"Randolph? I just met a guy by that name."

"That's my boy—and he's going to stay that way."

"You and him are—"

"Absolutely, totally. I took a call to a traffic accident and there he was. You could make a movie about the rest."

"I wasn't expecting to meet Marco Ambastilias."

"He's a bit of catch in my book and don't tell me he hasn't noticed you."

It had been a long time since Helen had talked to another woman about a man. Most other dog handlers were male and in truth, her closest friend was Lanza, and even he had balls. This girl with her exotic tattoo seemed open and friendly.

"Can you mix police work and personal involvement?"

"Of course you can. If you get a guy with a bit of a uniform fetish it saves a fortune on buying one from an online sex shop."

"So, no lecture on duty and moral ethics."

Kaitlyn laughed again.

"Sugar, you can beat yourself to a pulp trying not to have fun in this life. It's legal and you want it, so do it."

"Do what?"

"Take your chances or shall we say, open yourself to happiness."

For some reason, perhaps because she didn't know this woman, she allowed herself to share her feelings. It was a fair guess that Anna La Salle or Shannon Knightsmith had briefed her with what civilians called gossip.

"I'm assuming you know my husband died in Afghanistan. I genuinely loved him, never thought there'd be another man for me. Even kind of dreaming about another guy seems a betrayal."

She decided not to reveal her actions had gone far beyond dreams.

"Sure, you feel survivor's guilt in any case. What you shouldn't do is transfer guilt to your husband because he wouldn't have wanted you lonely and unable to love again. All you're doing then is blaming him for *your* fear of commitment to a full life."

Helen felt a surge of tears. Kaitlyn was direct but also accurate, although she didn't want to concede the point quite yet."

"It's a fantastic help to talk to you."

"Any time, provided I can hit you with my own worries and conflicts."

"Any time to you, too."

The car dropped her at Marco's house. Perhaps now she had a girlfriend. And now, she could begin—something.

CHAPTER FIFTEEN

This was crazy. She'd come to Marco's house, but she didn't live here. Sure, she'd been here the night before because she'd had to collect the parcel and keep on top of Cressida. The police bosses wanted her here, but did he? Did he?

He opened the door as she approached. His arms were around her.

"I hate this. You go off and do whatever you did. You didn't come back and no one tells me where you are. Now you're here, thank God."

"Thank you."

"For what?"

"For holding me, for caring."

"It's not a gift, it's a desire and I'm saying thanks for coming back to me."

She wanted to hold this moment. She was a plain foot soldier cop, rubbing shoulders with mega chiefs, let alone a world opera star. It had been quite a day.

"I came here because I wanted to be with you, not because my bosses want that."

"So, you can stay?"

"You really, really want that? Cressida may not want a police officer grafted onto her life."

"We can deal with that and I can see a difference in her since you've been here. By the way Simon Leonard called in to say that Lanza is up and eating. He's ready to go home."

"Then I'll take him home."

"Bring him here, if you have to do other work we can care for him."

"Marco, Lanza is *my* responsibility. A sick dog may make a mess, may be difficult, may not fit in with your own dog, Sam."

"I'll talk to Sam over a few beers. That's the way guys do business."

"Lanza has his own bed at home."

"First we get his bed, then we get the hero himself, like now."

"Now?"

"Did I ever tell you I wasn't impetuous?"

"And I never want to hear that. Let's go."

At the front door behind Marco, Helen spotted Cressida.

"Hey, Lanza can come out of the hospital. Shall we all go and get him?"

"Me too?"

"Of course you too."

Helen watched a smile bud and flower on the girl's face. Inclusion, that magic glue which could join together fractured worlds had shown its power.

Marco's driving was an aria of angry passion and the heartbreak of love denied. Cressida and Helen shared complicit glances at his black comedy of car control. They picked up the dog bed and some extra clothes from her house in Streatham and spilled out into the hospital. Simon, the veterinarian welcomed them in his office.

"His chest is still healing and will be weak for months yet. Plenty of fluids and let him do as much he wants to do; he can feel what he can manage. Needless to say, his working days are over."

The door opened and a nurse led Lanza in, holding him by a soft surgical neck brace. Helen knelt to hold him as he almost cried in happiness to see her. Once the licking of hands and faces was concluded she took him to the car where he sat upright and alert on the back seat, ears pricked, tongue flapping, eyes keen. Life could be shit, but it could also be so beautiful. Marco drove with a studied sedateness, obviously aware of his precious cargo. Lanza needed help down from the car and winced a little with some movements. All he had to do now was meet Sam the black Labrador. Cressida went inside and brought him out on a lead. Just by his tail wagging it was clear he was pleased to have a friend. All the same Helen knew that dogs needed to know where they stood in order of importance. Lanza sat down as the Labrador sniffed around him, signaling his lack of fear and concern. Some instinct must have told Sam that this older bigger dog was injured but proud. Cressida let him off the leash. In a flash Sam scampered indoors and came back with his rubber chewing ring, concluding by dropping it in front of Lanza. Without a growl or a raising of hackles, the two boys walked together into the house, Lanza holding the ring.

"Just like that, magic," said Marco.

"If only the world was populated by dogs," Cressida commented.

This was a good hurdle to clear, but Helen knew there was a long climb ahead.

"I can see he's very weak and only a shadow of himself. He'll need a lot of love and care."

Cressida smiled with a sudden warmth.

"I'll be here if you have to work. It's great for Sam to have a companion."

"There's no one who doesn't need a friend."

Once they'd installed the dog bed in the utility room and ensured the boys were settling in, Helen could relax. She sat with Marco in the lounge watching the evening London local news. A reporter was covering the two stabbing deaths but gave few details.

"This knife crime is terrible. The people you met today could have stabbed you," he said.

"All that stuff's just between gangs, I simply met them at Vauxhall tube station and said goodbye. I didn't even see a dinner knife and that reminds me I'm hungry."

"You smell the smoke? The barbecue is on in the garden. Grilled Mediterranean sardines with a salad tossed in olive oil and Balsamic vinegar di Modena."

This man, this lovely man was filled with passion, flavor and color. A simple meal was an act of passion. She'd fired the question before she'd thought.

"Why don't you sing again, Marco? You need to express what's inside you."

"Inside me there is only this little accidental family. OK, I leave you and my child and travel the world to sing into the eyes of famous beautiful divas."

His response almost stunned her. He had thought through her possible jealousy. Her life was piling up with guilt.

"Marco, you don't owe me any loyalty. Your life and talent are bigger than my little foot-soldier existence."

"Life and the mystery of space and time is bigger than all of us, but my feelings about you are between you and me."

Did he have feelings for her? Did she want that burden of responsibility?

"I'll be frank with you. My bosses want me to learn more about Cressida's circle of friends. Somewhere there's a Mr. Big who set out to ensnare these kids with hard drugs. I'll be straight with her and I'm being straight with you. Like you say, we're an accidental family, like guys thrown together in an army truck to get up to the front. When the war is over...."

"Then you're a cop and I'm a singer. I know you English love your class system but would we be jailed if we still kissed?"

She looked at his soft dark eyes and gave up. Simply gave up.

"I'll lock you up if you don't ever kiss me again," she said.

He pulled her to him and this time kissed her with warmth rather than heat, with love rather than erotic desire. His moods and tones were nuances of reflection and emotion. He stroked her cheeks and her hair, leaving her without resistance, her every thought just translating to words without her normal filters.

"Now I know what makes you so great. First a song is a passion, a regret or whatever. Then you add the gestures and the voice, but first it is the essence of raw truth."

He held her as if she had fused into his body.

"No one ever says these things to me before. Maybe the great directors, the very, very great only know these things. But, I can never hold them in my arms or kiss their lips. For sure I can't cook them sardines."

He kissed her once more and hurried to the garden. Sam and Lanza were making a sedate tour of the property. It was a warm evening in early June. These other innocents didn't know what dangers paced in the shadows, stalking their prey, counting down to their moment. And she could never warn them without betraying her true purpose. One day they would know she was lying to them and they would judge her for it. That didn't mean she couldn't live for the moment. A table was set in the warm late sun. Cressida arrived with a carafe of rich red wine and poured a glass for herself. She took food and garlic bread, only pausing her meal to stroke the dogs. Lanza had been trained not to beg at table but Sam was a gipsy violinist, who played the sad-eyed urchin. Lanza seemed to watch this behavior in amazement, drooling with temptation, glancing between Helen and his impertinent undisciplined house-mate. Marco refilled the wine as they let the sun slide down toward other dawns in other lives. Yes, where was there ever to live, other than in the moment?

She stroked Lanza's head, filleted the flesh of a sardine from her plate and fed it to him from her palm. He ate and repaid her with a look of pure sin and civilian ecstasy.

CHAPTER SIXTEEN

How the hell could it be that sexual desire could embrace her with everything else that was on her agenda? Marco had suggested a hot tub soak and she could imagine no higher bliss, although she'd only ever seen such things on TV. Cressida offered to stay with the dogs in case there was an issue. Somehow, caring for Lanza was giving her a sense of purpose. Helen almost felt a stab of jealousy as she watched the girl stroke him, and his evident happiness. She was a natural with animals and Helen knew that was a massive talent.

"Do you mind if I help to care for him? He's your little boy."

"Sharing and letting go are the greatest acts of love. Of course I don't mind. One love never replaces another. It adds to it."

"You say some weird stuff for a cop."

"What stuff should cops say?"

Helen chuckled, kneeling between Sam and Lanza, sharing her love with precision.

"Cops stick to facts."

"Sure. Lanza trusts you and feels secure. And that's a fact from a cop."

She kissed Cressida on both cheeks in the way foreign and theatrical people regarded as normal. She walked away to the house with both dogs looking up to her as if she were some great orchestral conductor.

Marco pointed to a kind of pagoda at the far end of his wooden decking.

"This is your doh-ray-me time. You relax and I sing."

"Marco, have you been rehearsing that line?"

"Of course. You think I don't practice?"

"I think I want you to perform all over me and tell me if you found the panties I left for you."

"Of course I found them. Now you want me to tell you of my disgusting passion for your human body and then express my spiritual need for your soul?"

"I guess I wanted to know if my sex scent made you want to fuck me?"

He was still seated in front of her at the table. He closed his eyes and let out a deep sigh.

"You're so real and so sexy. Yes, yes, if you want me to tell you."

"Did you hold them to your face? Did you want to come thinking of me?"

"Yes, of course…."

"I love that Marco. I'm feeling wet and horny thinking of that."

"Did you touch your cock? I'd love that—if you'd jerked off on my panties."

"Helen, look, well yes, I wanted to, but I wanted for us to be together again."

"As lovers, as scent-driven beasts?"

"Yes, not just that."

Maybe the wine, maybe her recent brushes with death and for sure her dangerous future had released all her anchors. From his face and from his breathing she could feel her own raw sex need was drawing a pure erotic response from him. Where was her behavior coming from?

"You want to fuck a hot pussy that's wet for you?"

"Helen—yes, but with…."

She knew he wanted to dress it up, as if life were on a stage. She wanted it real.

"With your big hot cock coming in my belly."

"But with more…."

"More?"

"More, like yes, you excite me but I want to express feeling for you."

Fuck. She'd taken him as the actor but the truth was that he was genuine while she wanted to believe that this could be only hard sex. That way there was no betrayal of her dead husband. Yes, she was falling in love with him. Yes, he had re-awakened her strong sexual desire. She just had to keep those two warring tribes apart. Marco Ambastilias couldn't be, wouldn't be reduced to meat. Yes, she was falling. If only she could keep it physical she could come out the other side in one piece.

"Can you express feeling by getting in that tub with me?"

"It'd be a great place to start."

She couldn't wait. She felt empowered by her wantonness and his sexual desire for her. Merely his presence turned her on. He was an artistic and creative hero of a man while she could play the warrior queen. It was only a role, but to play a part was not to be herself, not to carry her mental guilt into her bodily pleasure. They stripped off in the pagoda. Her nakedness had aroused him. He pulled her to him and kissed her lips, cupping her sex with his hand. Pings of pre-orgasm trembled through her thighs. Her hot wetness brought a groan from deep inside him. She glanced at his straining cock, the tip wet with his juice. She slid into the water looking up at him standing above her. The powerful jets stimulated her whole body.

"I'm a naughty girl, Marco. I'm feeling very cummy looking at your cock. I should stop, shouldn't I?"

A pulse of water caressed her clitoris. Deliberately she held her pelvic floor muscles, climbing the stairs to release. She brought up her hands and fondled her nipples. His eyes were on her, his voice came thick with lust.

"I want to see you...."

"You want to see me come?"

"Yes, do it, be naughty."

"I'm having sexy thoughts...."

She almost doubled over as the pulse of her climax shot spasms through her belly and into her sex.

"You're coming in my pussy, fuck, cum in me."

She abandoned herself to the pleasure of her own flesh and also the pleasure of whipping up his lust, to send him out of control. Aftershocks of orgasm brought bestial groans from her lips. Maybe in her loss of self she was ugly or feral. Her sounds made her feel wild but also free. She had closed her eyes, wanting him to see her animal surrender to pleasure and fantasy. She knew this vulnerable gift of intimacy was dangerous to her, took her too close to the sun where she could melt into him. She was calming now. It was only sex. She had control. It was only sex.

He had slipped into the water, taking her into his arms.

"That was very beautiful," he said.

"Me?"

"You and what you shared with me."

His huge hot cock was against her belly. Its presence made her long for him inside her.

"Sit on the edge," she said.

He raised himself on his strong, dark-haired arms. She cradled his balls and drew the head of his cock into her mouth. Powerful jets of water coursed against her sex as she ran her tongue around the rim. Looking up at him she watched his expression of desire and abandon. She could feel he was close.

"I want your cum in my pussy."

He groaned and pulled away, stood up and bent to take her hands. In an instant she was out as he bent her forward over a handrail. He was behind her, his massive dick finding her hot drenching entrance. His hand held her thigh as he drove into her, filling her to the limit with his flesh and his need to release. His lips came to her neck as he surged in and out of her, sending pulses of climbing ecstasy through her body.

She couldn't hold back. She was coming.

"Do it in me," she blurted in grunts.

She felt his tremble and his final thrust of pouring release.

"Helen, oh my Helen," he groaned, squeezing her shoulders with strong but tender hands. Still, he was hard and buried inside her, the jolts of his release endlessly throbbing in her squeezing sex. She craved his hot seed in her, could smell the muskiness of his ejaculation and her own wild fluid. A final shudder of his cock pushed her over the edge to another orgasm, demanding her body to suck his male juice into her flesh. He turned her to kiss him, pushing his hands back through her hair tightly as if to possess her. He looked into her face.

"No moment of my life has ever been like this, what I feel, how I want you."

"Oh, Marco—Marco, I'm trying not to let go."

She was looking up into his eyes. For now, it was useless to resist. In the morning she would push back. But not now.

She slept in his arms, letting go of all care and sense of self. She was safe and held. Inside her she carried his marker, his semen, in the way that nature had meant a man and woman to be. The fusion of male and female that was the only worthwhile truth beyond all the politics of gender and dominance. Male and female at their furthest points from each other defined a harmony of physical joy.

She awoke in the light of dawn. For a while she turned over in her mind how she would approach her mission with Cressida. She needed the girl to trust her but was deceiving her as to the true nature of the investigation. A mob of terrorists was on the loose and she needed to work fast. Why did Scimitar of Holy Vengeance want to insinuate themselves with a group of kids from wealthy and influential families?

She wanted to reach out for Marco, show him tenderness and affection. There could be no future here and she needed to keep a sense of reality. This man gave her great sex. Many women and probably even more men would just settle for that. She had to stop dreaming and thinking of him outside of the deal.

"Will you ever sing again?"

Her mind had just spilled out the question and she knew at once she would care about his answer.

"Ah, you're planning to nag me."

His tone was playful, but serious.

"Yes, would that be OK?"

"Tell me, Helen, would you be there with me if I did?"

"Don't put that responsibility on me. It would depend on my shift rota and if I could get a dog sitter."

"Maybe you could try to be there, if it were convenient?"

"Of course."

He pushed her onto her side and played kisses along her back and shoulders.

"It would be easier to admit you have feelings about this affair, my sweet lover."

"How do you know I have feelings?"

"Because I'm a human, probably made a lot like you. Didn't we all descend from the same two hundred women?"

"I'm a hard-core creationist."

90

"So, you're my rib."

"I took it to give more room for your lungs, so maybe you could sing a bit."

"I'm gathering you want me to sing."

She swiveled over to face him. She couldn't pretend she didn't care.

"Yes, for the world."

"There's seven billion souls in this world and I was just wondering about one of them."

"So, you stopped because you wanted to be with Cressida?"

"Yes, I wanted to be father to her. A real person."

"Now she knows the world is a poorer place because of her. I mean she's a kid and all that guilt is a bit too much."

"I'd be a fool if I couldn't see that for myself."

"So?"

"So, I'm enjoying not performing, not being surrounded by gushing pouting jealous egotistical insecure showbiz types. God, if only you knew how I love having you in my life."

"Soldier girl and cop is a long way from diva, I guess."

"And a long way from Hollywood."

She hesitated before answering him. Obviously, he was referring to his ex, Zelda Mitchell, who'd left him for a ballet director. Did she want to go there? She couldn't imagine why any woman would ever leave Marco Ambastilias but didn't want to express it.

"Cressida is no showbiz girl. You've got to trust her to see through all that tinsel. She's a natural with animals and she tells me she wants to do science."

"She needs someone like you to guide her."

"Like Maria in the Sound of Music."

"Like Helen Marx."

Well, that was a pretty direct remark which she couldn't bat away casually as if he'd asked about the weather forecast. After all, she was in his bed, had moved in her dog and was going to be squeezing his daughter for police intelligence.

"OK, like a plain little sparrow in a universe of peacocks. Marco, when this drug enquiry is over, when the investigation into the death of Peter Lodovitch is closed, that's an end to things."

"Things?"

"Yes, but not this thing."

She reached for his cock. He gave a groan of pleasure. He rolled her onto her back and eased his hand to her sex, immediately soothing and teasing her clitoris. His lips came to her nipple, pinging thrilling jolts to her hard little lady cock.

"I love it when you come," he whispered.

She was high and climbing, holding the ascent, holding and longing, feeling his hot cock swelling in her hand, feeling his wetness as her need stimulated him. Yes, her orgasm burst out of her pussy and her mouth.

"Yes, cum, fuck."

She was wet and craving his hot cock inside her. He moved above her and pressed at her entrance. She kicked off the bedding and raised her legs either side of him, spreading herself wide and open. He eased in to her, filling her and finding her sweet spot. He moved in and out tirelessly, driving her closer and closer, his balls rhythmic against her ass cheeks. She watched his face, the evident bliss behind his eyelids. His movement was faster now. She wanted to watch him come.

"I love it when you come, Marco."

He opened his eyes as she reached for his buttocks. She couldn't hold back. She had to let go her spasms of ultimate oblivion and abandon. His eyes were blurring into a loss of self, of surrender to lust. He was close. She brought her hand to her clitoris.

"Look at me. I'm a naughty girl—fuck, cum in me."

His eyes caught the movement of her hand. She was openly masturbating with a hot cock inside her. She loved his gaze on her bad-girl exhibition. She was shameless and brazen. She was beginning to come so hard as both his straining ruthless cock and her own touch fired her convulsion of joy. Marco gave a deep grunt as his juice poured into her open body. His cock was deep, deep inside her, the jolts of his release meeting the contractions of her pussy.

"Woman, Helen, I love you," he growled.

She folded her legs behind his back, keeping him inside, shuddering with pleasure as his juice flowed into the twitching heat of her belly. She wanted that hot cum inside her so much. God, she'd never felt this way. Her mind played a fantasy of his sperm shooting and oozing from his tip. This was total loss of control, a total letting go of everything. Her mind was spinning. Now she'd found this expression in her soul, how could she ever stop? And, had he said "Love"?

CHAPTER SEVENTEEN

In the kitchen, Cressida had already organized Sam and Lanza.

"He needs to eat and keep hydrated," she announced.

Her little boy was a good patient and already looking stronger.

"Shall we try him with a small walk on the downs?" asked Helen.

"Do you think he'll remember what happened to him out there?"

"Yeah, he'll know. He'll be fine if he feels secure."

Helen noted that already Cressida looked healthier. She knew a wounded dog needed to eat and the information appeared to have rooted in her own consciousness. They sauntered out of the back gate into a lovely summer morning of birdsong and blue sky.

"So, what are you going to do with your summer?"

"Maybe a lot of the usual stuff, you know, Royal Ascot, Wimbledon tennis, Henley Regatta, Goodwood Races, Garston Opera, a couple of balls and the normal royal garden parties at Buckingham Palace or Windsor."

"That sort of entertainment isn't usual for most of us. Either you can't get tickets, or you just aren't on the guest list. Do you enjoy that kind of event?"

"Who doesn't love free champagne, caviar and the whole royal family and government thing? A lot of honors and jobs are sorted out at these occasions. If you want to whisper in an influential ear, you just have to be there. For me it's where I get to see my friends. If you want tickets or passes we've all got loads."

"Let's see how my work goes, but thanks. It sounds so glamorous."

"It can be a drag but you get to dress up and like I say, mix with the top brands like Martell, Moet et Chandon, Bollinger."

"Afghan heroin?"

Cressida's face clouded with anger.

"That's cheap."

"That's a cop's view of the world."

"I know you want to find out how Peter died and who supplied him with drugs. You want me to inform on my friends, too?"

"I do want information, but I'm not looking to lock up anyone, except maybe some murderers. Don't you guys care about Peter Lodovitch?"

"I care, but some of these people are like, so up themselves that no one else exists."

"From what you know, how many of your group use drugs?"

"Like everyone, duh. Like you know we're generation K. Like festivals, like clubbing, everyone gets in a K-hole at some point."

"I'm feeling my age. Some police training course is telling me you're talking about Ketamine, like duh, it's a horse tranquillizer drug. And Peter supplied it?"

"Pretty much, that's it."

"You know, I'm going to make a guess here. I don't think you use it. I think you want to talk the talk but you've got too much sense to walk the walk. You have or had an issue with amphetamine, right?"

"Yeah, but I don't want that shit in my life. I don't, I don't. Why the hell do you have to be a cop?"

"What difference does that make?"

"I want to believe in you, trust you."

"I want that too."

Helen just launched the words because that was what she had to do. Maybe it wasn't a total lie? She wanted to identify and arrest terrorists but that didn't mean she didn't want to stand by this poor lonely kid.

"My friend Karine de Robinet is coming over this morning. I know her from my school in Switzerland. She's sweet, so please don't say anything to her about Peter. I won't mention Lanza and if she asks I'll just say you're Papa's girlfriend and you've got a dog. We'll probably go up west to shop for Royal Ascot."

"Sure, it would be great to meet her."

A cream-colored vintage Jaguar XK150 cabriolet pulled up in front of the house. The driver was a middle-aged man in a tweed jacket and peaked cap. A skittish girl jumped out. Cressida ran out to greet her friend as the car roared away.

"Daddy's getting ready for Goodwood Festival of Speed and of course the Silverstone Grand Prix. You *are* coming with us, aren't you?" gushed the girl.

Helen held back. Just as a spectator, she was beginning to get a flavor of the English wealthy upper class in their summer plumage.

"That'd be so, so fun, Karine. Of course, I'll be there."

Helen shook hands and noted the polite way that the young guest kicked off her trainers before running up the stairs with Cressida. Life had dealt her this hand of friends and she needed them like any person of any age.

She heard the tap of dog claws as Sam and Lanza wandered into the marble floored hallway. Suddenly Lanza whined, sniffing the trainers. He sat on his haunches, pointing his nose and let out a growly yelp that Helen knew so well. Explosives! Lanza was giving his crooked good-boy smile.

"I've got it covered," she said.

Christ, what could or should she do now? Was Karine carrying a bomb or had she been exposed to a trace of explosive chemicals? She hadn't seen a bag and the girl was only wearing very light clothes. A dog has three hundred million smell receptors giving them forty times the ability of a human. Lanza would pick up the merest trace. Helen's instinct was not to panic but probably that was only because she wasn't a panicky person. The two girls scampered down the stairs, carefree, hand in hand. A waiting Uber cab driver called Cressida's cell phone. Karine slipped on her trainers and skipped to the door.

"Ciao everybody. Back for dinner," called Cressida.

Now she had a problem. She had to check in with her bosses, but she also needed to think. Think Helen. Think! A scenario was playing in her mind. If Karine had received some drugs from a source who had been near an explosive, that source would lead to a terrorist. These kids and their families would be attending all the circuses of the great and the good. They had VIP access to all the inner circles and all the royal enclosures. What if the plan were to take out the government, the top bankers of the City of London and unthinkably, the Queen of England and her family? Could that be? Would anyone listen to a dog cop with a hunch?

She felt Lanza's wet nose nudging her hand. She smiled down at him.

"Good boy. I haven't forgotten your treat," she said, reaching into the pocket of her jeans. Sam's eyes did his gipsy violin pleading. How could she deny him? She was glad of a banal moment to think. She needed to talk to her bosses but she needed Marco not to hear. She walked through the garden gate and out onto the down land. Eventually DCI Shannon Knightsmith answered. Her tone was tense and hurried.

"Yup?"

"It's Helen Marx. I've got a bit of a lead."

"Is your dog on the end of it?" Shannon's manner was kind of witty but stressed. "Look, we've got a bit of a situation. There's been a failed bomb attack on a crowded tube train. The detonator worked fine but it looks like they used the stuff we modified. The bomber is burned but alive. I'm thinking aloud here. SOHV will soon figure out the trick and know it was you who handed over the parcel. Keep a low profile. I'll call you back."

"Please do, I may know what the whole plan is."

"Give me ten minutes. Get a coffee. I'm trying to stall the press and keep control here."

She turned to go back to the house. A tall broad man had approached from behind and blocked her path. She hadn't even heard him. He was unshaven but wore a crumpled linen suit, almost English upper-class style with a cricket club tie. One word flashed into Helen's mind—commando!

"The whole plan? I don't imagine I was part of it," he said.

"Who the fuck are you?"

"We can be friends, Helen. I'm Bastian Wolf and many of your guys know me. Let's say I represent Eastern commercial interests."

"Russia?"

"Let's just say a wealthy father of a murdered son."

She appraised this rock-hard bundle of muscle and self-confidence. His rugged face carried a couple of scars and something of a boxer's nose. His full head of fair hair was cropped and added to a cold brutality in his nature. His accent carried a trace of a Germanic tongue.

"So how do you know who I am and what do you want?"

"We'll get to that. First let me say how you impressed me with that package handover. I love a boat trip on your London Thames."

"You were there?"

"I was there. Now, there's been an incident with our SOHV friends. Some brainwashed kid burned his dick off at Oxford Circus tube station. He'd hoped for two hundred dead, so he didn't make killer of the month on the office chart."

"How do you know all this?"

"You may think your computers and cell phones are secure. There's guys in Moscow who eat digital code for breakfast."

Helen couldn't help some kind of admiration for this cool operator. She just knew his background was military.

"You've been hired to find who killed Peter Lodovitch?"

"I know that already. They got themselves stabbed at the cable car station."

"So, you're done, job finished."

"Not quite. There's a terrorist cell on the loose in London. They controlled those low-life crooks who murdered Peter. Would you like me to whisper something in your ear?"

"I've nothing to lose, have I?"

"Code Sirius."

Helen raked through her mind. Code Sirius was familiar. Yes, Anna La Salle had said that when she'd handed over the package to the army guys. Bastian Wolf seemed super-informed but probably he was bluffing.

"Means nothing to me. I'm a dog handler."

"It means that your own British government has authorized your agencies to work with us, Captain Marx. Me, I'm ex-Dutch Korps Commandotroepen. Colonel Wolf at your service, madam."

She was certain he was telling the truth, at least about himself.

"Nice to meet you. What the fuck do you want?"

"Since I arrived when you were about to tell your boss how you'd figured out the whole deal, I'd love to share in the moment when he or she calls back. If it's Shannon tell her I'm here. She knows me well."

From the house she heard Lanza barking and that would be

painful. The tone was aggressive. There was trouble. Should she run back and let this guy follow her? Sam had joined in the noise even though he didn't have any aggression. She had no choice. She turned and ran through the garden to the house. She saw Marco in the hallway, hands up. Facing him was an African guy holding an AK47 machine gun. Lanza was by Marco's side, snarling a warning. If she gave the command, he would attack and certainly die. He was too weak to fight but his stand-off growl had stalled the gunman, giving them this split-second chance. Could she demand this one last act of courage from him? A crack of a single shot from behind deafened her. The machine gunner collapsed as blood sprayed from the back of his head, a neat bullet entry point between his eyes. Bastian Wolf walked past her calmly, slipping his Walther PPK automatic back into his shoulder holster. He bent over the body to assess his work and search the pockets. With dexterous ease he neutralized the machine gun, removed the bullet clip and recovered the round in the chamber. He pocketed a cell phone, a set of keys, and a wallet.

"Not bad. Helen, this is Harum Jaba Mushti. I don't suppose he had the good manners to introduce himself."

Marco looked at her in perplexed horror and confusion.

"The doorbell went, I opened it and this man pushed in with a gun." He stared at the body and at Bastian. "Who is this man? Who the hell are you? Why are you in my house?"

Helen reached out for him. She had to remember that Marco knew nothing about SOHV and she couldn't tell him. How could she explain without some outrageous lie? In any case who was this Dutch commando? Her cell phone was ringing. She could see it was Shannon.

"Sorry about that earlier. We're stable now. What's up?"

"I don't know where to begin. Do you know Bastian...?"

"Bastian bloody Wolf. I've heard he was here. He's an evil bastard, but he'd always be first on my team list."

"He's here. He's just shot a guy dead in Marco's entrance hall."

"That sounds like Bastian. I'll be with you in twenty minutes. Give him a coffee and tell him not to touch anything."

Marco walked tentatively to the body pooling blood onto his floor.

"Helen, I just don't understand anything. This man is dead. Shouldn't we be calling someone?"

"The police are on it. My boss is on her way."

"Who's this man? Why is he here?"

Bastian had made friends with the two dogs. Clearly this kind of deal was just a day in the office.

"Sir, Mr. Ambastilias, I came to meet this gentleman on the floor. I have contacts who told me he was coming. I thought maybe I could help."

How could she expect Marco to understand?

"I believe he saved our lives," said Helen.

"So, you gave the drugs back to the dealers. That was supposed to be the end of it. This guy seems more like a terrorist or lunatic."

She shot a glance at Bastian. He picked up her meaning and stayed quiet.

"So, who are you? Are you a policeman?"

"I'm a concerned citizen, sir. I work with the police but today I represent Mr. Ivan Lodovitch. You may know his son was murdered."

"You carry a gun?"

"Yes, that was a lucky chance for you, wasn't it?"

"Shall we get a coffee?" asked Helen. "My boss will be here in a minute."

CHAPTER EIGHTEEN

They went through to the kitchen. She calmed herself and made a cafetière of strong coffee. At least it took Marco's eyes off the corpse and gave her time to think.

A maroon BMW 740i pulled up outside behind an unfamiliar white Ford Mondeo which Helen guessed belonged to the dead man. She opened the door, aware of the growing buzz of flies around the body on the floor. Marco had fallen into a state of silent anguish. Suddenly he spoke.

"Cressida and her friend are up the West End. If we're some sort of target so are they."

Helen pretended not to have heard him He had a very good point. Shannon walked in and shot a glance at the bloody scene.

"Jesus Christ! Bastian you're a pro but the entry wound is just a tad to the left."

"I noticed that myself. Shannon, great to see you again."

The two of them hugged and exchanged continental cheek kissing. She pulled back and adopted a senior and serious manner.

"Mr. Ambastilias, I'm so sorry this has come to your home and family. I'm Detective Chief Inspector Knightsmith and this gentleman is known to me. He has lawful authority to assist us."

Marco spread his arms and appealed to heaven.

"Look, I'm a simple man. This is murder, this is crime, this is madness. There's a body on my floor, my daughter is at risk out there. I know Helen is a cop, the rest of you could be anyone."

Shannon reached inside her grey business style suit and snapped open her police warrant card.

"We'll deal with the body and then we'll be out of your hair. By the time Cressida gets back there won't be a trace."

"How do you know where she is and when she'll be home?" Shannon gave him a warm smile.

"Sir, there's a lot of officers on this enquiry. She's being monitored."

"And this man you call Bastian. What, what, what? What the fuck? There are laws, there are inquests, there are courts and judges."

"All taken care of, sir."

Marco's attention fixed on Helen. His dark eyes pleaded for her to help him. Surely, he had the right to know the truth?

"You're my dear friend, I trust you so tell me if I can trust these people. Cressida had some drugs which Peter Lodovitch had left with her. We gave them back, so what does anyone want now?"

"I don't know the whole story, but yes, you can trust these guys. We're fighting some bad, bad people here."

"Yes, I can see that. I want to help you, of course. If I have to stand up to violence I'll do it, but I must protect my daughter. Thank God she wasn't here to see all this."

Helen's heart seemed to weep inside her. The police needed to keep the lid on the situation, at least until all the terrorists had been identified. She had no choice but to mislead him. Soon enough he would know how she had treated him. She took his hand and looked into his face.

"I'm so, so sorry Marco. I thought we'd put it behind us by handing over the parcel."

"Parcel? You mean the drugs?"

Her heart skipped a beat. Marco was an artist working with words and meaning. He'd picked up the glitch of her reluctance to lie to him."

"Sure, the drugs, of course the drugs," she said, unable to hold his eyes. She looked away to Shannon who was on her cell phone, seemingly organizing the recovery of the body and a clean-up operation. She turned to Helen.

"We've got a team meeting at the Yard. We'll give you a ride." She paused and tweaked an eyebrow at Bastian. "I guess you've got transport."

"You guess right. Tell Anna I'll call her. Maybe she'd be free for dinner and a catch up."

"I'll tell her."

Helen watched in amazement and confusion. These guys seemed to be some sort of all-powerful family. If Bastian had dinner with Deputy Assistant Commissioner Anna La Salle, he had the inside track to government and who knows what else. He knew who she was, knew her history. He knew about Marco. And he'd just shot dead one of the world's most feared terrorists like a regular day at the office.

He did the cheek kissing with Shannon and reached out his hand to shake with Marco. Helen found him smiling at her and kissing her cheeks.

"We're comrades after all," he said with a wink.

A black Ford Transit van had pulled up outside. Two guys walked in, nodded, and bagged the body. A Crime Scene officer put the AK47 machine gun in a paper sack, while a couple of men in one-piece yellow overalls spread a powder on the congealing blood. Within a couple of minutes, the floor and walls were clean, and the body was gone. Bastian tossed the keys for the Mondeo to a guy at the door and the vehicle drove away. He handed the terrorist's cell phone and wallet to Shannon.

"Don't say I never give you anything. It's good to share so when you've stripped it fill me in."

Then he strolled to the door and away into the road. This wasn't police procedure but a Detective Chief Inspector was letting it run.

Shannon spoke directly to Marco.

"Sir, once again our regrets at this inconvenience. I can promise you this is an end to it. We have a fix on Cressida so don't worry. I need Helen for a while but she'll be back later and will be able to give you a lot more insight. Try to relax and of course don't talk about this business to anyone."

Marco puffed out his cheeks and let out a long sigh.

"That guy came to kill me or all of us. I understand the difficulties of your work and of course I trust you. Look after my daughter and please, please send Helen back to me, that's all I ask."

"That's a promise, Mr. Ambastilias."

Marco was half smiling, studying Shannon's face.

"Do I know you? Did I do a charity concert at Fleetworth

103

Green and you were there with some aristocrat business guy who put up a load of money?"

"You have a good memory. Yes, that was my husband. It was a great night and we made a huge wedge of cash for back-street kids. The TV and DVD money still pours in."

"Next time I do it for cops."

"Do it for our dogs. Lanza's attack bark saved us," said Helen.

"OK. If I sing again it will be for all dogs who serve—even if it's by just giving their love."

His arms were open, his honest smile was full of passion and generosity. How could a woman not love such a man? How could a woman deceive such a man? She hated herself, but loved him totally even though she would never be able to express it to him.

"OK guys, it's a wrap here so let's go. You ready Helen?" said Shannon.

"Sure. Marco, can you keep an eye on Lanza?"

"Of course. You can repay me with a hug."

His warm open expression and soft eyes drew her in to him. His arms folded around her. "Keep safe and come back."

She eased back from him. Truthfully, she wanted to get away before she was obliged to mislead him again. She wanted to regroup, clear her mind and develop some sort of strategy.

"I'll be back."

She slumped gratefully into the front seat of the BMW alongside wheel ace Kaitlyn. Shannon slid in the back blowing out her cheeks.

"Shit, that was so fucking close," she said.

"I'm confused and bemused. Who's that Bastian guy and how did he get into the picture?"

"We had a track on Mushti, but he slipped us. We guessed he was on the way to you. We knew Bastian was close by so Anna called him in."

"He appeared from nowhere."

"He was in a fox hole somewhere in a clump of brambles. There's nothing he likes better than a night in the open. Just so you know, he's a really close friend of Anna La Salle. They worked together on some massive job in France."

"But he's not a cop?"

"No, but he's in the World Intelligence Forum loop. He has presidential authority here."

"Isn't he working for the Russians?"

"Forget all that trashy newspaper politics. The fight is against terror. End of story."

"So, you're saying he or someone expected some action at Marco's house."

"Anna expected it, so she deployed Bastian. Believe me that's like having Saint Michael and all angels on your case."

"Shannon, what the hell am I going to do with Marco?"

"If I were you I'd lie back and enjoy what he'd like to do with you."

"We—I'm—deceiving him and exposing him and his daughter to danger. If that machine gunner had opened fire...."

"Relax, if you work hard you get better luck, but it was close I'll concede that. Now, let's get professional here. We're cops and we do whatever we have to do to protect this city. Scimitar of Holy Vengeance know there's a problem with their explosive. We've put a block on main stream media pushing out the Oxford Circus failed bomb story. We've got to expect some amateur cell phone footage on YouTube. There's statements from Transport for London going out to say there was a small electrical fire on a train. That should pre-empt any drama. News from up the road is that they've scooped several hard-core terrorists by tracking the explosive."

"How do you track it?" asked Helen, feeling dumb and ever further out of depth.

"Right, this *is* top secret. That package was fixed up with a radioactive marker. The Americans have satellites usually picking up traces of Russian submarine waste water and North Korean activity. If Kim Jong Un goes to a nuclear test site, the CIA can track what happens to his shit for a week. Like I say there's carte blanche presidential authority on this job."

"This is England."

"The world enemy is terror. Now tell me what you phoned me to say. You think you've got a lead?"

Helen took a deep breath. For sure she was going to look stupid, so she might as well jump to her conclusion.

"They're going to attack a series of prestige targets and maybe even the Queen. They've cultivated a bunch of rich and well-connected young people who have access to all the royal enclosures and inner circles. My guess is that these kids have paid for their drugs with VIP passes and first-class tickets. I think Royal Ascot could be high on the list."

"Christ, yes, that makes sense. They could even plant explosives on these kids themselves and remote detonate with a cell phone."

"Lanza picked up a trace on some trainers belonging to a posh kid called Karine de Robinet this morning. That's the girl who's out shopping with Cressida Ambastilias."

Shannon pushed back her wild black hair, a broad white smile on her face.

"But you didn't tell her, right? I think you and that mutt have cracked it. It makes sense of several other threads coming in. We need to share the news. Let's get to Scotland Yard."

CHAPTER NINETEEN

The day became a blur of expert reports and intelligence briefings.
Police and other agencies had identified three-quarters of the
terrorists and knew where they were. Their leader, Kashi ben
Quaffir had gone to ground. Police and spy chiefs now believed the
plot was to assassinate the Queen, her family and the government
as they attended high profile events. Two issues hung in the air.
Did Scimitar of Holy Vengeance have access to other explosives?
Could the combined law and order forces of the free world let the
show go ahead, in order to draw out and terminate Kashi ben
Quaffir, and crush religious terrorism for at least a decade? Helen
thanked heaven that such decisions were not on her desk—not that
humble dog cops had desks. She was getting a coffee in the
corridor when she was called back into the conference room. A
grave-faced grey-suited Dickon Maltravers gestured everyone to
sit. So, this was James Bond's boss, in real life.

"Everyone, it's going to be on the news but there's been an
explosion at Brussels airport. There are many casualties. What the
media won't know is that the chemical signature of the explosives
was the same as the material we intercepted in London and
neutralized. Sources tell us that the idea of the terrorists is to draw
forces away from London. We mustn't take that bait. With luck the
media frenzy will take some heat off us as well. The day after
tomorrow Her Majesty the Queen will be attending Royal Ascot
races where she has three horses due to run. She has been warned
of a security threat but says her people wouldn't expect her to back
down to terror. Ladies and gentlemen, a decision has been made to
allow her to attend. She knows what is at stake. We also can't
overlook that the new American princess, Meghan Markle, Her

Royal Highness the Duchess of Sussex, will also be there. Current media attention to her would make this a huge terrorist coup. International authorities believe that the termination of Quaffir and his outfit is worth the risk. Split to your teams, and leaders be ready for a briefing with the prime minister at 9 p.m."

Oh my God. Helen let her head sink into her hands. This was the decision of the World Intelligence Forum, the guys she'd met in Anna La Salle's office. Few people in the room even knew of their existence, yet by chance she had the inside lane. Stupid personal thoughts bubbled up through her brain. Marco. How the hell could she pile more lies into a relationship with a man she had fallen in love with? A man whose imprint she secretly craved in her belly.

She looked up to see Deputy Assistant Commissioner Anna La Salle at her side.

"Hey, some guys get all the luck. You're going to the races with an opera star. Tomorrow you've got a crash firearms course. Your army scores were sniper level so it's just a familiarization with the Glock 26. Kaitlyn will collect you and drive you to a couple of boutiques for all that hat and dress stuff. You and Marco will have passes to The Paddock and the Royal Enclosure courtesy of Sackman-Platinum Bank."

"I know Cressida plans to go with her friends but Marco tries to stay out of the public eye."

"Well then, honey, you've got a mission to convince him. If he thinks it's all about protecting his daughter, he'll be right at your side. I'm sure you've got wiles to oil any stiff wheels."

"So, what is my mission?"

"Be there and look the part. We believe that Badu al Bagwandi has your photo from footage taken at the cable car station. His comrades will be looking for you and everyone in the world knows Marco Ambastilias. His presence there will send a message to the terrorists that no one is on to them. They'll drop their guard. We have to do everything we can to put the odds in our favor."

"I think I understand what you're saying," said Helen with a cold shudder of realization that a few extra bodies would soak up a few extra bullets.

"The Queen of England and her family are the targets. The

more we can confuse the terrorists, the better. With Marco alongside you the whole show looks genuine and as if there is no enhanced security assessment. Bastian Wolf will be close but obviously don't acknowledge him. No enemy knows him because no one has ever come back to tell the tale. Relax and have a great evening."

"Do you think I can convince Marco this is all about some drug dealers?"

"He's not a cop. Helen, this is as serious as it gets, so do it. Think of the bigger game and just do it. If you have to lie, lie big. We all believe in you. You won't be alone. A Rolls Royce limo will pick you up at eleven o'clock. We've scheduled a tailor to come to the house tomorrow morning to fit Marco while you're at the firing range."

"Sure, I won't let you down," she answered, accepting that her own life and feelings had to be a low priority. She'd been a soldier at eighteen and a cop at twenty-five. She didn't live to express herself. Maybe she could tell him the truth but then she knew he wouldn't let Cressida go and there was a chance the story would get out. Simply he didn't have the security clearance. And she had to follow orders.

He opened his arms to her in his usual passionate generosity of spirit as she walked in. Sam and Lanza greeted her with licks and wagging tails. For a few seconds the world slipped away, and she enjoyed the simple joy of coming to a place like home, not that this was her home or ever could be. All the same, the illusion of peace and affection was delicious. Why, in the obvious failure of all other systems couldn't mankind settle for sharing and love? Marco handed her a glass of wine.

"How was your day? I used to think those dreadful maestro conductors and all those spiteful theatre critics were as bad as life could be. Then I meet you and see I knew nothing of this harsh brutal world. You, my angel, accept your torment as your duty."

His face was so handsome and yet so kind. Her lies and subterfuge had brought death and violence to his home just a few hours ago. And even yet he was holding her, making her feel secure against his chest, serving her wine and thinking only of *her* life. His was the voice that the world thought of as opera, as

109

passion and soaring desire for love. How could *she* be here in his arms?

"My day was great because I've come back here."

"Really? Really? Even though I'm just a fake performer. How could you guys respect someone who acts and sings with no real threat of death or tragedy?"

"Because, my dear Marco, the real-life muddy puddle reflects the unreachable sky. For those of us who cannot fly, a man like you gives us wings."

The words had poured out of her. Not her own words but those of a dead hero who would never come home. She pulled away in tears. It was her own meaning, yet she had stolen some kind of poetry from his grave.

"Helen, please. Your soul is sensitive and beautiful. Thank you from my heart for what you say."

"Marco, I'm repeating someone else's words. I'm the fake. I'm in a mess."

She just had to hold it together. She believed what she'd said but had remembered a moment with her dead husband to find the words. She was in love with this man but could never give him that truth. She was misleading him into danger because it was her duty. For Christ's sake, this story should be a freaking opera. She took a deep breath and looked down at Lanza. Poor boy, she'd almost forgotten him. He was looking healthy and at a glance almost his old self. She could see some movements hurt him. In the closed world between dogs it seemed as if he and Sam had formed an equal bond. As a police dog he had never had the freedom to make a friend or play with his own kind. His life had been dedicated to the service of human beings. It was a wonderful thing to see him free in his own universe of body language, smell, and the remembered inner call of the wolf pack. When she spoke to him he glanced at Sam to let him know he was on the team. Lanza was a wounded leader and Sam his youthful deputy dog. If ever there was justice, it was that her brave boy had found true happiness.

"Is Cressida back?"

"Sure, she's in her room trying out stuff for Ascot. She wants to impress Prince Harry."

"Do you think she'd mind if I popped up to see her outfit? I'm not really girlie, but I do have a weakness for hats."

"She'd love to show you. Now I get the chance to cook without a woman looking over my shoulder."

She kissed his lips and thrilled to the slide of his hand down her side, brushing her breast. Even with her mind a mire of guilt and contradiction, his touch was arousing. She allowed the warmth of temptation to sink into her soul as she climbed the wide marble stairs. Cressida's door was ajar.

"Hey, can a cat look at a queen in here?" she said with all the warmth she could find.

"Sure. Come in and tell me what you think."

Helen stopped at the door, almost gasping at the innocent beauty and poise of the girl. Since Cressida had become head nurse to Lanza, she herself had begun to eat properly.

"Wow, you're going to break some hearts," Helen said.

Cressida smiled and performed a one-legged spin, billowing out her pretty summer dress, a slim-fitting cream design with black spots by Jenny Packham. The dress had gathered fan-style ruffles at the shoulder and hip, giving it a 1940s feel. For the obligatory hat, she had chosen a natural straw boater with a striped straw twist by Rachel Trevor Morgan. She conveyed the confidence of wealth with the elegance of a butterfly. A shudder went through Helen's heart as she imagined the horror that could unfold among such beautiful people as they gathered at Ascot Races.

"You know you mentioned some of your friends had given away passes? Do you know who has them now?"

"Peter Lodovitch was always wanting them, you know for his contacts."

"Did you give him any?"

"A few, the British Formula One Grand Prix and Wimbledon Center Court I think. He really, really wanted the Royal Enclosure passes for Ascot, but just no one's going to get mine."

"Do you think any of your friends gave any away?"

"Does it matter?"

"It's nothing illegal. It's just about security."

Helen realized she couldn't seem too concerned, after all it wasn't as if they were talking terrorism here.

"I'll ask around, but I don't want anyone to think I'm working with the cops."

"That's cool. Anyway, I'll be there with your papa."

111

"Are you sure, he hasn't said anything?"

Cressida's face expressed an amused frown. Helen knew she could use this. She knew she could persuade Marco simply by telling him he could help protect his daughter.

"Look, between us, he doesn't know yet. This is my one chance in a lifetime to go to something like this. Maybe you could soften him up a bit, you know for me."

"I'll try. You've not seen the kind of frenzy that goes on around him. Junior royals want selfies, and every journalist wants an exclusive on why he quit. His life, his existence, is like a shadow across everything. This is the tragic Marco Ambastilias, the man with the voice of a god and the mystery of—"

"The pearl in an oyster." Helen finished the sentence, knowing that his duet with Fynn Bravel from Bizet's Pearl Fishers was the biggest classical music seller of all time.

"Yeah, you know your stuff, Helen. You don't need me to soften him up. He's in love with you."

"Fuck off!"

Cressida widened her eyes and laughed.

"It's true."

"I'm sorry I used such plain language."

"Don't be. I like your style and I like Papa to have someone like you. I want him to go to Royal Ascot and I want him to pick up his life again. I can't bear the guilt of denying him to the world."

"He doesn't want that either. I'll talk to him about your feelings if that's OK with you. How can he swan around the world knowing that his own child is—"

"Now I'll finish your sentence. Anorexic and drug addicted, that's what you want to say isn't it?"

Helen was in expert territory here, but there wasn't one in the room.

"You like it direct, so yes, those are big issues. He wants you to be healthy, believe in yourself, have a realistic body image, and not resort to slimming drugs. You say he loves me, but what am I? I'm thirty-five. I'm no super model."

"You're beautiful."

"And so are you, Cressida. I'm sure I'm wrong to say this, but I want you to see that the world is not just about your personal vanities and self-image. Other people's lives need you to be OK with yourself and able to contribute to a community of life. You've made a real bond with Lanza and believe me you have a real talent with animals. Don't neglect your own desires and self-image, but make things outside of yourself your focus."

"You're saying I'm too up myself."

"I'm saying that the whole picture of life gets drawn by a community of people. Be there, be strong, get a pencil and remember it's not all a fucking self-portrait."

Cressida pulled a tight-lipped frown.

"I suppose that's like all your army motivational attitude?"

"That's like there's a hidden roadside bomb and if I don't find it, a soldier dies, loses their limbs or goes home to a wife without their dick. That's like kind of motivational."

The girl slumped down on the bed.

"I don't want to be a lightweight."

"And you're not. You're confronting social issues I never dreamed of. Be young, be gorgeous and help me get your papa into that Royal Enclosure."

"Why do you want to be there? There's not going to be any drug dealing. There'll be so much security that no one would risk it."

"Of course not, but we need to identify the network of people behind the business. Anyone with a pass in someone else's name will be under suspicion. Then we can start looking at them more closely."

"A lot of passes are in big business names anyway."

"Narcotics is one of the world's biggest businesses. They don't call themselves Global Junkie Inc or Snort and Crystal Associates."

Cressida giggled. "You cops have some kind of cynical humor."

Helen took her hand and smiled.

"I'm so happy you're feeling and looking better. I know it's tough for you, blaming yourself for your papa's situation. We can work on that together. Maybe he's using the parental guilt thing to try and heal you. The only way forward is for you to get on top of your life and set him free."

Cressida returned her smile. Helen took that as her answer and

113

left her to enjoy some more mirror-time. Just maybe they were building a bridge that would hold. They wouldn't know until a storm broke.

CHAPTER TWENTY

Marco was in the lounge watching the TV news with Sam and Lanza either side of him on the sofa. Images of the Brussels airport attack rolled and rolled on the screen. It was the familiar carnage with the worst images filtered out by newsroom editors.

"These guys had guns like that man had this morning," he said in a matter of fact tone. "Does every thug have a Kalashnikov now?"

Her heart sank. She would have to lie to him.

"Pretty much. The Yugoslav war in the nineties pumped a lot of guns onto the open market. Then there was the IRA campaign and Libyan support for terrorist groups."

What she'd said was accurate but such a weapon would be extreme overkill in the world of average drug sellers. The news was reporting a small fire on a London tube train at Oxford Circus with some blurred amateur footage of some smoke and flames. Anyone with experience would understand what they were seeing but police news management had the initiative for now.

"Marco, I'm going to be at Royal Ascot Races the day after tomorrow. I'll be keeping close to Cressida. Maybe you'd like to keep close to me."

"Helen, it's a madhouse there. There's the royal parade in open carriages and every species of celebrity. Everyone wants to see Princess Meghan and Prince Harry. Cressida has a pass from a friend whose mother is a lady in waiting to the Queen, but even if I wanted to go I couldn't get in."

"I've got two passes as guests of Sackman-Platinum Bank."

"Those guys are brash greed-monsters. I've heard they're the place to go with dirty money. How or why would they invite you?"

"Some of their top people know my bosses. They heard about Lanza, I think."

"So, it's just for pleasure. You're not expecting gun toting drug dealers to pop up next to Prince Charles?"

She was in so deep she just had to keep digging.

"Of course not, but Peter Lodovitch handed out passes he obtained from his young clients, so we'll be taking the chance to identify any Mr. Big who has a nose in the drugs trough, that's all. No one will know you're going to be there. By the time the media can react we'll be on the way home."

For a moment he stood and looked at her from a small distance. His gaze was taking her in. She felt herself in the spotlight, naked and yet special all at once.

"I'd go anywhere with you, you must see that. If you're going to be in danger how could I sit at home?"

"I didn't know you'd come for me because I know how ordinary I am. I'm a gal hiding behind a famous dog."

He nodded and gave her an open grin. "So, I'm a singer hiding behind the genius of composers like Verdi, Beethoven, or Wagner. So, both of us little creatures can meet as equals, certain that the world and its history is bigger than us. That thought kind of makes me feel secure."

"So, you'll come?"

"Yes, but only if I can kiss you this moment."

She had no desire to resist. His arms folded around her as his lips pressed softly to hers. Just maybe if she kept her eyes closed nothing would exist beyond this feeling of security mixed with awakening desire. The coming night could be a last chance of an innocent encounter. Soon enough some new scene of horror would unfold and he would know she had deceived him. The truth about Scimitar of Holy Vengeance would hit the news screens. How could he accept that a man had been killed in his hallway that morning by a non-police agent, but the cops had shrugged and cleaned up the mess? She knew the sad and agonizing answer. He trusted her because he was an open-hearted man who wanted her inside his life. Because he was in love with her.

Promptly at nine o'clock, Kaitlyn collected her in a silver Range Rover Vogue. How this world of service and luxury could seduce.

"I've fixed a dress fitting at the Nigel Rayment Boutique. They've got an amazing collection of hats and frocks and there'll be something perfect for you."

"I feel like a celebrity."

"Tomorrow you will be, believe me. My man, Randolph, will be there representing Sackman-Platinum Bank. He wants a selfie with Marco if you can fix it."

"No problem. I get more butterflies worrying about all the posh people, royals, and stars than I do worrying about terrorists."

"I know what you mean. Although, Christ, this is a high-risk game. Anna La Salle asked me to bring you up to speed with where things are as of this morning. We know nearly all the hard-core terrorists and where they are. The leader Kashi ben Quaffir is completely off radar. His deputy Badu al Bagwandi has also gone to ground and may have organized the Brussels airport attack. The problem is, that there are so many sleeper low-level soldiers who can be used as bombers or gunmen. These guys are clean skins and while Quaffir is alive and can poison their minds with videos on the internet this nightmare will never end. The bosses are playing for high stakes here."

"The World Intelligence Forum has decided that it's worth risking the Queen of England and members of her family in order to cut the head off the snake?"

"Helen, when you're a Brit you think cute little tourist England is the world. These guys enslave and ruin the lives of millions. They create poverty with their religious wars. They abuse women, they murder any opponent in the name of God. The president and a host of world leaders have taken this decision. This is our chance and we're not going to blow it."

"You drive a Metropolitan police vehicle, but who do you work for, Kaitlyn?"

"I was a street cop like you driving high speed and pursuit cars. One day I got tied up with Randolph Quinn. As you know he's a big wheel with Sackman-Platinum. When all this is over you'll get a proper briefing, but just accept we're all on the same side. My pay cheque is from the bank. My bosses are the World Intelligence Forum. We get to travel a bit but it's great to be back in London for a while."

"Where's home for you?"

"With Randolph, but I guess that's Rome, when we're off duty."

Helen settled back in the luxurious vehicle. It was as if she'd fallen down a rabbit hole into a new universe. They hit the M25 orbital motorway. Kaitlyn floored the pedal with obvious joy in her heart at the speed. These guys just did whatever it took.

The training center was a way outside London at Gravesend. Kaitlyn dropped her at the entrance where she was met by an instructor in overalls. He was a no-nonsense kind of guy with a deeply serious manner.

"You're getting the Gen 5 Baby Glock 26. We've got to keep it slim for concealed carry. With a twelve magazine you'll get a bit more handgrip for single-handed fire. Check?"

Helen slipped back into military mode.

"Affirmative."

"We'll practice plenty of magazine changes in case you get into a proper shootout. This weapon's new to us, but she's sweet. Are you used to Glocks?"

"Negative, Sig Sauer 9mm. Glocks came in after my time."

She spent the morning firing round after round. Now and then her mind switched to what she was training for. She was going to be at Royal Ascot Races, maybe in a gun battle with ruthless terrorists. How she hoped she was just going to sip some champagne, lose money on some horses and admire the hats of the aristocracy.

"You're a top shot Helen. I'd want you on my side if it got rough," said the instructor.

"Thanks for the compliment."

"I'm Inspector Tom Ryan. If by any chance you see me tomorrow, you don't know me."

Helen took a deep breath. She was a pawn in this game, but obviously hundreds, if not thousands, of officers were being mobilized. Of course, all the crack shots and snipers would be there. No one would be closer to the action than her.

"We're going to set you up with a thigh holster. At Ascot the skirt length has to be modest so it's ideal. You just pull up your hem, draw, and you're in business. Just remember you've got no body armor so don't give the guy a second chance."

For a moment her mind flashed back to Lanza. She needed to lighten up.

"Do they do fashion designer ones?"

"Of course. We're fitting you with a lace stocking-top model. It'll take the Baby Glock and two spare clips."

"I feel sexy already. At least any groper would be in for a shock." she said with a nervous abandon.

Her afternoon was as alien as a trip to the moon. Kaitlyn handed her a Sackman-Platinum infinite wealth card to pay whatever it cost to create her look. First up was a trip to Nicola Clarke at John Frieda for a hair fix. Helen had never dreamed of being a client with the likes of Madonna and Cate Blanchett at a West End salon. The exclusive area between Carnaby Street and Marylebone intimidated her with its flavor of wealth. The mysterious Mercedes limos and the cool, fragrant females crossing the pavement made her feel plain and awkward, like a starling among swans. With her new nearly blonde hair she felt more the part as she stepped into the Nigel Rayment Boutique near Marble Arch at the top end of Oxford Street. The dress code for the Royal Enclosure was strict, allowing no extreme creations. Gentlemen had to wear morning dress with top hat. The shop interior was opulent with a passionate rococo flourish to all the fittings. She couldn't tell the assistant that she would be carrying a loaded firearm on her inner thigh, so pencil-style dresses were definitely out. In the end she chose a perfect Veni Infantino design by Ronald Joyce. It was a crepe and lace dress with pleated skirt, an appliquéd bodice and a cute matching mikado jacket. She chose a color coordinated swooping brimmed hat in navy and pale rose. She had to admit she liked her own look—no—she adored her new look! For shoes she selected some navy-blue satin peep-toe pumps with a moderate heel. Even with everything else on her mind, she wondered if Marco would enjoy a private viewing of her outfit, both putting it on and taking it off. The thought sent a teasy little ping to her sex. This coming night was almost certain to be her last with him. First, she had a final briefing at Scotland Yard. She went straight to Deputy Assistant Commissioner Anna La Salle's office where Detective Chief Inspector Shannon Knightsmith was already seated. She recognized the tall distinguished man in his mid-fifties who stood and introduced himself.

"Such a pleasure to meet you directly. Miss Marx, I'm Dickon Maltravers, from MI6. I have overall responsibility for tomorrow's operation."

Helen swallowed. She'd seen him at briefings, but it was hard to believe she was in a personal meeting with such a man. Anna La Salle spoke first.

"The good news is that we have identified the hard-core terrorists who plan to act tomorrow. In a coordinated attack we will take them out long before they get anywhere near Ascot. We know they have a second source of explosives which they used in the Brussels bombing. However, they spread the stuff from your parcel around the group and retained it long enough for us to get a fix on them using the radioactive marker technology. Your presence at Ascot with Marco will create a major stir, which will confuse any freelance terrorist who happens to get through. Our hope is that both Bagwandi and Quaffir will surface once their operation launches. Your job, Helen, will be to keep close to Marco. This will be his first public appearance in the spotlight in three years. Scimitar of Holy Vengeance know he is somehow involved in the fake-explosive trick you helped us to pull on them. The royal family is the principal target but the both of you also present a great temptation. Don't worry too much because the whole group are identified and will never get there."

Dickon Maltravers cleared his throat.

"We *cannot* rule out the possibility that there are clean-skin guys brainwashed by Quaffir who would be unknown to us. I believe you know Bastian Wolf. He will tell you he's working for the Russians. Trust him and let him guide you if things get complicated."

"Complicated?" she echoed.

"He will maintain an outer secure area around you. If he identifies a target or targets, open fire without hesitation, no matter how they look or how they are dressed."

She nodded in response. She'd seen Bastian in action and if she trusted anyone it would be him.

D.C.I. Shannon Knightsmith continued the briefing.

"Charles and Sophia of France will be in the Royal Enclosure. There will be a big buzz around them because of the semi-scandal of her being so much older than him. They've been briefed to make themselves known to Marco, and Sophia will be at Bastian's disposal if there is a need. She'll be carrying."

"Sophia of France will be armed?" said Helen in astonishment.

"Just like you. She's an experienced woman with one hell of a story. Trust her completely. No terrorist will expect a royal to take them out. Effectively she gets a free shot."

Helen let out a long breath. That morning at dawn, when she had chased a suspect with Lanza, was making Alice in Wonderland look like a stroll in the woods.

"OK, there's a Russian agent and the Queen of France armed to the teeth at Royal Ascot Races in the presence of the Queen. If they start shooting I join in."

Shannon laughed.

"That's pretty much it. Just get Marco Ambastilias back onto the world stage and let the rest fall into place. My advice is to relax and have a great evening. As always, it's crucial that no one outside of us knows what this is about. We can't allow the bad guys to get wind of anything."

"I understand," said Helen. She just couldn't let her own emotions interfere with her duty. For a second she let her head sag forward a little. No one can hide their body language. As she looked up she caught sight of the others exchanging serious glances over her. Anna La Salle smiled quickly. Helen knew there was something between these people and she was outside the loop.

"Helen, the press have received a tip-off that Marco will be there," said Anna.

"There'll be an absolute feeding frenzy," Helen replied in a reflex, imagining the scene and his reaction. "I told Marco there'd be no press."

She glanced at Shannon who looked away. Dickon Maltravers didn't flinch. To him this was work and personal relationships were of no account.

"Helen, *we* told the press, I won't deceive you about that. There's no reason Marco will ever know that unless you tell him."

She stared into his face. His expression was implacable. Her years as a soldier and as a cop had conditioned her to follow orders from above. In this instant she was a woman—a woman in love with a wonderful man whom these people didn't even know.

"You bastards! You know that if Marco is there and the whole of the world's press are tearing at him, he'll be the biggest terrorist target on the planet. The royals have so much protection that they'll never get close so Marco's a fall guy if anyone gets through."

Dickon Maltravers almost smiled.

"Well said and well analyzed. No one *is* going to get through. Every possibility is possible of course. That's why we have duty and orders. Let's see how the world looks this time tomorrow."

Anna La Salle stood up signaling the end of the meeting. Helen guessed that the decision had been made over her head.

"I'm sorry, Helen. All the same I know you'll step up and do what you have to do. My gut feeling is that nothing will happen. Enjoy the day. As the mysterious beauty on the arm of Marco Ambastilias, I think we can predict quite an experience for you. Tell them you're a public-relations officer from Sackman-Platinum Bank. They'll just swallow that since the bank is sponsoring the Platinum Cup race where the Queen has two horses. By the way, your hair makes you look even more gorgeous. Enjoy."

Anna reached out and took her hand. "Like Dickon said, the world will look a different place this time tomorrow."

Helen couldn't blame her boss. She had so much on her shoulders. Shannon was a higher rank but still was no more than a foot-soldier in an operation like this.

"I'll do my best, ma'am," she answered, using Anna's formal title under police regulations. She preferred to swallow the truth from this woman as an order rather than a personal betrayal.

Shannon changed the tone. "I'll be in the area myself tomorrow with my husband. It may help you to know he has no insight into our operation. I'll introduce him to you and Marco of course. Your Rolls Royce will be at eleven o'clock."

"I'd never asked you about your husband. I guess from what you say he's not a cop."

"He sure ain't a cop, thank God."

For some reason Shannon's deception of her own man made her feel better about her personal situation. It was shit, but at least they were smeared with the same stuff.

CHAPTER TWENTY-ONE

She piled her bags and hat box in the hall as she entered. She could hear Marco speaking on the telephone. His cell was ringing, unanswered. She walked through to the lounge to see him waving his free hand in the air and speaking Italian or Spanish. He gestured for her to answer the cell.

"Hi, you've reached the number of Marco—" she began.

"Madam, hi, this is the newsroom of CNN. Can we get Marco on here?"

"He's on another call."

"We'll hold, but hey who are you? Can you get us up on a video call to go live?"

"Live to whom or what?"

"The world. What else? Are you involved in getting the world's greatest tenor back into the public arena?"

"No, look maybe you can call back?"

She terminated the call. At once the cell started to ring again. Marco rang off on the landline call and immediately it restarted. He slumped down with his hands to his ears.

"The nightmare has started again, Helen. Somehow the media has learned I'm going to be at Ascot. My agent wants me to do a small press release and put it up on YouTube. Then he can just refer everything to that. As long as they have something visual to go with the story they'll shut up."

"I'm so sorry—"

At once he stood and crossed the room, pulling her into his arms. His deep voice resonated in his chest as he spoke.

"Helen, this isn't your fault. This has been my life since I was discovered in Naples as a boy. Before now I had no one I trusted to share this madness. With you at my side everything is different."

"I'm not worthy of your trust."

"How not? You're not chasing fame or money. You would die to save the other guy. Believe me, you have a soul I can trust. I'm going upstairs to my office to make a press statement. My agent will tell me what to say. Fix yourself a drink and think how I'm going to kiss you. And then I'm going to show you my top hat and morning suit. All this was beginning to get to me but now you're here the world has flowered again." He strode away with a boyish grin. "Marco is coming back to life because a woman is squeezing his heart. If the world wants to know this, I'll tell them."

She watched him bound up the stairs. How could her presence seem to bring him such joy? Maybe everything would unfold peacefully tomorrow?

She poured a glass of wine as the dogs strolled in to greet her. Lanza was gaining strength with every day. While she'd been in a constant whirl, Cressida had cared for him and monitored his medication. Caring for a helpless animal had drawn her focus away from herself. What a mess she would leave for this family when everything came crashing down.

She showered in the ensuite of the master bedroom and spread out her outfit. So many thoughts, desires and conflicts collided in her mind. Never had she felt so wanted and yet so alone. The thought of Marco was enough to turn her on. Since the death of her husband she had rejected all thought of a man with a face or a name. She had soothed her loneliness with honest masturbation, using it as a way of losing herself in pleasure and in a blank blur of anonymous sensation. This man had taken that from her. It was his face, his arms around her, his kiss, his cock spilling hot cum into her belly that crowded her thoughts as she slipped into an escape. She snapped back her mind, trying to fix on anything—anything sexy. She had the one very secret little grenade she could throw into her battle for her own independence. She flashed her mind back to a night at an army transit camp as a cadet when she'd shared her tent with another girl. The night was hot and heavy. A sound had awakened her, a sound of sexy pleasure in the half light. The other girl was awake and had let slip an involuntary sound into the night. Helen feigned sleep and watched the girl languidly fingering her pussy, slowly ramping up the tension, obviously aiming for some result but not to be discovered. The air was a sigh of musk and need. The sight and sound of oozing lust had shot a jolt of juice and excitement to her sex. The other girl had begun to focus, was feeling those first teasy shocks. Helen had been in this place herself, but had never gone beyond. The sheer shameless desire and passion of the other girl drew her hand to her own clit. The other girl was going for it now, focused, holding, climbing, holding, biting her lip, holding her breath. Then her tent mate let out a grunt and bucked forward with several strong spasms. Helen found she was holding her own breath, almost in sympathy. The girl subsided, sighed and lay back. As she turned her head she caught her open eyes. Helen smiled, embarrassed but fascinated. Her mate smiled back and slid her hand back to her pussy, circling her clit, making a sticky tick, tick sound. She looked across and nodded an encouragement, a female complicity. So, it was OK. This girl was inviting her to share something, whatever it was. She pulled back the covers and followed her companion's climb. Suddenly she was in a place beyond those teasy shocks, somewhere with a summit, somewhere with a fall or a release. She needed to be there. The other girl was there already, bucking and sighing almost like pain. She was at a plateau, holding, holding. She pulled herself tight one more time. Her hand was in a frenzy. Then, she crashed through that barrier, into waves of pleasure, trying not to cry out, like trying not to sneeze or yawn in class. She looked to her unwitting instructor. Still her hand soothed into her wet groove. She knew men had one big shot, but no one had talked about girls. She wanted it again, to be at that place of joy and oblivion.

"Do it again. I'm doing it too," whispered the girl.

Maybe her temporary friend was a lesbian? Maybe she was a horny girl open to her own needs and aware of human desire. Maybe she simply liked to be watched? For sure she'd led her to a life-changing discovery. One more time she turned to watch as she tried to match the journey, pausing, pulling up, moving on, moving on, starting to slip and yes, yes, yes, coming and feeling the flooding joy of her own hot juice. OK, another young woman had shown her the journey and the mental final climb. So, who could have done that job better? She was as straight as anyone and never had to tell a soul how much that lesson could always turn her on.

Without fantasy, her first climbs had failed. Her own touch and control in that situation had formed her in a certain way. She could give herself up to a man, but a woman had taken her innocence with merely a smile and open compassion.

The next day the other girl had moved on to her own unit and they had never met again. That night was a secret, but one that could block her mind whenever she couldn't bear to fantasize about her dead husband who could never touch her again. Until now. Until Marco.

Her hand was between her thighs as she sat at the dressing table. Her hair looked so feminine, so sexy. She pressed a little on her groove, finding a joyful moistness of desire. Marco was in his office and the bedroom door was closed. How she wanted to feel sexy, to shut out the horrors and fear about what lay ahead and what had already happened. It wouldn't hurt to prime the pump a little, maybe not to come, but just to arouse her need. She leaned back on the chair, watching her own face in the mirror as her finger circled her clit. She could see her inner lips, glistening with her juice and rhythmically clicking as she caressed her button. Her own face was focused and serious in the mirror. She was a naughty girl, climbing and climbing away from all her cares. She had to stop. She was a naughty girl. She brought her other hand to her soaking entrance, slipping in her finger, then two fingers. Marco's cock was inside her, she wanted his cum deep and deeper in her belly. Her legs were shaking, her nipples wanted his lips, tremors rippled through her abdomen. Her orgasm was on the horizon, like a teasing storm about to burst its liquid on parched earth. She glanced at herself, her face pretty but almost ugly with uncivilized sex-need. Her nostrils had flared in her animal longing to release. She closed her eyes, increasing the speed and pressure of her fingers. His cock was spurting, she was jerking off his seed. Her clit was his cock soaked with cum.

"Fuck, fuck my cunt Marco, do it in me." she growled out as her orgasm exploded. "Fill my pussy, cum fuck."

Her juices gushed and yet she didn't care. Nothing had ever happened at that intensity before. Her twitching pussy needed more. Her nipples pinged shocks through her belly flesh to her sex. Hands were caressing her from behind, teasing her breasts, pulling them up and outward in a delicious pressure. Tremors of her climax still fired through her. Warm lips were on her neck, a hand was easing her chin to the side to receive his kiss. His kiss. Marco's kiss. In her oblivion she hadn't heard him come in. Her inner thighs were soaked, the perfumed boudoir air was heavy with woman lust-musk. Still pulsing with pleasure, she felt shamelessly for his tongue, exchanging heat and wetness in an abandoned kiss, thrilling to his response.

"I was being naughty. You make me lose control," she whispered in a thick lazy voice, her eyes blurred and unfocused.

He didn't speak but came to kneel in front of her chair, looking up at her with his kind dark eyes pleading for her. Pleading for her to open herself to him as a woman and as a being. If she loved him she'd warn him of the danger ahead. She couldn't let this man love her and yet her soul and her sex longed for him to fill her. His hand stroked up her thighs, his thumbs sliding on her juice. He brought his fingers to his mouth and kissed the wetness. He groaned in passion and animal instinct. His eyes were on her blood-engorged sex. He stood and raised her up. The bed was spread with clothes. He gestured for her to lie down on a thick-pile rug. Her clit ached for release as he sat facing her, holding her ass cheeks in his big strong hands, her legs over his shoulders. His hot tongue swept from her entrance to her hard little woman cock, drawing her in with a mind-blowing kiss. Her view was of the chandeliered ceiling, the feeling was a shameless abandon, a deep pulsing thrill sending her higher and higher until she could hold back no more. As she came his tongue fucked her pulsing entrance. She could only cry out as spasms wrenched through her belly, setting free her need to come in pulses of juice.

"Fuck me. I want your cock," she shuddered out.

He held his weight above her, his hard bursting cock gliding inside her. He let out a deep groan, driving in to the limit. His balls made a rhythm on her buttock cheeks. She had to come. She had to come. She brought her hand to her clit. The thrust of his cock on her inner wall and the nerve pulse at her own touch, drove her over the cliff in a double sensation of soaking ecstasy.

"I'm a naughty girl," she blurted out as she jolted out her orgasm.

He brought his lips to hers as he fucked her harder. He was getting closer and now she wanted him to come. She wanted him

127

to come hard and to build a vision in her own mind of him coming helplessly. She wanted him to jerk off onto her sex, to watch his cum squirt onto her drenched triangle

"Do it for me on my pussy. Cum on my pussy. I want to see you jerk off."

He smiled as he pulled out and knelt between her legs. His powerful hand ran up and down his wet straining cock, dripping with clear pre-cum. She brought her hand to her pussy lips and began to masturbate hard, fixing her wanton eyes on his. His belly tightened as his first jet of semen shot onto her feverish hand. His cry was deep and satisfied as his man juice poured onto her pulsing groove in a hot torrent. He brought his tip to her clit as his last ooze of fluid met her last wave of orgasm. She lay back, exhausted and floating on a buzz of animal abandon. He moved to her side, stroking a hand down her cheek. God, she'd wanted to come as if she was squeezing out man cum from her clitoris.

"Marco, I lost it there."

"You didn't lose me. You're pure hot woman. No man could ever, ever dream of more."

"Really, you don't think I'm a wanton sex monster who likes to touch herself?"

"Any time you feel wanton, tell a man who wants to come just watching or even thinking about it," he chuckled. "You've been alone out of respect for your dead man. How do you think I've coped with sexual need?"

How strange it was to be so open and so intimate with this man. She'd shown herself to him without restraint in her most private and vulnerable behavior. She knew his longing for her and in that security, she trusted him to want her as she was. Just absolutely totally as she was. Now of course her mood had to change. From now on it was work. Once she'd cleaned up again she could try on the outfit and at the same time find a way of him not detecting her thigh holster and firearm. Hopefully he wouldn't want a quick fondle in the Rolls Royce on the way to Ascot.

It was after dinner when the Ambastilias family tried on their outfits for the Royal Enclosure. The sight of Marco in his morning suit made her gasp. He was a big man and the formal clothes added to his aura of power and confidence. The top hat provided a period

Victorian Barnum flashback. His double-cuffed shirt and dove grey double-breasted silk waistcoat accentuated his natural sense of theatre.

"The tailor assures me that Princes Charles, Harry, and Andrew will be wearing double-breasted waistcoats," he said with an amused grin.

They took advantage of Simon Leonard, the veterinarian who had come to pay a house call on Lanza. They all posed for photos while he snapped away. Behind her smile she wondered if she would ever see those pictures. Before bed they watched the late news. She prayed there would be no drama involving Scimitar of Holy Vengeance. There was coverage of the Brussels bomb and the hunt for a ringleader. Her ears twitched to the names Quaffir and Bagwandi on the lips of a translated Belgian police chief, but the story went no further. The bulletin arrived at the last item which is often a light story about a cute dog that adopted a duckling or a guy who'd found a box of gold coins under his floorboards. The female presenter gave the familiar intro.

'And now for something different. Ladies look up. ITV has received world exclusive news that the world's most desired opera singer who's been a recluse in hiding for three years is coming back. The gorgeous Marco Ambastilias is resuming public life at Royal Ascot tomorrow. Our reporter asked him why.'

The scene changed to Marco in his office.

'So, you're coming back, Marco. Could I ask you why and why now?"

Marco smiled broadly to camera. He was so handsome and so confident that he could hold an audience with an eyebrow or a flick of his hand.

'What other reason than love? I stopped because my heart was cold, the arias were only words and notes. I sing of love with a heart of love and that power has come back to me.'

'That's so wonderful. Can you tell us more?"

"If I start to talk of music, passion, and love we would need a long show. I have re-found love in my daughter and with a very special woman. I will sing again and you will see the expression of this love or at least you will see my humble attempt to demonstrate my emotions."

The scene cut back to the studio anchor.

'I can't wait for that moment, folks. Wow! Big Marco's coming back. See you all tomorrow at ten.'

For a moment she sat in stunned silence. Marco took her hand.

"I wanted to say your name and tell them about Lanza and how we met. Maybe I assume too much?"

"I'm glad you didn't do that. We've not discussed our future—except with the world's media."

Helen didn't want to say too much while Cressida was still downstairs. She waited until the girl had done her two-cheeked kiss with her papa. She turned to go, but then came back and hugged her with an almost desperate grip.

"Everything is so different now. Now we can move on. I can't wait to show you to all my friends at the races."

Inwardly Helen sighed. She'd been engulfed. In any other woman's life this would have been the happiest ever time. In a short while she'd come a long way with Cressida, even though she knew that Lanza was the main healer. She'd come a long way with Marco, to the limits of her sexual passion, to the outer edges of orgasmic ecstasy. Emotionally she just couldn't go there. Yes, yes, yes—she was in love with him, but she could leave the words unsaid even if the meaning was burning into her soul.

"It'll be great to meet them," she answered. Perhaps nothing would happen. Perhaps Marco and Cressida would never know she was letting them walk into an open-ended risk of injury or death. She *could* warn them. She could simply defy her orders. The press were expecting Marco. Cressida's friends were expecting her. If they pulled out there had to be a risk that someone would smell a rat. Her bosses were right. The security operation against the terrorist cell could end religious terror for a generation. The public news that the great Ambastilias would be there would encourage these maniacs to go ahead, sure there was no one on their case. A trap was set and all of them were in it. The boss from MI6 had said no one would get through. At least he hadn't given her an order to trust him.

CHAPTER TWENTY-TWO

How precious were these minutes of the dawn. He lay beside her, cradling her head on his chest. These really were the last shreds of innocence. Her body was a blur of fulfilled joy, her belly caressing, grasping his hot seed, the taste of each other's juice mixed on their lips. Her marriage had never been like this and yet she would love that poor dead warrior until she died. In her blind raging passion for Marco she had let her focus slip from Lanza, acknowledging that Cressida had replaced her. Here in the warmth and protection of one of the world's most talented men, she had to admit she was pleased with the exchange. She wasn't proud of herself, but a woman who couldn't live with her own selfishness would never have the claws to fight for a man whom other women wanted. A woman who couldn't draw blood for a man, couldn't see love as his child's selfish sucking mouth at her breast. There was a boiling savage need inside her, and no other man but Marco would ever know her heat. She was in his bed, feeling more protected than the jewels of a queen, but what did she know of him?

"How did you get to be an opera singer? I guess you didn't do X-Factor."

His voice was a deep, good-humored chortle in his chest.

"I love that show. There's people there with more desire and talent than me. OK, short history. I was a poor stupid boy in Naples, running errands for some Camorra guys. This is so corny, it has to be true."

"Camorra?"

"*Si, La Mafia di Napoli*. One day I went to collect a payment from a guy at the opera house, the Teatro San Carlo. He was a man who wanted a favor for his son. He'd crashed a car and was with a

131

prostitute. My boss was able to use influence with the media, you understand. The young man was a rising star of politics. I go to meet this man and his assistant tells me to wait. In the big hall they're rehearsing an opera, *Il Trovatore*."

"Verdi," she sighed.

"*Si*, the famous *Anvil Chorus* you say in English. I'm waiting and the guy isn't coming and so I'm singing along at the back. My mama send me always to the church choir. My papa was a mid-level capo with the Mafia."

"I'm guessing all this drugs and crime stuff isn't a surprise to you?"

"No, the surprise is how much you police of London put into something that is routine in every city of the world."

This was not the time to tell him the truth. Anyway, she wanted to know his story.

"We're algorithm cops, study the brush strokes, miss the picture. So, you're singing along…."

"*Si*, and some guy sitting in the dark in front of me comes back and asks me if I want a job. Turns out he's the director and they need an extra tenor in the crowd scene because some guy is sick. For sure I said yes."

"And then?"

"I get a few parts and all these big shots get excited and I go to music school and learn more and people who know ten languages and have gold and silver on their pizzas want to be my friend. All kinds of women want sex with me."

His sudden harsh language shocked her.

"This sounds totally overwhelming for a teenager."

"Yeah, but my passion and my gut is of the streets. Let me say this to you. A Hollywood star and the world's greatest divas are frail, vain, and cold compared to you. When I sing, it's sex. If it's not sex, it's not connecting with the secret joy inside a human being even if they don't orgasm in their theatre seat. They don't call it a climax for nothing, Helen. That high note, that searching elusive longing is that need to build and release. All the greats knew this. You can talk about teenagers and yes it was difficult, but I had tough friends and family around me. Until a man really helplessly loves a woman, he doesn't know the power that his need for her brings him. Only in longing for love does a man know his

132

endless strength. I tell you now, you have given me back my desire, and nobody, absolutely nobody, has heard my true voice simply because I didn't know it myself. Now, I know that power in my heart. I will give that truth to the world."

His arm was tight around her. His total love was protecting her. Oh, to stop life at this minute.

"Hey, that's too much of a speech for a regular dog cop."

He laughed softly.

"Too much of a speech for a Mafia boy-soldier with acne who got lucky. Enough words. When I sing again, you'll know in your heart what there is in mine."

She'd been ready for a couple of hours when the black and white long-wheelbase Rolls Royce Phantom pulled up. Cressida had already grabbed a ride with a mob of young friends in a stretch limo. The Baby Glock pistol was snug in her thigh stocking-top holster. She was carrying four spare magazines, just in case. The weather was perfect and she looked fantastic. The uniformed chauffeur opened the rear-hinged back door. Even though he was a cop armed to the teeth he looked absolutely genuine. Marco settled beside her, fabulous in his perfectly fitted morning suit. He took her hand.

"You look so beautiful. There's going to be kings, princes, and sheiks all over you. How does a man like me make sure you stay with me?"

"Marco, I'll be pushed aside in the press scrum."

"No press in the Royal Enclosure, just fame, wealth, and beauty."

The sleek surging power of the car soothed her a little. Money was so, so seductive, seemed to make every obstacle in your path move. They were approaching the race course. It was obvious at once that such a place was a security nightmare. The main Ascot High Street ran a few yards from The Paddock and parade ring. Normally she would have been concerned about finding a car park. This celebrity life took away all such cares. The chauffeur dropped them at the main entrance and cruised away. As their feet touched the pavement there was a shout.

"Marco—hey Marco, who's the beautiful girl?"

Helen watched as news of his arrival spread through a tidal

wave of paparazzi and reporters. It wasn't quite noon and the royal parade in horse-drawn landau carriages wouldn't be until 2 p.m. Until then the press were on fame and fashion patrol. The return of Marco Ambastilias was a gift from heaven. Within seconds they were in a jostling mob with microphones and cameras. Green-vested security guys moved in to assist them. Helen caught the eye of the inspector who had led her firearms tuition. OK—the security guys were all armed cops. The press didn't give up.

"Hey, gorgeous, give us a smile. What's your name? Hey, over here for the Express. God, you're gorgeous. Over here, over here."

"Hey, guys, give us some space and you'll get some shots," said Marco. "This is Helen."

"Helen, who did your hat? How old are you? You look about twenty-six to me. That OK for you?"

She had to laugh at these persistent guys and allowed herself to relax, glad at least that no one had jostled her enough to detect her firearm.

"Twenty-six is just fine with me," she said, secretly enjoying the flattery and posing hand on cheek in a coy expression.

"The hat, who did the hat?"

"Veni Infantino,"

"How long have you known Marco?"

"About a year."

"Where are you from? Where are your folks? What do they do? Are you related to royalty?"

The questions piled and tumbled around her as she threw out random answers into an ocean of faces and voices. Marco had raised his voice.

"Guys, you want to know if I can still sing? If I show you, you'll leave us to enjoy the races, OK. Do we have a deal?" Lenses snapped to his face. Microphones jabbed towards him. "OK, I give you *E lucevan le stelle* from *Tosca* and I hold my own beautiful Tosca in my arms."

He opened his embrace to her, his hands beckoning her to come to him. How could he have such confidence in himself? Could he still sing? With a busy public street just a few yards away, he was going to sing one of Puccini's greatest arias above the noise of traffic to the world's press. He was a showman and a total star. The mob fell silent as he took her in his arms.

"*In bocca al lupo*" he whispered into her ear. Then holding her with his soft dark gaze he began to sing in a voice of such aching tenderness that she felt spontaneous tears in her eyes.

"E lucevan le stelle…."

There was no other sound for her in the world. The press guys sucked in this exclusive with incredulous joy. As he sang she translated the words of the second part in her head.

'Oh! sweet kisses, oh, lingering caresses,

Trembling, I'd slowly uncover her dazzling beauty.'

In her mind a full orchestra played, dubbed in by her memories of listening to recordings when her husband had been alive. This was a sweet agony of guilt, a torture of love for this man. What else could a man offer his lover but this? And what was she giving him in return except deception?

The press stared in stupefied silence for a second when he finished by drawing her lips to his in a tender kiss. Then there was a shout, a cheer, and calls of "Encore, Bravo, Maestro."

Marco held up his hands.

"That's a wrap guys. We had a deal, remember."

There were a few stragglers but they respected his generosity. Already the images would be beaming up to satellites from the media trucks. Big Marco was back and for the press there was the Prince Harry and Meghan show still to come. For now, their editors were placated.

Helen took a deep breath. She mustn't lose her focus. So far everything was calm.

"That was so wonderful. Thank you," she said.

"Thank you for being with me and for falling into your role."

"Did you think I wouldn't?"

"In the case of a woman a man never knows. It's always a walk on thin ice. If you melt her she is no longer there. If you do not warm her, she is cold."

"Perhaps some females aren't so difficult."

"For sure, and it is because they are in love themselves."

She had no words for an answer. She took his hand and kissed his lips. The guards swept them through the security checks and they were free to mingle with the great and the good of the world. Every time he stopped, some gushing fan wanted a selfie with him.

135

He took it all in good humor, signed hats, posed, and postured to order. Beautiful fragrant women visibly paraded themselves before him with pouts and eyelashes in a show of practiced coyness. He responded with charm but never let go of her hand or held anyone's eyes but hers. Among the racegoers she spotted DCI Shannon Knightsmith who flicked her eyes towards the ladies' bathroom. She excused herself from Marco and strolled to Shannon who took her elbow and spoke in her ear like a girlfriend sharing a risqué joke.

"It's all gone down. There's some mess, but all the terrorists with VIP passes we identified have been taken out. There's been raids and arrests all over Europe and in the States. Two bits of bad news. Quaffir and Bagwandi are still missing. Less serious is that the press know about Scimitar of Holy Vengeance and there's questions about what the police knew. There's been a couple of suicide bombs and a couple of shootouts. It's all over the news and everyone here has a cell phone. No one needs to know that Royal Ascot was the target, always remember that."

"So, the threat is over?"

"Nothing is over while the leaders are still on the loose. The main plot has been busted. We knew who those guys were and what they intended to do. Anything further is pure gut instinct and freestyle, honey. Stay off the champagne and stay alert. The bosses say it's all over, but something tells me not to relax until Quaffir and Bagwandi are locked up or dead."

Helen nodded. Her heart gave a little flip of joy all the same. No one had gotten through. Shannon smiled, giving her elbow a squeeze.

"Hey, that was a sweet show out there. It's keeping the terrorist story off the top of the news. We're booked into Raymond Blanc's Panoramic Restaurant for lunch. We're at a table with Charles and Sophia of France. I've just seen their chopper come in. See you there."

They parted, Helen's heart pleading with the heavens that the threat was over. Now maybe there was a chance for her. Lunch with the French royals seemed like just a small blip on her radar of worry. Marco would take all the heat and attention and she could simply enjoy the view of the racecourse and maybe some lobster. She just had time to return to Marco and make their way to their table. A surge of tough-looking suited security guys were guiding a young man and a beautiful older woman through the doors, blocking all other diners, no matter their status. They were speaking in French. When the couple were at a window table, set for six, they dispersed to different corners, always watchful. She saw Shannon and what looked like her partner ahead of her and took Marco's offered, gentlemanly arm. At the table Shannon introduced Charles and Sophia, the controversial new royal couple of France. He was about twenty-five while she was about forty, but stunningly attractive with black hair, dark eyes, and a fine long aquiline nose that screamed aristocracy. Charles was boyish and handsome. Obviously, he'd been briefed about her and her story.

"The French nation send all their hearts for your little boy, Lanza. A hero Belgian Shepherd police dog called Diesel died in a gun battle in Paris with terrorists. It was a stray bullet in a battlefield situation. Our people cry for him, you know."

"Yes, the British people send our sympathies in return," she said.

Shannon introduced Sophia who almost winked. Helen had been briefed that this other woman was armed and up to speed with the whole situation. Her impression was that Charles knew nothing. Finally, she shook hands with a very tall, strong, good-looking guy introduced as Spencer, the Earl of Bloxington. She hated to ask but he appeared to be Shannon's partner, lover, or husband. This was a bizarre set-up. At a table on the far side of the restaurant she saw Cressida with a group of friends. Seated at a table for two, close by, was Bastian Wolf accompanied by the guy called Randolph Quinn from Sackman-Platinum Bank whom she'd met in Anna La Salle's office at Scotland Yard. Watching these people was like looking up at the night sky and trying to draw the shapes that the ancients had seen as gods and animals. She could see the dots, but couldn't join them up.

She skipped the champagne but feasted on lobster. This life of ease and luxury could sweep her away. At one time it would have worried her, but for now she was soaking it up, for it was certain not to last. No one wanted to miss the arrival of the Queen's carriage procession. The Earl of Bloxington swept up several bottles of champagne and carried the crate down to the rail under the grandstand with a view along the straight mile of perfect green grass. Marco shook hands, spoke in German, Spanish, and Italian, to a never-ending presentation of fans. He seemed so much in his element. Could this life at this intensity ever be for her? Every minute of calm brought that possibility closer and closer. She dared not let her mind jump that gap of a few hours.

A mile away at the entrance to the course, the crowds were waving and cheering as the horse-drawn landaus swung in through the golden gates and onto the main green-grass racetrack. The royal party had dined at Windsor Castle before making the traditional regal journey to the course. The procession of four open carriages approached the packed grandstand, the Queen's led the way, pulled by two pairs of Windsor gray horses. Accompanied by her second son, Prince Andrew, she was unmistakable in a bright yellow hat and a floral dress. In the second carriage was Prince Charles with Camilla. Everyone knew that the whole world wanted to see only the third carriage carrying Prince Harry the Duke of Sussex and his new American bride Meghan, Duchess of Sussex. In a Philip Treacy hat and Givenchy dress she looked stunning and elegant. A military band played the British national anthem, "God Save The Queen," as gentlemen removed their hats in respect for their monarch. The carriages turned into the tunnel under the grandstand to go through to the Parade Ring. Passes to this area were difficult to obtain but all of Helen's party were admitted as the Queen stepped down to mingle with the exclusive guests in a reception line waiting to meet her. This situation truly was a security nightmare. Many of the liveried footmen were special forces guys. Glancing around, Helen spotted several CIA and FBI types whom she'd seen at Scotland Yard. She brushed down her dress, checking her weapon. Two uniformed Metropolitan Police horse officers sat astride their mounts. Everything was calm. She checked the gun again. Everything was calm. Marco was at her side, his hand around her waist, marking her as his. From the corner of her eye she saw Bastian Wolf leave his seat in the banked seats overlooking the scene. Behind him was the main Ascot High Street and an entrance into the course. She picked up a sound, a noise like some kind of car accident, a blaring horn and a roaring diesel engine, maybe a truck. No one around her was taking any notice but Bastian was running towards the entrance gates. More than likely it was just a routine vehicle collision on a busy road.

The engine was louder, Bastian had drawn his gun.

This was a truck-attack and it was time to move.

She ran, following Bastian and noting Shannon to one side of her. They reached the road. About three hundred yards away, a monster semi-trailer truck had crashed into a number of cars and was heading for Bastian, who had taken position in the middle of the street. Dressed in his top and tails he calmly took his stance and fired six shots into the black-masked driver. Still the vehicle advanced. Helen drew her weapon and placed a clip through the windscreen into what looked like at least two other guys. Now there was a storm of fire from other positions. The truck swerved and crashed into more cars and a street lamp. A hand was on her arm. She swung round to see Marco.

"Jesus, what the fuck?" he shouted.

She nodded and pulled another clip from her stocking, reloaded and retook her combat stance. This was not the time to chat. Bastian joined her, speaking calmly.

"We've got the fire power, but there might be a bomb and more armed guys in the back."

Uniformed cops were clearing the area. Shannon had a police radio. For sure the royals would have been led away to the grandstand. With luck no one had really taken in what had happened. The truth would come out but not before the police had control. Around her, police voices were telling people to move on and that it was a traffic accident. Lines of vehicles were starting to form. Her job here was over now since there were firearms guys and snipers everywhere. Still she watched the trailer which had curtain sides that could be pulled back. The fasteners along the bottom were loose. She knew that at any minute there could be a hail of bullets from inside. She spotted a slight movement. Bastian was alert to it and called out.

"Hold fire. If we shoot through the fabric we'll hit other cops."

In a bound he jumped onto the truck cab and scaled his way to the roof which was a light, semi-opaque, plastic covering. He stayed out of sight, looking along the length of the vehicle.

"Time to show yourselves boys," he called out, throwing his top hat halfway along the roof. Gunfire erupted upwards ripping his hat to pieces. Suddenly the curtain pulled back to reveal four masked men, two with AK47 machine guns. One of the unarmed men leapt to the ground and headed straight for Helen. She saw at once he was trying to operate a contact inside a heavy winter coat. She'd seen this before in Iraq. As she was about to place a head shot, Marco stepped forward and drove a crunching fist hard into the terrorist's face. He fell to the ground holding his head. In seconds, officers overpowered him. At the same time snipers took out the three others on the trailer in a choreographed ballet of blood.

Helen was stunned. Maybe Marco had no idea that he'd just floored a suicide bomber. Why the hell had he involved himself?

"That was crazy," she said.

"Not as crazy as a woman with a gun in her panties. Are you OK? You must have been expecting this."

She didn't answer. She had no answer.

"That was quite a punch," she said.

"You think the Mafia in Napoli give someone a little slap? I'm thinking you knew this was coming. This isn't about a few kids buying drugs is it? That guy in my house was one of these types, wasn't he?"

The game was up and he was no fool. Again, she deflected his question.

"Maybe you should check on Cressida. I'm going to be explaining a lot of stuff and writing half a book before I can get away."

She avoided his eyes, turning her attention back to the scene in front of her. Almost certainly she'd killed at least one guy in the truck cab. Marco touched her arm.

"We'll talk later. I'm asking why you have a gun and a spare magazine under your dress. I'm asking myself why you don't mention it."

"I'll explain it all. For now, I've got to focus on my job. Please Marco, I know what you're saying and we'll talk later, OK?"

"Yes, of course. Call me as soon as you can."

His tone was serious and cool. She knew that as he turned over all the events in his mind, he would see the whole picture. The news channels would all be full of the operation to take out

Scimitar of Holy Vengeance and the various battles that had taken place. In short, he would know he'd been deceived right from the start of her relationship with him and Cressida. For now, she had no feelings. She was a cop. She had one final thought.

"Marco, I'm sorry in ways you'll never know. I know it's not your responsibility, but please care for Lanza until I can see you again."

As he looked back at her she, could see the sadness in his face. He spoke slowly.

"Of course. Do your work, come back to our home and trust us to care for him."

What a fucking mess, but amongst it all, Marco Ambastilias was a totally good man. And PC Helen Marx loved him totally. If she told him now, it would have the flavor of lies and manipulation. The words boiled in the cauldron of her heart, but choked in her throat.

He turned and walked away.

She watched the official machinery take up the routine of aftermath. Bomb guys, drug and explosive sniffer dogs, coroner's officers, photographers, CSI, ballistic specialists, and of course media spin professionals. Now she had a role to play and it didn't involve any kind of personal love story.

CHAPTER TWENTY-THREE

The cop stuff was easy. She wrote her reports at a desk in Anna La Salle's office. She'd heard the advancing truck, had opened fire. She'd watched the suicide bomber running at her and had taken aim, but Marco, the world's greatest opera singer had banged him on the chin before he could detonate his bomb. If you wrote it quickly it kind of sounded sensible. She'd fired at two targets but only post-mortem examinations of bodies would reveal who had fired the killing shots. With every word of her report she thought of him, that man who had been her lover and now must be seeing her full betrayal of his trust. It was 11 p.m. when the weary troupe of cops and international agents assembled in the conference room. Dickon Maltravers opened the briefing.

"Gentlemen, we have something of a triumph and something of a disappointment. The triumph is that no innocent person was killed or injured and that Her Majesty the Queen's horse won the Sackman-Platinum Cup. The royal party passed a calm day undisturbed by ghastly religious lunatics. A further triumph is that twenty-one senior members of Scimitar of Holy Vengeance are dead. Gentlemen we have cut the body from the snake but not the head. Neither Quaffir nor Bagwandi have surfaced. These guys are slick and devious. The CIA and FBI have intercepted traffic to indicate that these masterminds knew we had identified all of the VIP pass-holders. All they could do was to draw on clean-skin local boys to mount a low-tech attack with vehicles. Ladies and gentlemen, these leaders sent their own comrades to die knowing they'd been uncovered, hoping that this truck could crash the fence into the parade ring and attack our Queen and her family. The plan was to machine gun the crowd and detonate homemade suicide vests. We intercepted a second vehicle some miles away in which seven men were armed with axes and butcher's knives. We're all familiar with that tactic from the London Bridge atrocity. While Bagwandi and Quaffir are at liberty and alive, they have thousands of young unknown martyrs in our community to send against us. With social media speeches and propaganda, they can incite and excite wave after wave of attack. Families will lose sons and daughters whose minds have been poisoned by these psychopaths. Our operation will continue until we eliminate our targets. Once again, I must stress that no one must know what we know. These guys monitor every bit of news and every straw in the wind. The fact is that at this minute we have no fix on our enemy."

Helen took in the information. Even now she wouldn't be able to talk to Marco about the police investigation. It was a job for her to see what use she could now be to her bosses. As the room emptied, Deputy Assistant Commissioner Anna La Salle remained and took a seat next to her.

"You did well, and by accident your man Marco did brilliantly. That guy who ran at you should have been shot dead but now we have a prisoner. He was a young man who everyone thought was just a trainee bus driver. Our experts believe he'll crack."

"I'm guessing there'll be specialists with some colorful interrogation techniques?"

Anna nodded seriously. "Between you and me, there's a guy from the French Foreign Legion and a couple of American Special Forces operators who are very experienced at putting questions in the right way."

From her own military involvement, Helen knew the prisoner had no chance, particularly since he wasn't a hardened soldier. As each minute passed, her thoughts turned more and more to her own personal situation. Anna placed a hand gently on her shoulder. The touch and warmth of another human being opened her emotions in a rush of uncontrollable tears.

"It's obvious you'd formed a bit of a thing with Marco. How does it stand between you now?"

"Nowhere, bloody nowhere. He saw me pull a gun from under my dress and then go back for another magazine. He knew straight away that I was set up for something but hadn't told him. I let his daughter carry on without telling either of them of the danger. It's possible they'd have just gone ahead anyway but the point is I lied and lied, telling him it was about a couple of drug dealers. He'll never trust me again."

"Believe it or not I had a situation with a guy when I was a young cop. I fell for him but didn't explain what I did for a job."

"Why not?"

"Cos I thought he might be a crook and I could lock him up by staying undercover."

"What happened in the end?"

"I married him."

Helen had to smile. "So, was he a crook and does he know you're a cop yet?"

"He was a bit of a cocky rule bender and yes, he found me out. It was rough for a while."

"He forgave you?"

"Forgive is a difficult idea isn't it? To forgive you kind of step back from a feeling of resentment or anger. Marco's a proud man so he'll be feeling angry that you fooled him. That's the area I'd work on if I were you."

"I never fooled him. He kept saying it was all overkill for a couple of regular hoods."

"So, he doesn't have to feel that anger. If he loves you he'll understand, and if you understand the life of a cop, you're a crook, or you're sleeping with one, or both."

"We know he's not a crook," Helen answered feeling almost a glimpse of hope.

"Give it a bit of time. For now, I want you to stay on the squad if that fits with you. As our man just said, you can't tell Marco about Quaffir and Bagawandi. Things slip out, even from cops. Our only hope is to make them think we've lost interest and don't even know they're in the area. The news shows will be telling the world that all those guys from the truck are dead. I need you to tell Marco that after he punched the suicide bomber, a police sniper took him out because he tried again to detonate the bomb."

"Please no. You want me to lie again."

"No, I'm telling you that's what happened. You're merely telling him what your boss told you."

"Yeah, sure. Once you've smashed the car up, why worry

about a scratch on the paint?"

"Exactly. For now, keep a low profile and work with DCI Shannon Knightsmith. There'll be masses of paperwork to complete and there'll be a big routine investigation by the complaints and discipline team, to tie the dead bodies to the right gun. Just take the next two days as leave. I'm keeping Bastian close to the Ambastilias family, but they won't see him."

Anna La Salle stood and went back to her official life in front of the cameras and critics of the world. She was a woman with kids and it seemed she'd known love. A bigger world turned on.

Helen had few other choices. She was a dog handler without a dog and a woman in love without a lover. No matter what, she was a cop with a duty and if that didn't define her life, then nothing did or ever would. It was half past midnight, surely too late to call Marco. She loved him enough to be inappropriate and rude.

"Hey, I'm sorry it's so late."

"Don't be sorry, I've been thinking of you."

"Do I need to ask what you've thought?"

"This terrorism thing is all over the news. Helen, there were gun battles and suicide incidents all over London. There's hundreds of cops and international agents involved. The BBC and CNN are saying there was a plot to take out the royal family and that police swooped to intercept them. You knew, didn't you?"

"I knew."

"So, you let me go there while you have a secret gun? I'm a fool who doesn't know his woman has a gun in her pussy. I am your man and your lover and if there's danger I would always be there for you. Why not trust me? Why let my child maybe die because you don't tell us?"

"It wasn't in my pussy. That's not a police territory. If you want to know that's only for you because I love you."

"Now you say this because I find you out. Before, you stay cold in your words and hot in your actions. I long for you close to me as a woman but the trust in you as a friend is gone."

She could hear the hurt in his voice. Her mind swept back to Anna La Salle's advice.

"Marco, I didn't fool you. You said to me time and time again that you couldn't believe all this was to catch a couple of drug dealers."

"Yes, I thought this, but passion for a woman blinds a man. He wants to trust and believe. All you modern women say men are selfish sex monsters and bullies but I tell you, a man who loves a woman is helpless."

"I don't really want this conversation on the phone, Marco. I love you but I did deceive you because those were my orders."

"In my life no orders overrule a man who loves and protects his family. You'd come into my life and you belonged there with my child. I would have held you there in my arms forever. You made choices and in life you live with them. I will never deny you love, but the trust is broken. You're the only cop I've known and I believe your own truest love must be your work."

"And your work isn't important to you? Don't you sing love into the eyes of a woman you don't love, in order to do your work, to create a bigger art for others out of love? Isn't that a lie for a greater cause?"

She heard him sigh deeply. She allowed him time to respond.

"In pure terms you're right. Many things are happy lies. A woman may want the joy of her child but not reflect on the pain of birth even though she knows it. She has that balance and that choice and that is what you denied me."

Her response was hot and without thought.

"The only child I'd ever want would be yours and no one ordered me to tell you that."

"And that I believe, because I have held you as my lover. Before you're my lover you're a cop and that person hasn't loved me."

It was hard to argue. She'd known all along it would come to this. She wanted sleep and oblivion.

"I'll come over in the morning. Let's make this simple, OK?"

"Sure. Ciao, Helen."

She clicked off. At least at the death of love she'd told him she loved him. Like a cathedral in a landscape of ruin, those words stood proud. She got a lift in an L-district response car back to her small police house in Streatham. Without Lanza the place seemed big and empty. Soon she would have to make a decision about taking a new puppy. That would commit her to a period of years as a dog handler. She poured a very large whisky, sloshed in a shot of

146

tap water and threw it down her throat. She'd eaten little all day and the hit was instant. At least she could still sleep.

CHAPTER TWENTY-FOUR

The Uber cab dropped her at Marco's house. As Cressida opened the door Sam and Lanza bounded out to greet her. The girl looked disheveled and hungover.

"You OK?"

"Yah sure, like you know we partied on Bollinger until three. I dragged myself out of bed to give Lanza his meds."

Helen touched her arm. "Thanks for the way you've cared for him."

Cressida shrugged. "I love him so it's easy. I hear there was a lot of police action stuff."

Marco appeared in the hall. He looked tired and strained.

"Hi," she said.

"Hi, come through. I'll fix some coffee. How was your night?"

"It was official. The more the mayhem, the more the dull bureaucracy."

She wanted to hug him, tell him she loved him. She held back, uncertain of his mood.

"How's that guy I punched?" he asked in a flat tone. "The news hasn't mentioned a prisoner."

"I'm afraid he got hit by a stray bullet in some crossfire. Anna La Salle asked me to explain to you."

"Jesus, that was careless wasn't it? Maybe some agent like that Bastian Wolf executed him?"

"They didn't tell me the exact details."

The lie soured in her mouth. How she hated this.

He sighed and poured out two coffees from an Italian espresso pot.

"Helen, you know things can never be the same between us. I

know you had orders and you can't choose what you do. If I'd known the danger you were going into I'd have been there with you. I would never have let my daughter put herself at such a risk. You could have trusted me enough to have warned me."

"But what if Cressida had kicked up a fuss or warned a friend? Everything was set up to take out the terrorists who planned to get into the racecourse with VIP passes. We had to make everything look completely calm."

"Including getting me there to add a bit of showbiz spin?"

"Yes, I'll admit that."

"I think your bosses tipped off the press I would be there."

"If they did they didn't tell me."

He slumped down on the sofa.

"You told me time and time again that this was about drugs. I said to you it seemed overkill. I didn't know you had a gun in your panties."

"It was a thigh stocking-top holster."

"I'm looking at you now and feeling desire for you and loving your beauty and your courage. But, I can never trust you again. What is true? What is a lie?"

"My feelings for you are true, Marco."

"Until last night you'd said nothing of feelings. Then you find love suddenly like a band-aid to patch up the mess."

"I wanted to tell you the whole picture, but I couldn't."

He got up and paced the room, a buzz of anger around him.

"I can't blame you, to be fair. In the Mafia they have the *Omerta* rule of silence. I learned these things as a boy. Tell me now all this horror is over."

How could she answer him while the two leaders were still at large and dangerous? She couldn't tell him the truth but just could *not* lie to him.

"As far as I know it's finished, but the bosses don't tell me everything do they?"

"You know Helen I just have a feeling that there is more and you're following orders. Look at this from my shoes. A man was shot dead in this house. A truck full of terrorists die in front of me. The news is full of stories about this Scimitar of Holy Vengeance and you knew. Tell me now if this is all over."

The words wouldn't come. She couldn't lie again. He

continued, his eyes locked on to hers.

"I believe you don't want to lie to me and I respect you for that. I desire you as a woman and love you because I'm a fool. Tell me now there's no possible chance that some religious maniac is going to show up at the door with a knife, gun, or bomb. Tell me all of them are dead and the police are going back to chasing speed tickets and telling tourists the way to Buckingham Palace."

"No one could guarantee something like that," she answered quietly.

"Helen, I hear you and your reluctance to answer me is a loud message. I thank you for that. Cressida and I are taking a lazy drive through Europe, so we can carry Sam in the car. We leave this afternoon. Our destination is Naples. I still have a home there. I have no plans to come back to London at present."

"So, I won't see you again?"

"I think not."

His eyes were heavy with sorrow. She couldn't hold back her tears. He sat down and put an arm around her. "You gave me back my passion and desire Helen and I'll always love you for that. I must keep my child safe. You have other loyalties and I could never live with that."

"I know, I knew it all along. I'll need to get my suitcase and take Lanza."

She stood and went upstairs. Her case was in the corner where she'd put it the evening she'd arrived. She called Kaitlyn for a ride rather than argue with an Uber driver about taking Lanza. She remained seated on the bed, not wanting any more futile conversation. She heard a car pull up and saw the Range Rover Vogue on the drive. Sam and Lanza waited with wagging tails for pats and scratched ears. She went to the kitchen, collected his bed and his medications. It seemed that neither Marco nor Cressida wanted to say the final goodbye. Helen opened the tailgate. Sam jumped in and performed an excited spin. She pushed him out, helping Lanza to make the jump. She closed the door and saw Sam's sad eyes looking up at her. He gave a small whine, his tail still. He stood on his hind legs against her, seeing Lanza behind the screen.

"See you later Sam," she said, throwing in her suitcase and the dog bed. Still there was no sign of anyone. As she paused at the door, Marco ran out, taking her in his arms.

"Maybe in life we don't have too many choices. I choose to go now because I have to go. But I choose never to say goodbye even though we don't meet again."

"OK. No goodbyes."

From the corner of her eye she saw Sam, his rubber chewing ring in his mouth. She recalled how he'd brought it for Lanza the night he'd arrived weak and in pain from the hospital. He dropped the toy at her feet and simply sat down. She picked it up and bent down to hug him.

"He'll never forget you, Sam."

It was done. Kaitlyn started the engine and was fastening her seatbelt. Helen swung into the seat as the car pulled away. She took a deep breath.

"You needed to get out of there honey. Much more of that and I was going to start bawling myself."

"I was expecting it to end like this all along, so it shouldn't hurt, should it?"

"What do you mean "end"? Nothing's ended in his mind. He's completely in love with you."

"So what? He has to protect his daughter and can't forgive me for putting her at risk. To be honest, I'd feel the same."

"Give it a bit of time. Love's like a bloody ticking clock in a quiet house at night. The more you try to ignore it, the louder it gets."

"I'm a digital kind of girl. I've never had a ticking clock."

"You have now."

Her house phone was ringing. Only police called that number. It was 7 a. m. What the fuck?

"Yeah, hi?"

"PC Helen Marx?" said a young male in a casually superior posh voice.

"Who is this?"

"I'm Olly from media management. Like you know it's just so great to speak to you. That dog of yours is just so perfect. We all love Stanza."

"Lanza"

"Hey, forgive. I did poetry at uni. Yah, that's perfect. Lanza—

151

how is he?"

"Olly—who the fuck are you and how did you get this number?"

"Anna La Salle gave us the nod. Look, everyone hates cops, right? You know, twenty terrorists shot dead and religious prejudice and stuff. No one hates a hero dog. We need a counter story. The press are so on top of us. Cops are racist killers. You know the routine. We want to strike back with canine bite. The hero police dog returns to duty. Can you get yourself dressed and brush up Dansak?"

"Lanza. His name is Lanza."

"Sure, that's our boy. We love him. We really love him. We've got slots on daytime TV. The nation is going to eat this and lick the sugar off the spoon. Has he got scars? Can you see the wounds?"

"My friend, he'll never return to duty. He stopped a bullet in his lung and lost two ribs. If it hadn't been for Simon Leonard, he'd be dead."

"Hey, give me that name again. He's going to be up there in lights."

"I can't say he doesn't deserve that. Lanza deserves his place in the hall of fame. Why the fuck do you need me?"

"Look, Helen, maybe this is a bit showbiz, but work with us. TV Britain have organized a poll of viewers. Since midnight seven million people want Lanza to receive a special royal medal of honor. They've sent a request to the Queen and to the prime minister at Downing Street. All the popular newspapers have signed up. Facebook is on fire."

"This is incredible. I love my little boy, but all I can do is hold his leash."

"Hey, the world has seen you with Marco Ambastilias. God, you're a camera magnet. Miss World Cop, celebrity boyfriend, and hero dog. You can change the way the world sees cops, Helen."

"If you're on the level I guess this is what they call public relations. So far, we've kept it secret that I was a cop. Are we dropping that story?"

"Wow, yes. The media will eat this. Your eyes met over a dying dog. We're going to run with the truth, which is breaking new ground for us. Be ready in an hour. A car will take you to the

TV studios. First up is an interview with BBC World. Then you're on with Morgan Spiers and he's like mega, even though he says it himself.

"You want me in uniform?"

"Hey, that's a male fantasy angle. We'll work with that."

"I'm going to check you out with Anna La Salle. If you're kosher, I'll be ready."

"Be there, Helen. That dog's going to howl out a big message."

She sank back onto her bed. This was crazy. She called Anna La Salle. She sounded weary and harassed.

"Sure, Helen, just do it. The police press guys wanted a good news story, so I threw you to the lions. There's nothing to be gained now by not telling the story straight. Pull this off and you can go anywhere. If you can deflect all these media bastards, please, please help me."

While she dressed she clicked on the TV. In that instant she realized how much pressure her bosses were having to take. Police had shot dead twenty terrorists, maybe more. There were rumors of Russian agents with guns alongside London cops and American Special Forces. Ambitious camera-licking politicians were demanding resignations and public enquiries. As she pulled on her uniform she remembered her dead man. A man she respected and would have honored all her life. Terrorism had made her a lonely widow at the age of twenty-seven. Lanza and her police career had given her back a life. She had never fought back until now. Terror had cost her two lives, but now she would play to win. Chance had dealt her a hand and she knew her role. She thought of him—of Marco Ambastilias. Even in a few words with him she had seen the confidence of performance. He had sung for her in the street and the world had stopped to applaud. She had shared honest sexual passion with this man as his equal. Now she would step out with Lanza and just maybe she would change the world. Not with lies. Not with bullets. But with the truth about loyalty, duty, human dignity, and love. Let that big shot opera guy see her on her own stage of real life, dealing with the stories of real pain. Maybe he did love her? Maybe others would see her and love her too? Maybe he would see that too? Maybe he would see into his own heart and see a reflection of hers? She wanted to be no other woman and she

153

wanted no other man. Fate had dealt her a hand and an audience fell silent for her to perform. She could do this. Her man had shown her the way and his woman would seize it as it her own.

She could tell Lanza was subdued and if he could speak she knew he would reproach her for taking him away from Sam. All the same, he sensed he was going out to work. A police dog unit drove her to the BBC studios in Portland Place. A makeup guy dusted her face and it was *lights-camera-action.* Over and over she smiled at the red light and told the world the tale. Lanza sat proud beside her. His time with Sam had shown him some casual, human, Labrador-ways but he was perfect. Helen pulled back his fur to show his scars where his titanium plate held together his sternum. She moved on to studios on the South Bank near Waterloo. He spent an hour on the sofa with Morgan Spiers for his hit breakfast show. Next up was a show called *"Femme Fatality"* a kind of loud bunch of celebrity women talking about their love affairs, world politics, dramas with fit of bras and passion for homemade pastry. They patted Lanza but seemed far keener to talk about Marco Ambastilias.

"He's a gorgeous hot guy. Are you an item?" breezed Cynthia Sirocco, the soap actress and cleavage promoter.

"We're friends," Helen replied.

"Yo! I'd like a friend like Big Marco with his hand on my ass in the Royal Enclosure at Ascot."

The other women shrieked with outrage or glee or both.

"That'd be sexual harassment in my black book, Sugar," yelled Michelle Mabelle the feminist novelist and campaigner.

"I said *my* ass," bellowed Ms. Sirocco at full volume and an edge to her tone. "I was talking *about my ass,* not out of it."

The others shrieked again. A cat fight was in the air. She guessed this was good TV.

Lanza sent out expressions of puzzlement at this bizarre circus, lolling out his tongue and glancing between the overly made-up faces of the women. The conversation moved on to Twitter-politics and a luxury vegan cheese called *"Squeeze"* made of recycled waste paper pulp. Helen was so glad to escape. Her driver took her to Scotland Yard for lunch where Lanza would be accepted in the canteen. As she stepped from the vehicle a young male civilian greeted her. She shook his hand.

"I'm Olly from media. We spoke this morning, yah?"

"Yes, it's been quite a day so far."

"Helen, you're sensational. The world isn't just licking the spoon, they're eating the jar. This afternoon we've got the papers and the mags for photo shoots on the steps outside, with the Scotland Yard sign. We've got the dog doc coming up for the session. Everyone, just everyone is so, so proud of you."

"They should be proud of my little boy."

"The world's just loving, uh Mario."

"*Lanza*—his name is Lanza."

"Yah, yah, that's it. Your dead hero husband named him. I tell you, there were tears enough to flood London when you gave them that angle."

Helen had to laugh. Her life had hardened her to take nearly everything on the chin. This young guy was modern and politically correct. All the same, he was far more cynical than her.

"Olly, it's not an angle, it's the truth. I understand what you people need and I'll step up to that, as Lanza has always stepped up."

"That's perfect. Anna La Salle and just all the bosses can't believe the heat you've taken off them. We could pile dead terrorists in Trafalgar Square today and it would be inside page stuff."

Her lunch was punctuated by a chain of admirers. A woman turned up with an ink stamp pad and took autographs of Lanza's paws. A police publicity official talked to her about T-shirt production. This was how the modern police had to be. Everything was lived out in a screaming muddle of competing opinions. There was no right or wrong. It was a simple struggle for media control and manipulation, second by second, minute by minute, as the news channels and internet platforms churned out endless conflicting propaganda. Terrorist maniacs and cute dog videos jostled for dominance and it never stopped. Never.

She took a deep breath as Olly led her out to meet the press on the steps. It was great to see the hero dog-surgeon, Simon Leonard, again. He was a real caring person who did a real job. Normally, no one knew and he'd never sought fame.

The frenzy started.

"Helen, give us a sweet smile. Now go cute, make some eyes honey. Wow, that's the shot. Hey, you're a stunner. They're calling you the sexy widow of Wimbledon, Helen. Is Marco going to change that? Give us a big wet kiss on Lanza's nose. Hey, that's cute. Give us a Lady Di big doe eye. Wow, now chin on fist looking distant wistful. Yeah, you're so gorgeous."

Something had happened. Suddenly she was officially sexy and beautiful. Strangely, the more others reinforced that idea, the more she actually felt that way. It was wrong and it was egotistical, but she was loving it. When the press scented a trail, they themselves were a pack of dogs. "There's a rumor you carry a gun in your panties. Take your hat off, wow, let your hair fall free, now go over the shoulder looking back."

For half an hour she did everything everyone asked. It was useless trying to answer individual questions. One thing made her stop the action.

"Ladies and gentlemen, I need to get Lanza some water."

She could see the poor boy had had enough. It was a relief to go back inside and let him lie down in a conference room, where interviews with a couple of celebrity magazines had been arranged. A pretty young woman posed the first question.

"You and Marco share a love of dogs, don't you?"

"Yes, he has a Labrador called Sam."

"Fantastic. He's in love with you and that love has brought him back to the world stage. This is a fantastic story."

"I can't speak for Marco."

"It must be a collision of worlds—the cop and the opera star."

"Until I met Marco, my best friend was a dog. A man is harder to handle but you do have a bigger vocabulary of commands."

The woman laughed.

"I'm going to splash that quote."

And so it went on until, at last by late evening she made it through the door of her little house in South London. She fed and watered Lanza and clicked on the news. She poured a whisky and threw in some ice. Watching TV was like looking in the mirror. All she saw was herself. Terrorism and the search for Quaffir and Bagwandi didn't feature. She needed to sleep and not think of that bloody man.

CHAPTER TWENTY-FIVE

The whisky hit her hard, but she was awake by two o clock in the morning. A day lay ahead, but she had no idea where her life, or career was headed. For the moment it seemed she was a sexy cop icon. She'd liked her look on the screen, and clever editors had done everything to make her more than she, or any real woman, could actually be. In truth, she was alone, without a friend or lover. Maybe she could down another whisky? She didn't want to start that route out of desperation again. If she thought of him, her loneliness softened into his face and his kind dark eyes. A flash of sexual imagery fired across her mind like a shooting star. She'd stored that moment of him pulling out and jerking out his cum onto her clitoris as she masturbated, their eyes fixed on each other, each of them shameless in shared need to tear down the fences and see the ecstasy the other brought to them. It was naughty, it was a bad-girl thrill to show herself to him. Bad of her to ask him to do it. Delicious to have that moment in her small library of abandon. She needed to sleep, wanted oblivion, didn't want that man to control her fantasy. She went to her drawer and found her little buzzy silicone friend and lube, just in case. She flicked back to that sexy night of her first hard orgasm, that other masturbating girl. Her hand teased along the edge of her sex, tantalizing her triangle. She was a TV star, she was beautiful. Her hand eased to her clitoris. She didn't have to come. This was just a distraction in a sleepless night. She clicked on the buzz. The feeling was comforting, not so sexual. She was wet, she was moving faster and pressing harder. It was good to tease her entrance with her *friend*, good to think of his hot cock hard and harder in her pussy. Good to squeeze her tube around his longing cock, needing to spurt out his juice into her belly. Her flesh needed to seize his hot cum. She wanted to see his soaking cum pour out onto her naughty pussy. She wanted him to jerk his cum onto her clit, to flow into her juice as she let go. She needed to come, needed to feel his heat in her groove. She was calling out, flicking out her orgasm from her hard woman shaft as he held his tireless spurting cock against her clit and fingers.

"Cum, fuck, do it," she groaned as she released her own juices into her pressing hand and pulsing filled belly. The aftershocks bubbled out through her throat. Even though he wasn't there, Marco had made her come harder and wetter than she had ever managed alone. To love a man and come in a fantasy of him was not masturbation. It was fan fiction. She slept in the sticky sweaty arms of a man who wasn't there. God, she'd let go without shame or restraint. That buzzy cock had been that man. The fact that he existed on this earth was a joy. The fact that she wasn't with him was a torture.

Another day dawned. A shower was urgent. Although she was an officially beautiful celebrity, she had no idea what her next orders would be. It was 7:30 a.m. and her cell was ringing. It was Deputy Assistant Commissioner Anna La Salle.

"Helen, great job yesterday. We may need more today—no, we *will* need more. Just to let you know we've had a car ram-attack on Parliament a few minutes ago. Some clean skin inspired by Quaffir wiped out some civilians in Parliament Square. Excuse my French but this fucking nightmare has hardly started. I'm sorry. I'm rambling. Look, some guys have asked me how it stands between you and Marco. So how does it?"

"Anna, ma'am, I don't know. He's pissed that I misled him. He's gone off to Naples with Cressida."

"OK, I'll pass that down the line. I've a gut feeling that some guys well above my pay grade are going to be wanting you to see him. I'm a dumb cop at the end of the day. It's all about PR if you know what I mean. If we fly you to Naples is he going to spit in your face or take you in his arms?"

Helen thought for a moment. She was officially hot and sexy. She was a somebody. Whatever they were cooking up she had the balls for it.

"Bit of a mix. Perhaps he'd take me in his arms and give me a wet kiss."

"In your shoes I'd take the flight and some mint gum. I'll pass on your analysis. Meanwhile do what that creep Olly dreams up. He's a sick prick but Christ he can spin the angles."

"Semper fi, Anna."

"Until this latest jerk crashed into the Palace of Westminster you'd taken all the heat, Helen. Cute journalists are speculating that there's a puppet master and for fuck's sake we know they're right. Between you and me, the Americans have locked up a top aide to Scimitar of Holy Vengeance in Oklahoma. This guy is gay and has everything to lose cos SOHV don't do same-sex love. He's talking to their special interrogators if you understand me. They've got footage of this guy going oral on his man friend. He confirms that Quaffir and Bagwandi are in London and looking for their chance. They want a world-shattering spectacular. They're going to hit us hard, Helen, and they have thousands of followers. We're running over six hundred terror plot investigations at this moment. There's eight million souls in London. With you on the team, I don't feel so alone."

"Anna, I'll do whatever I have to do, you know I will."

"I know your professionalism. By the way I saw the ballistics on the truck cab. Bastian nailed his man with five out of six shots. You nailed one guy with three bullets and the other with two, that's not bad out of eight bullets."

"I was nervous. You know, stage fright."

"You're a star. Let's stick together and beat these bastards, no matter the cost."

Olly had organized another day of dog and mistress media scrums. She hadn't switched on her laptop or checked her Facebook messenger. Who was going to say anything she wanted to hear? By the end of the day she'd given an interview to a magazine called *"Fur and Feather"* and posed with a German weightlifter who sold chemical supplements for vegan pets. She'd been invited to go on a show called *"Paws For Thought"* where celebrities worked out what animals people from the audience had at home. If this was fame she'd far rather be a kennel maid. It was late afternoon when she checked her in-boxes. Her eyes zapped to one small SMS message.

"*Che bellezza*! Saw you on TV in my hotel room in Dijon, France. Had to tell you. Marco x"

What the fuck was this? Why tell her that? But Christ, he'd seen her and responded. How could he say things were over and then tease her with stuff like this? Should she reply? God, she wanted him and could never deny that within herself. Deep down she hadn't wanted to stop him and Cressida leaving London. He'd asked her to promise no more terrorists were going to turn up at the house. In reality she thought it was quite possible, merely in revenge, if nothing else. Until they reached Naples no one knew where they were and once there, any terrorists would probably have to deal with the Camorra mafia. So, should she reply? If she did, what should be her attitude? She thought back to her situation, before she'd taken that call to his house in the middle of the night. All her life had been response to demands, requirements, and the desires of others whom she always regarded as more important than her. Marco Ambastilias had changed the way she saw the world. Sure, he was a great singer and he believed that, because if his belief faltered, he wouldn't launch into an aria knowing that any human can fail. Now, she had killed, she had posed for the cameras, crossed and uncrossed her legs on those TV sofas. She had truly made love and knew the power of her own sexuality. Marco wanted her, yet she did *not* have to knee jerk her joy back to him. If she was right, he'd be in touch again, soon, and by then her longing for him would demand release. All she wanted now was to take Lanza for a walk on Streatham Common. She'd stop for some fish and chips soaked in salt and vinegar and crack open a couple of beers. The streets of London, the red double-decker buses and the black taxis, flowed in her blood. Life could offer opera houses, lobster, caviar and champagne, but nothing could replace the flavor of home. She awoke the next morning, alone and tearful. She checked her cell. Nothing. Nothing. Fuck you, Marco!

Kaitlyn collected her at ten o'clock. Lanza was well enough to leave at home for a few hours. She took a deep breath and stepped out to meet another day. She dressed in a fun, simple red and black jumpsuit with revere collar and wrap front from New Look. Her hair was still in its Ascot style and the TV makeup staff had tweaked her look to perfection. Soon enough she'd be back in a

160

hasty ponytail under a police cap.

"Just how many meetings and briefings can a girl take?" she commented, as they parked in Scotland Yard.

Kaitlyn sighed. "I know what you mean. This is a small chat and I'm going to be there myself because Randolph is kind of running this deal."

"He's your boyfriend from Sackman-Platinum Bank?"

"That's my boy, so no pouting, leg shows, or Lady Di eyes."

"Why are these bankers involved? Maybe I shouldn't say, but Marco hinted they can manage dirty money."

Kaitlyn gave her a hard stare. "It's OK to think that, but now's not the time to explain. The point is that they're the world's richest people. They have infinite wealth and I know that, cos I've seen it."

Helen decided she was well out her depth and was grateful for the strong coffee poured by DCI Shannon Knightsmith. In the room were the dashing Randolph Quinn, Anna La Salle, and Dickon Maltravers from MI6. Anna took the lead.

"We had an attack on the Houses of Parliament yesterday. It was a low-level vehicle assault by a guy who'd come in from Sudan, a complete nobody and he didn't succeed. We know from his internet use that he was directly radicalized by Quaffir. We know he met Bagwandi in Birmingham two days before he came to London. The terrorists are just ticking over, sending out mosquitoes while they're waiting to get re-armed with explosives and heavy weapons. Thousands and thousands of shipping containers enter the UK every day. We have a huge coastline and numerous small airfields. Guys, once they source the stuff, it will come in. The Americans are giving us every shred of intelligence they're picking up. Scimitar of Holy Vengeance are looking to buy."

Dickon Maltravers looked up and spoke calmly in a deep voice, glancing over the top of his half-spectacles.

"Thanks, Anna. These bastards stay just ahead of us. No cell phones, no internet, no faces on streets. They planned the Royal Ascot attack for about a year. At the last minute we took them out but still they tried a desperate plan B, which so easily could have succeeded. The prisoner from the truck is talking and we're a lot closer. He has revealed that Quaffir and Bagwandi use landline telephones and move in stolen vehicles on false number plates. But, they move when they want to. Our prisoner says that the Royal Ascot attack presented them with such a tempting target they just could *not* resist. Can you believe open horse drawn carriages in front of a crowd of thousands? A parade ring a few yards from a public road? There are few such targets unless we give them one so big and so soon, they'll have to take risks."

Next to speak was Shannon. "Right, we've all seen our TV stars Helen and Lanza. We've all seen the glossy coverage of Marco Ambastilias and the love of his life—the very same girl. Our terrorist friends have a very real personal motive to take out both of them but that's too obvious. Our friend Mr. Randolph Quinn has suggested a project which we believe will uncover them. It will be that juicy cold plum in the fridge that you just had to eat."

Randolph beamed a perfect smile and pushed back his dark wild hair. He was just so hot.

"The bank sponsors many events and sporting contests. Sackman Platinum prides itself on its attachment to culture, education, and the arts. Is that enough of the PR and marketing shit?"

Kaitlyn laughed. His eyes shot to her with a deep smile. These two knew each other deeply and enjoyed it.

"OK. We city slicker big shots are going to promote the return of one of the world's greatest performers. Guests will be stars, presidents, royals, and any possibly famous or important person who will accept free tickets, flights, accommodation, champagne, and blah, blah, blah. It will be a gala concert for Lanza, but more than that. It will be a fundraiser for all the working animals of the world. The tourist elephant in Thailand, the laboring donkey in Romania, and on and on. Sackman-Platinum have set up the *Lanza Foundation* and will match pound for pound, dollar for dollar all the public donations. In the interval a special guest will present the World Gold Medal for Animal Gallantry to Lanza. Guys, the greats of the world are fighting for that honor. The president of the United States of America is on the list and a heap of other leaders, Hollywood legends, and royals. Marco Ambastilias will sing the top arias in the world amongst a glittering array of divas and performers. The TV rights are sold, the recording, distribution, and

162

DVD deals are done. Needless to say, the generosity of the bank has been covered with maybe a slight profit. This is the biggest and best show ever to have happened in this universe."

Randolph Quinn was irritatingly shameless about wealth and grasping his share.

"And perhaps the biggest ever terrorist outrage," said Helen.

For half a minute nobody replied. Once upon a time she would have shrunk down in her seat, embarrassed to have spoken.

Dickon Maltravers was smiling. "That response my dear shows the power of our strategy. That's exactly what those evil bastards will think."

"As far as I know, Marco has no knowledge of this plan. Where would you hold such an event?"

"Our enemy is here in this city. We have secured the use of Bloxington Manor at Fleetworth Green on the edge of London. A stage will be erected in the middle of the lake and the show will have the fabulous manor house as its backdrop. His grace, the Eleventh Earl of Bloxington has connections with the police and has put the whole estate at our disposal."

Helen thought back for a moment. This was the big man with the crate of champagne at Ascot who was obviously very close to DCI Shannon Knightsmith.

"I imagine you'll have to inform Marco?" Helen said.

Anna La Salle spread her hands and looked to heaven. "We're sub-contracting that job to a specialist. Mr. Ambastilias has just arrived at his villa in Naples. You're on British Airways 2610 out of London Gatwick at 3:25 p.m. to Napoli Capodichino. He may be a gentleman and ask you to stay. If not, Sackman-Platinum will fix you up. They have a big operation in that city. I must stress we need him signed up to this project without delay. We're surfing a wave and we need to use it."

"No one's even asked me if I have a passport."

"If you haven't, you will have. In any event you'll be travelling first class with diplomatic authority and covert protection."

"You mean Bastian Wolf?"

Shannon cleared her throat and reached across to touch Helen's hand.

"Not exactly, Bastian is in the Naples area. He shadowed

Marco out there. Mr. Ambastilias is a top asset."

"I feel like a whale," Helen began. "Just now and then I pop up for air and get sight of you guys. Then it's back to the depths. Just tell me what I'm allowed to tell him."

"Nothing's changed. You want him to agree to this concert because of your caring for animals and what happened to Lanza. Once you've asked him his own agent will get a call from Sackman-Platinum. Believe me the voice of money speaks very loud. Don't miss your flight."

"Who's looking after Lanza?

Shannon Knightsmith replied. "The Earl is a big dog fan. Lanza's getting a break at Bloxington Manor. I kind of love him too. I hope you think we're suitable.

"Of course. You? The Earl?"

"He's my husband."

Helen shook her head. She was beginning to catch on that these guys were a kind of club. She knew the bank and the World Intelligence Forum were connected. They had wealth and power. They operated on some kind of international level with presidential authority which put the might of the USA and seemingly Russia, behind them. The enemy was big crime and for now, big terror. She could work with that—whatever it was.

CHAPTER TWENTY-SIX

The Airbus 320 climbed away from London, turning south to fly across France, towards the Mediterranean coast of Italy. She ordered a bottle of Chianti red wine with her in-flight meal of *filet mignon* and salad. The wine warmed her heart as she read and re-read the message on her cell screen.

'Even my view of the Bay of Naples doesn't replace you in my thoughts. I wanted something that wasn't yours to give. That was my mistake and my sadness. You didn't reply yesterday but I know you're working. I'll call you this evening. Please pick up. Please.'

She simply loved him and this time she'd simply tell him. Maybe she could be in his arms before he placed the call. Even now she had to deceive him if she followed her orders. Any leak, even by the most innocent accident, could alert Quaffir and Bagwandi. Looking from the window, her heart bursting with need for the man, her determination softened by the wine, she feared she would tell him. There could be no love without trust and in her bones, she knew he would die for her. She also knew that he would never expose Cressida to risk. Keeping her away from the event would be impossible and sharing the truth with her was just too dangerous. Until she felt his lips and his hard need for her, she didn't have to choose her path. She closed her eyes and lay back against the luxury seat. That hard cock pulsed into her belly. His seed fired into her flesh and juice. She crossed her legs, enjoying her wetness and semi tremor. His eyes were dark and kind, closing in joy as he let go in her, sharing her trembling abandon. Her nipples ached for his lips. Her life had been so tense and she'd hardly thought of her own body. When this was over she'd go back to the gym and work on her weight and shape. For now, she'd finish the wine.

As she entered the terminal, two large men in sharp blue suits gestured for her to leave the line for immigration controls. They exited by a side door and swept her into the rear seat of a deep blue armored Alfa Romeo Stelvio. A familiar tough-looking man turned and smiled.

"*Benvenuta*, Helen."

"Bastian—can I simply say what the fuck?"

"There's some local boys around your Marco. I just came for the ride and a little chat. Take my cell number and call me if there is any issue. I have some sudden international bank business, but I assure you the villa is totally secure."

"Are we talking police here?"

"Not exactly—"

"Camorra Mafia?"

"No, good guys on our side. The chief is Giuseppe Pino who's ex *Gruppo di Intervento Speciale*. He's a pro bodyguard with Sackman-Platinum. Helen these gentlemen know about secrecy and silence. *Capisce*?"

"Aren't you working for the Russians?"

"I'm a freelance. The enemy is terrorism, not Russia."

The car had moved off. At least Bastian's presence gave her a sense of security. If you counted fatal shootouts, he was her closest friend. She hated to admit it, but she absolutely trusted him.

"Where are we going?"

"You're going to Via Alessandro Manzoni where the world's greatest opera star has a villa overlooking the bay of Napoli. It's to the north of the city in Chiaia-Mergellina. He's not expecting you. If I were you, I'd enjoy a pizza Neapolitana. It has to have tomatoes from the slopes of the volcano Vesuvius and buffalo mozzarella cheese. There's no other place for pizza. I recommend a Barbera d'Alba wine. By my side I have a couple of bottles as a gift for Marco."

"What sort of man are you, Bastian?"

"A woman always says all men are the same. The only man who is different is the man she loves."

Just for a second she glimpsed a soul inside Mr. Bastian Wolf. He called her cell to give her the number. The car pulled up and he was gone, striding towards a powerful motorcycle parked in a bay.

166

He picked up a helmet from the back rack, fired the motor, and rode away into the hot melting turmoil of Naples. Bastian Wolf travelled fast and light. A few minutes later the car stopped at the gates of an imposing villa. The high walls were of stone. So now what did she do? She wasn't expected. On the seat beside her were two bottles of wine in an expensive paper carrier. On the gate pillar was an intercom. It seemed like the place to start. She pushed the button. Maybe he had servants? A male voice answered but the sound quality was poor.

"Pronto?"

As she wondered how to respond, she heard the lock release on the two high ornamental iron gates. In the distance a door opened at the back of the villa and a man started to run towards her. Her heart thumped, her soul sang. She stepped inside and took a few steps forward into the arms of her man, her lover. He held her tight, smothering her hair and head with urgent kisses.

"Helen, Helen, how can this be?"

"Maybe it isn't, maybe I'm dreaming. I got on a plane and I got off when it landed."

"This shouldn't have happened. I should have stayed in London. Cressida goes back to university in September in any case."

"I misled you Marco, but it wasn't to make a fool of you. I had orders and couldn't tell you the whole story."

"Let's not think of the past. Let me hold you."

His strong arms pressed her into his chest. The sun was still warm in the still evening air. There was scent from the lemon trees that grew in the garden. When he let her go they walked hand in hand to the villa. The interior took her breath away. The ornately tiled floor and sweeping staircase provided an air of art nouveau elegance. A fabulous grand piano seemed to beg for hands to caress it into life. Beyond she could see to the front of the building, to a terrace and balcony looking out over the Bay of Naples and the imposing volcano Vesuvius. Sam appeared in a frenzy of excitement to see her. He sniffed her, looking around as if to find his friend Lanza.

"Still he looks for him," said Marco.

Suddenly she felt a tear on her cheek. He put an arm around her.

"I don't know if I'm sad or happy," she sniffed with a smile.

"Believe me, in art the two are the same. Come and see my poor little view."

He took her hand and led her through to the balustrade at the edge of the marble-tiled patio. Dusk was settling over the deep blue Tyrrhenian Sea while lights were blinking on in the city and down the coast towards Sorrento. It was a fairy tale of magic with the heavy scent of oleander filling her senses. The crimson, purple, and deep pink of the bougainvillea flowers added to this crescendo of life. From the house came the sound of the piano playing. It was a delicate tune she knew at once was Mozart.

Marco breathed out deeply in a groan of appreciation for the music.

"Cressida is very gifted. Since you and Lanza, everything has flowered. It's the *Romanza in D minor*. As I say, beauty, vulgarity like in golden cupids and what Italians call *la tristezza* are difficult to separate. I think she doesn't know you're here, so she plays a minor key to find warmth and maybe love in sadness."

His deep eyes were fixed on hers. How she loved this artist of a man. How she loved the tough guy who had stepped in front of her to confront a suicide bomber with his fists. Could she risk losing him again? She had already closed her eyes as his fingers stroked down her cheek, still wet with tears. His gentle hand raised her chin to meet his lips in a kiss of such depth and softness that she melted into him and the perfumed night. This was the kiss she had never known but had always craved. Sensual but not sexual, it had lifted her from her body. To kiss a man like this was to know him and to know his wordless love. The music had stopped. Still he held her, his eyes closed. There was a sound from the house. She looked to see Cressida bounding towards her, Sam in tow. She stepped back from Marco and opened her arms to her.

"Helen, my papa didn't tell me. I'm so happy."

"Me too. He didn't tell because he didn't know."

He beamed and threw his arms around both of them.

"Where's that wine you brought me? Who's hungry for pizza Neapolitana?"

"That's an offer no one can refuse," said Helen.

Marco pulled out his cell and spoke in Italian at the speed of a Ferrari. Ten minutes later, the food was at the door, the glasses were filled and a table set on the terrace. Consciously she stored this moment, maybe for a day when she was old, reminiscing with her and Marco's children, maybe for a day when her cop's life was bleeding out in the gutter. Soon enough the urgency of the moment would kick back in.

"So, you come to save us in our emptiness. Thank you, thank you," he said.

"The emptiness was mine."

Cressida sensed the deepening of the conversation and headed back to the piano. He pursued his theme.

"Truly, truly? There's no other motive?"

"No, no. My bosses have a crazy plan to present a medal to Lanza and for you to do a concert. That bloody bank wants to sponsor it."

"That Sackman-Platinum outfit? But why?"

She looked down at the floor, her judgement possibly blurred by her emotions and the wine.

"I'm longing to tell you the truth. I can't lie and honor you with the love I want to give you. I have orders and possibly many, many innocent lives depend on what I might not have the strength to keep from you."

"Then don't tell me. I would never ask you to make that call for a guy who's only a singer after all."

"I didn't come out here to sign you up for some mad showbiz project. I came out here to be with you."

He leaned back and smiled.

"Helen, who is completely free in this life? You're part of a police machine, I'm part of an entertainment machine. Tell me what this concert is about and I'll make my own decision. I'm no fool, I hope. I believe that your bosses and beyond may want to bait some sort of trap. Since that Royal Ascot incident, I've been thinking and it's almost obvious. I've no fear for myself and what sort of man wouldn't share a danger that his lover faced?"

"I love you," she said.

"So, we share the same emotion and we share the same future. Somehow, I will keep Cressida out of the line of fire, even if I trick her and lock her up. Tell me your plans for the show."

She watched his face as she outlined the event. A range of expressions crossed his eyes and his mouth. Of course, he would

169

have worked it out and she respected him more for having done so. She finished simply.

"You're right about the reasons behind this. Are you certain you don't want to know who the targets are?"

"I'm certain even though I'm longing to know from your lips. I understand your responsibility and your duty. I'll say that I've read every bit of coverage of these events. This Scimitar of Holy Vengeance have been linked to the Brussels bombing and to Ascot. You understand that the foreign press often say things that your government and the Americans can't control. French media have mentioned this Kashi ben Quaffir. I'll not put that question to you so you won't have to answer."

She didn't take her eyes from his.

"Thank you."

"No thanks needed. What sort of man would love a woman who betrayed her trust and duty? I'll say one thing and then leave it forever, or until all this is over and I get the whole story. This psychotic murderer Quaffir is the enemy of our civilization. There would be no opera in his world and no women cops, or wine, or love. If I were to die to defeat him it would be my greatest joy."

She nodded. She had no words but found herself in tears. This was a truly noble man.

"Now I start to plan the program and the other performers. Also, I love this *Lanza Foundation*."

"I hope Cressida will get involved," she said.

"Yes, an ambassador," he beamed, his hands reaching up to heaven.

She took a breath. Maybe now she could almost think of a future, a future with him.

I'd love her to be there when Lanza gets his medal. More than anyone she brought him back to health. I do know she can't be there."

"Never say never, Helen. I don't want you to tell me of your police plans. In London I was like a little boy lost in Oxford Street. A nice policeman tells me the way and I do as he says. Naples is my town and we have our own ways."

"Marco, please, no Mafia."

"Sometimes my enemy's enemy is my friend, *has* to be my friend. Big governments talk about Russia and Mafia and want everyone to worry about these bad, bad men. For sure, some are bad but none of these guys stop me going on the metro, a horse race, or singing a few songs. Helen, the enemy is terror with a capital T. These religious tyrants strut as if there were no other ruthless people on this earth to stand up to them. To them we're all cowering victims afraid to strike back. Me, Marco Ambastilias, I believe these people disrespected me, my lovely woman, and my child. You, the police, and your security people have a mission. I know nothing and I will do nothing but sing in your concert."

"I can't ask more than that."

"Don't worry, all these great matters of the world are so much bigger than us. I'm a backstreet Neapolitan kid who could sing a bit and got lucky. You're a Miss World beauty queen who got derailed by your love for dogs. Somehow, we find each other in all the chances and throws of dice in a universe of happenstance. Let's accept the gift of love and share it in this beautiful life."

"Yes, yes, nothing but that Marco."

"If you want that here and now I will never waver, you understand. Wherever it goes, whatever we have to do, I am yours alone, and there will be no one, or nothing, to keep us apart. *D'accordo*?"

"Si, si d'accordo, Marco."

Looking out into the deep night over the bay of Naples and the sprinkled sparkling lights of the city and coast, still with the dark ominous Vesuvius volcano brooding in the distance, she didn't know where her mind should be. His next words snapped her back to reality.

"And as soon as possible, you will be my wife."

For some unknown time, her mind whirled. When she re-focused she heard her own voice.

"Yes, yes, yes."

Her animal gut was lurching, that hot flesh that had craved his flowing joy of seed in her belly. That seed, that meaning of the man to the woman. That echo of the creation of life itself. She heard his voice pulling her back from her own ecstasy.

"Here's your ring. You will never take it off. It is Italian by Buccelatti, maybe old fashioned because it's ruby red with the heat of blood and the passion of theatre."

She looked into the palm of his powerful hand. The ring was

171

an orgy of sensual longing fulfilled by beauty. It was a white and yellow gold band set with diamonds with a huge central ruby.

"This is all so fast and it's so beautiful. You bought this even though we were over?"

"Like a bullet is fast. If your little adventure at Ascot had gone wrong, life would have been over. I believed we were meant to be that's all."

"I love you, Marco. You're this big cosmic fact that I've run into and can't escape the gravity."

"So, you marry a fat guy, eh?"

"Fat, thin, just you. For an opera singer you're a skinny rabbit."

He threw back his head and laughed.

"Sure, a rabbit in your headlights. So, you have that ring in your hand. If you put it on your finger, that's it, no going back."

She slipped on the ring. Truly it was the most beautiful thing she'd ever seen. She held out her finger to show him.

"You like?"

"I love. Now you're mine."

He stood and took her hand leading her back to the balustrade. Now the night and the sea were black. His lips were gentle but searching. With her eyes closed she let her spirit drift and mingle with the scented breeze. This was flesh made spirit. This was love.

CHAPTER TWENTY-SEVEN

Already she adored Italy. In the morning her first thought was of Lanza. She would need a pet passport to bring him out to Naples. She called DCI Shannon Knightsmith.

"Hi. How's my little boy?"

"He's great. I'm going to adopt him because his owner ran off with some sexy guy."

"No way. That sexy guy's going to do the show. Can you pass that news up the line?"

"That's great, cos we're already building the stage and bringing in the sound equipment. We've got four days."

"Four days?"

"That's how long a news story stays hot. I'm guessing you haven't seen the world news this morning."

"No, what's up?"

"One half of our problem is resolved."

"Resolved?"

"Badu al Bagwandi. He's been found dead in a waiting room at Birmingham bus station."

"What? Was he waiting for a bus?"

"We believe he was trying to hide in plain sight. License plate and facial recognition on the motorways are risky for these guys. It looks like Quaffir ordered him back to London to get ready for the concert. When you work quick you work careless."

"Has the concert been announced?"

"Yeah, we knew you could turn Marco. It's called having faith in your staff."

"Jesus, you guys are chancers. So how did he die?"

"Here's the show-stopper honey. Looks like his take-out

falafel was dosed with a Russian nerve agent, Novichok 9."

So, it was the Russians? Why not just shoot him?"

"It's a message. Bagwandi worked for them as a well-paid agent in Afghanistan before he turned bad and moved onto Holy Vengeance with Quaffir."

"Do we know who did it?"

"I can guess. Whoever, he's a real pro."

"Bastian Wolf? I saw him in Naples yesterday evening. He shot off on a motorbike saying he had some business to do for Sackman-Platinum Bank. Are the police chasing him?"

"Helen, maybe the cops are happy to blame the Russians. Maybe the Russians are happy to take the blame? It's not a bad idea to let rogue agents know there's always a ruthless threat out there in the dark."

"But Quaffir is still holed up and potent?"

"Yup, in opera, it's not over until the fat lady sings or in chess, while the king is still on the board. He's alone now but still has his clean-skin cast of thousands to direct. He can't plot and plan long-term, so he's under pressure. He'll know that whoever got Bagwandi is good enough to get him too and perhaps his game is up. For sure he'll go out with a bang, so don't miss it. Both you and Marco are booked on Alitalia AZ 204 out of Rome Fiumincino this afternoon."

"Why Rome?"

"Cos there's no Alitalia flight from Naples and the Italian government want him to fly the flag. The media coverage starts as the plane touches down. Welcome to showbiz."

"Sheesh, I'm stunned. By the way, I'm going to marry him."

"This story builds and builds. Can we get Lanza as best man?"

She ended the call with a wry laugh and sat down, staring into the thick, black coffee in front of her on the kitchen table. Marco moved behind her and stroked back her hair.

"There's a frenzy ahead of us for a few days. Then it's about us."

"My boss just told me we're heading back on a flight from Rome this afternoon."

"*Si*, my agent tells me already. Once we're back in London I need to work with musicians and I need to rehearse. Great performance is an art—the art of hard work, you understand?"

"I sure do understand that. This isn't the time to talk long-term."

"We talked. We marry. The rest is babies, pasta, and love."

"You're a chauvinist."

"Now at last you see me for what I am and you change your mind."

"I want you as you are."

"And I want you as what you yourself want to be. You think I want to hide you at home and dress you in black?"

"No, it's just my lack of skill with pasta."

"I've seen you with a gun in your panties. A bit of tagliatelle is nothing after that."

She couldn't help but laugh and love him more. So how the hell did they get to Rome? First Marco had to organize Cressida. He called her to the lounge. She seemed serene.

"A guy will come and help you. Bring Sam and drive back to London in the Alfa Romeo," he told her.

"Papa, you trust me with your car? Why do we go back to *Londra*?"

"*Si*, I trust you and you share the drive with your assistant. We go because I sing for Lanza and all the poor working beasts of the world."

"And you trust me with this tough guy and this tough guy with your little girl?"

"I do."

"Do we have tickets and bookings?"

"No, that sort of data is too loose. Use cash for gas and take the tunnel from Calais. Buy tickets for cash at the terminal."

"So, you choose some bodyguard. Maybe I don't want to go to *Londra*?"

"You do. I heard you have bewitched some boy at Royal Ascot. I drive, but I hear him begging on your phone."

"You listen to my calls?"

"*Si*, because I'm your papa. You think I think you play that sad longing Mozart for me last night? You're playing what is in your heart. It was sadness and longing and it was beautiful."

Cressida smiled. For sure she had a hot date in London, and Marco knew it.

"OK, what do I call my guard?"

175

"You call him Mr. Wolf."

Helen gulped. How the hell had Marco formed a bond with Bastian Wolf? He'd see him at work and that would impress anyone. She had to suspect that Bastian had terminated Bagwandi, but had put the Russians in the frame. He could easily be back in Italy with no trace of his night's work. Devious masters on a mountaintop controlled him. She turned and smiled at Cressida.

"Trust him. He's the best," she said simply.

The white Fiat Tipo S station wagon ate the tarmac of the autostrada A1. The Carabinieri driver was fast and professional, assisted by his four motorcycle outriders, blue lights flashing, sirens wailing. They swept directly onto the tarmac of *Leonardo da Vinci Fiumincino* airport and boarded the Alitalia A321 Airbus without the bother of standing in line for passport checks or security searches. If Helen were a terrorist herself, she'd pose as a celebrity or politico. Thinking back to Royal Ascot, the bad guys had already figured that one out. Even her short acquaintance with this lifestyle had softened her resistance to it. Ease, power, and luxury are good for the soul. It's easy to be nice when someone opens every door ahead of you. Much more of this and she'd be hooked. They stuck to San Pellegrino sparkling water and tomato salad for the in-flight meal. After all, they were on their way to work.

Once they entered the arrivals hall, they were confronted by a wall of sound. There was the world's press but also a mob of fans in Lanza T-shirts bearing his photo and the Sackman-Platinum logo. Officials led them through to a packed conference room. Question after question crashed over them like Pacific surfing waves.

"Marco, should the Russians be allowed to come after the poisoning incident?"

"I want everyone to come. I'm not a politician."

"Is this the biggest classical music event the world has ever seen?"

"Yes, it's even bigger than that."

"Helen, what's your ring?" called out a young American eagle-eyed female in the front row."

"It's simply beautiful," she replied.

176

"Looks like forty thousand dollars' worth of Buccellati genius. So, when's the wedding?"

"Not before the concert," said Marco with a careless flourish of his hand. "Now, who of you want a song dedicated to your wife or your mama, eh? Speak with my agent and he'll put names in a hat."

"How's your voice, Marco? Some critics suggest you can't just crank it up without months of practice."

Helen watched his face. Although a broad confident smile dazzled the crowd, there was just a little catch in his speed of answer.

"Hey, I could do it now, but if I did, who would come to the show, eh? Always remember the thrill of the tightrope walker is that he might fall. That stuff's dangerous, so I chose an easy safe job. Be there and you'll see."

The pack swallowed the meat he'd thrown them. Helen knew from a few things she'd read herself, that her big man couldn't just rely on belief. They posed for more shots and let the journalists drift away to meet deadlines. He was a pro with these fellow pros.

"If you stumble, the bull will attack you," she said, taking his hand.

"Yes, and more people are killed by gentle cows than by fearsome bulls. It's a well-known fact."

"I didn't know that."

"It's well known by people who are in the buffalo cheese business. You have to be so careful not to grab the wrong thing."

She laughed, knowing that he'd deflected a genuine fear.

"We're together in this, Marco, I'm not watching a circus. I'm watching the man I love."

He looked at her and sighed.

"Thank you, I know that. I've got two and a half days. I'll see you at the perfect dinner you cook for me. My agent has fixed rehearsals so now I get my humble throat out of my big boastful mouth."

He held her and let his eyes burn into her. This feeling and this look was now her life. It was all she thought of and all she wanted. Maybe he wouldn't be able to get his voice in shape? If he was humiliated and failed would he blame her for having encouraged him to do this? Would she ever live down the guilt?

177

CHAPTER TWENTY-EIGHT

"Relationships aren't all they're cracked up to be," said a familiar female voice at her side.

"Shannon, hi, yes. Did I look complicated and concerned?"

"Yeah, for a girl who's going to marry a dream, you're like a girl having a nightmare."

"I'm sorry. I don't think I'm seeing anything properly. Everything's been out of control since I met Marco."

"I do know the feeling. I was a gutter girl who married a bloody earl for Christ's sake."

"And he's turning over his castle or whatever, for this concert."

"Yeah, and he loves it. I'll drive you out there so you can pick up Lanza. I outrank you remember, so I could demand to keep him. My stepson Ben is on holiday from Sandhurst and he's been by his side every day around the estate.

"He's a soldier?"

"Yup, it's the tradition of the Chamberlain Knightsmith clan, ever since the first earl fought with Charles the First in the English Civil War."

"What's he like?"

"Helen, I think I can read your mind. Yes, I've seen Cressida Ambastilias and I've mentioned to my husband that she's a very attractive and well-connected girl. I'm afraid the aristocrats don't like to be beaten around the head with the love word. Of course, he married me for love, but I confused him with wild animal sex which made it seem like hunting."

Helen almost gasped at her boss's directness.

"Did you mention her to your stepson?"

"I was going to, but I found he already had her on his radar after the Bollinger champagne bash at Ascot. It seems they exchanged personal tokens."

"Tokens?"

"Panties for boxers apparently. I didn't enquire further and I've not seen any illegal fabric in his washing. God, I wish I still had that honest filthy lust. Mind you, his room smells like a zoo."

Helen giggled. "Cressida is a wonderful pianist."

"OK, it's a deal. I'll get a marriage contract drawn up ready for the concert."

They drove to Bloxington Manor in Shannon's old Landover. The village of Fleetworth Green was like a throwback to the days of red phone boxes and straw-thatched pubs.

"The royals visit a lot. They love this place kept as a haven from modern life."

The truth was that everything exuded money. They swept in through the coat-of-arms-decorated gates into a fabulous parkland. In front of the massive Georgian manor house was an enormous lake, reflecting the building, blue sky, and green summer trees. Builders and technicians had created a huge stage in the center, reached by a bridge. The concert would begin at dusk as a light show played on the house front and water. TV and film crews were everywhere, like ants on a discarded picnic doughnut. Satellite trucks were parked in careful rows.

"It's breathtaking," Helen said.

"Yeah, it is. Marco is just so massive and so missed. Sackman Platinum are putting in eighty million dollars for the set-up but the TV rights and sales of merchandise will pay back double at least."

"The connection between this bank and the cops bothers me a bit...."

"Yeah, I get that. Just trust and don't ask. I've been where you've been and I'm a straight cop. Trust, accept, and you'll learn when the time is right."

"God, all this rests on *his* shoulders doesn't it."

"Short answer—yes. Long answer, yes, and he'd better not fuck up. The fact is that when these special guys draw that last deep breath to hit the big note they don't know if it's there. It's the same for Indy car racers going around the outside on the last curve. It's the win or it's the wall. There's men and women in all types of

179

lives who have that quality. Even cops love those guys who rent a shop opposite the bank and drill a tunnel under the street over Christmas. Risk can get you fame and wealth. It can get you dead."

"He hasn't sung at all. I read the internet and the magazines. It's like taking off with not quite enough fuel and hoping for the right wind."

"Blah, blah, blah—you're right. Now forget it. This morning I had a meeting with Dickon Maltravers and Anna La Salle. Information from the prisoner from Ascot is helpful. Quaffir knows the game is up. He could live as some old man in a farm cottage in Uzbekistan or maybe Alaska. He wants a spectacular to compete with Bin Laden. He has an elite team of a couple of men. They're untried and have no battle experience. On the other hand, they're fanatics. All his old friends are dead following our operation. He's still not broken cover but we're onto his sidekicks. We've got a tracker on a vehicle and a distraught sister who wants to save her brother by informing on him. This shit breaks good families. We don't know what he's going to do, but we'll know when he's on the move. We don't know if he has explosives but there's a lot of buzz around grenades on the low-life wires. He's having to improvise and that means dealing outside his cult and as we all know, the voice of money speaks very loud. We have access to infinite wealth."

"Sackman-Platinum?"

"Fine citizens and taxpayers, Helen."

They strolled into a wonderful conservatory of plants.

"This was an orangery when King Charles the Second was here with his lover Nell Gwynn. He stayed here because the local bishop objected to him consorting outside of marriage. He had at least twelve bastard children and they still own half of England."

Just then Lanza seemed to have heard the tread of his mistress and came bounding towards her. His health, power, and joie-de-vivre was like an operatic aria in itself.

"I knew you were fickle, Lanza," said Shannon with a warm smile and coquettish shake of her head.

Helen hugged him with a deep joy from inside her heart.

"He could have died. It was just luck and medical genius that saved him. Now my little boy will be a star for the world. He won't care, he just wants to love me and protect me. He was dying for me

180

and he only asked for a pat or a word of friendship. I know he won't live much longer relative to our lives. I lost my husband to religious nuts when Lanza was a pup. I lived an empty life, but with a full heart. Why can't these murderous terrorist bastards see what they destroy? Do people with no compassion deserve our care and justice?"

So many conflicts, fears and guilts jostled in her mind. This simple unconditional love had sliced her open. Her emotions poured out. She sobbed and almost howled into Lanza's fur.

"Good question. For me, no. Give me a straight shot at these bastards and they're dead. The world is going to honor one dog in the name of all dogs like him. A world out there does care. The president of the USA will be there, the heads of most world governments, Hollywood, and the royals of everywhere will be there. King Charles and Sophia of France have agreed to join the board of the *Lanza Foundation*. We can't get enough parking for the limos, we can't land enough executive planes and helicopters, we can't anchor enough luxury yachts. And they're doing it for Lanza."

"And all this is to draw out one terrorist?"

"Just think what one maniac like him can do. We've all seen it, honey. A world is doing this to honor sacrifice and loyalty. The cops are exploiting this to put this shit back ten years. Children in many lands will grow to have children because poisonous bastards like Bagwandi and Quaffir didn't destroy their innocent lives. And don't expect any thanks. It's a job and we do it."

"You're strong and certain, Shannon. I needed you tonight."

"Yeah, and it's all down to my addiction to Yorkshire Gold tea. Fancy a proper brew?"

They sat with their big steaming mugs. It was so English in the beamed kitchen, lined with copper cooking pots. She felt secure although the history of Bloxington Manor had many stories of religious and political turmoil.

"What's my role on the night?"

"Simple, you're Lanza's wardrobe assistant. We'll arm you as before but no one is going to get near you. The American president will have the firepower of a small army. There's a team of seals out there checking the bed of the lake. There's SAS dug in behind every tree. If anything kicks off, the most dangerous thing will be

181

crossfire. The whole show is being staged by Vandervell O'Brien, the movie director. Last gig he did was the French coronation and that was incredible. He'll tell you when and where to be. There's rehearsals all day Friday."

"I haven't got a thing to wear."

"You'll be in Met police uniform honey, with all your medals. The bosses won't miss that bit of PR."

"It saves the hassle I suppose. I wouldn't have minded one last blast as being beautiful civilian me."

She fell silent and finished her tea. There was something she wanted to check out.

"Shannon, Marco is using Bastian Wolf to guard Cressida. Is that a police deal or something he's fixed up himself?"

"You didn't ask him?"

"No, it got buried. I was happy to see a top man on the job and I trust Bastian. It's just that Marco is an artist...."

"He's an artist from a poor, tough family. You saw the way he decked that suicide bomber. OK, the bank, the Camorra Mafia, the Russians, the FBI, CIA, the Metropolitan Police, MI6, and on and on have different agendas. Scimitar of Holy Vengeance is the common enemy. Our civilization cannot live with this horror. You've met some people from the World Intelligence Forum I think?"

"Yeah, in Anna La Salle's office."

"Once Quaffir is terminated, the alliance splits and it's business as normal. For now, the WIF are running the show. Anna La Salle set up Bastian to guard you and now Cressida. They have a big history together from the French terrorist trouble."

"Did Bastian kill Bagwandi with the Novichok?"

"You saw him in Italy that evening. How could he have got to England and made it back by morning? It must have been those bad-boy Russians, don't you think?"

Helen watched a mischievous flicker in Shannon's eyes. "The big factor is that Quaffir knows there's a wolf creeping up on him. He has to move or die."

"What do you think he'll do?"

"I think he'll wait until the peak of the concert when it's live to the whole world. I don't rule out him putting a plane down into the stage. There's a no-fly zone enforced by our own Tornado fighters. The Americans are flying a Boeing E3 Sentry at altitude and some F35s to take out any strangers. There's ground-to-air missiles all around London. We figure he could steal a small plane, but he's dead if he comes within fifty miles."

Helen nodded, thinking back to the unexpected truck attack. In truth everyone knew there were too many angles to cover.

"And Bastian will be there?"

"For sure. If all else fails, nothing will get past him."

All she had to do now was look after her dog and marry her international superstar lover man. She'd start by getting home and fixing him a dinner. For years she'd only cared for herself and so far, Marco had cooked fabulous food for her. Despite everything that had happened, this next obstacle could be the most terrifying.

CHAPTER TWENTY-NINE

She didn't rule out a take-away Chinese chow mein for two. She could hide the packaging and flap about over a wok as he came in. That would be cowardice in the face of the enemy. Pasta was out for a guy who probably hand twisted his own fusilli. She knew how to crush garlic, she knew how to slice a potato and he sure wasn't a vegan. Shannon lent her a hard-worked olive green Range Rover to get herself and Lanza home. As a civilian dog he rode on the front seat, snout out of the window in an ecstasy of scent and breeze. From the house it was a short walk to the supermarket. Supplied with a bottle of Barolo wine, two juicy ribeye steaks, Maris Piper potatoes, French beans and a pack of fresh peas in pods, she was ready. She set about preparing finely sliced potato stacks cooked in butter and garlic. She steamed the peas and beans. When her man came through the door he could choose how he wanted his steak. He was there. She remembered his Italian expression.

"*In bocco al lupo,*" she said, going to greet him.

"Hey, La mia donna parla Italiano."

"*Si,*" she replied, not sure what he'd said.

He smiled but she could see he was tired, almost exhausted.

"You got Lanza. That's marvelous. Your cooking smells great."

"Marco, you seem a bit down. Was everything good?"

"*Si, si,* good, but I'm not used to working at that level. The best news is that I can sing and sing big."

"Can you eat big?"

"I could eat you. I see you, and my tiredness falls away."

In the past she'd waited for his kiss. This time she pulled him to her and thrilled to the feel of his flesh.

"How do you want your woman? Succulent and wet? With creamy pepper sauce?"

"You read my mind."

She fried the steak while he opened the wine and watched her from the table. He ate hungrily, reaching out to stroke her hand while he chewed.

"You need some TLC. I'm going to put you in a bath and relax you," she said.

"I should say no. I should say I would feel so selfish, but if that's a genuine offer, I couldn't resist."

"Do I look like a tease?"

"In that case, take me. I'm yours."

The bathroom was spacious with a modern central Carron Celsius duo bath. Marco selected some music and turned up the built-in wall system. The piece was from Wagner's Valkyrie sung by Johann Manstimme, the German star, who would be performing at the concert. She let the water run and took off his clothes as he half hummed, half sang along to the melody.

"It's sexy," she said, her voice dusky and thick with her own lust.

"Winterstuerme is wonderful and this man has made it his own. The sexiness builds into pure animal beauty. I admire Johann so much."

She pulled off his pants and paused to tease his cock with a gentle, stroking squeeze. She felt it surge and twitch. Her mind flashed to her vision of his jetting seed.

"Now you sit down and relax. I'm only touching your back because you're too tired for action. Just think of the music and close your eyes."

"The music is about two people about to make beautiful love—Siegmund and Sieglinde. It's a very naughty love if you know the story."

"I know it. Gods and magic don't have the same rules."

She soaped his back, kneading the muscles of his neck and shoulders. He groaned in bliss, singing more powerfully in between exclamations. Easing down each arm she saw his thick cock, hard and stiff with longing. The sight flooded her own panties, pinging her own tight little shaft. As she massaged his triceps she let her elbows pressurize her breasts. She was beginning to feel the need to come.

"I'll do your front and legs if you lie back."

His face was calm yet questioning. He lay back, offering her his dark-haired chest, arrowing down to his massive hot straining dick. He moved his own hand across his groin almost unable not to satisfy his own need. She soaped down across his pecs and belly. He was firm and so, so, strong. His tip was wet and releasing clear cum. She ran her hand across his pubic bone, splaying her fingers through his soft dark pubic hair. She moved to his thigh, massaging out the tension. Then she did the calves and feet, standing, looking along the length of him.

"I think you're done," she said in a slow, husky voice, as if some devil was talking from her throat. His balls were tight, his cock rigid. She saw torture and longing in his face. She was bursting to come herself, so she knew his torment.

"I think you've made me very wet looking at you. I'd better check."

She pulled off her T-shirt and cropped leggings. She brushed her hands down over her breasts. She looked to her ivory silk panties. "Look, I've almost wet myself. There's a big dark patch. Marco, I've been a bad girl in my pussy."

She ran her hand down over the fabric.

"It's so slippery. I keep being so naughty. I don't seem able to stop."

He was squirming, still not touching himself. She saw his hand move.

In that instant she stepped in, crouching next to him in the soapy water. She drew his pulsing juicy cock into her mouth, swirling her tongue around his oozing tip. She held the base with her hand, masturbating him while she licked the sensitive underside. He was so close and she wanted that juice. She pulled her panties aside and straddled him, plunging his hot shaft to the sucking peak of her tube. She moved up and down, watching his closed eyes, watching the first convulsion in his shoulders as his cum released into her belly. Now she let go, pulsing her own deep orgasm onto his shaft.

"Fuck. I'm doing it on your cock. I'm coming on your cock," she whispered. Her mind flashed to her vision of his cum pouring out onto her pussy. She couldn't stop her voice, couldn't stop pushing out her own release. She couldn't stop, wanted to let go with animal lust. Still he shuddered out his pleasure into her, still she let herself grind her clit and hot soaking musk into his man muscle.

He reached up to her cheek, pulling her lips to his, joining their passion with hot tongues.

"My sweet woman, my sweet lover," he groaned.

"Naughty woman. I've been a bad girl again. When we were apart I had my toy and I did it thinking of you in my pussy."

"God, you're so fucking sexy."

"I shouldn't tell you, should I? I shouldn't want you to know. I should feel dirty."

"No, I want you to share all your sexiness with me."

"Like I'm touching myself now, feeling all your cum on my little button."

She slid her hand into her soaked panties and stroked her convulsing lust out of her clit, kissing out her soul with her tongue, mimicking her orgasm against his.

"Yeah, fuck, I'm being bad again, Marco. I just love it."

"I love you, Helen. You've got so much humanity and passion in your blood."

"You, you've set me free to be your true lover. I want to let go all inhibition for you, to show you myself as a woman."

"When I sing for the world, that quality will be in my soul."

"You'll sing such beauty for a secret naughty girl at home?"

"I tell you my lover, this world has yet to see me sing of love and passion. Simply I didn't know it."

They slept the sleep of the just and the sexually exhausted. Her body melted into him as he spooned into her and squeezed her shoulders.

"Soon I'll repay that massage. I feel so good," he murmured in the half light of dawn. Then, the day swept them up and he was gone again to rehearse. For Helen, there was a pause in her life although she would have to return Shannon's Range Rover. She saw Lanza's ears go up and his eyes snap to full alert. She tensed as the front door opened and Cressida strolled in with Sam. The dogs greeted each other with excitement and evident delight.

"Weren't you driving from Naples? I didn't expect you until

187

tonight."

"We drove in shifts. Well, that Bastian guy drove all night. He's a machine."

"It's great to see you. You must need to sleep."

"I'm good. I've got a bit of a date so I wanted to get back. Bastian said he understood and just did it."

"That's our boy. Where is he?"

"He got out down the road. A black Cadillac limo on diplomatic registration plates picked him up."

"Like I said, that's our boy."

Helen made some coffee as Cressida made a fuss of Lanza.

"So, this date...?"

"It's cool. Just a boy."

It seemed intrusive to push further if Cressida didn't want to give details. She decided to change the subject.

"I've got to drive down to Fleetworth Green. The Knightsmiths lent me a car last night. I can fix a police ride back."

The girl spluttered into her coffee.

"Fleetworth Green, Bloxington Manor?"

"You know it?"

"That's where I'm going."

Suddenly Helen realized that Cressida's date was with Ben, Shannon's stepson, with whom she'd apparently done an underwear exchange at Ascot races.

"They say Ben's very handsome. I believe he's on holiday from Sandhurst Military College. Maybe I'll get to meet him too."

"Helen, it's not serious."

"But worth a non-stop drive from Italy."

The girl smiled. A new happiness radiated from her. She was young, but just maybe this was her first true love. If he was really a dish he'd be a catch equal to her. Obviously, she knew about her papa's concert, but not his plans to keep her away.

"It's going to be quite a show. My only function is to wear a dull police uniform and introduce my dog."

"Papa's being mysterious again. He's worried about trouble and he doesn't want me to be there."

"He loves you. I know that can be a two-edged sword."

"He doesn't want me to see Ben or any boy. He says young men are sex mad."

188

"He could be right. No, he is right."

Cressida reached out and took Helen's hand.

"Please help me. I want to stay with him tonight. He has to go back to the army and then he'll join his regiment in Iraq. There's a big last push against the terrorists. When we went to Naples, I thought I wouldn't see him. I couldn't believe it when you came and gave me this chance to come back. Please, Papa doesn't have to know does he?"

In an instant Helen's heart opened. Her mind flashed back to those last hours with her husband before he'd left to die in Afghanistan. She thought she'd forgotten, but bitter tears ran down her cheeks. She didn't want to lie to Marco, but she would not deny this girl.

"Drive the Alfa Romeo down behind me and I'll bring it back. I'll tell your papa that Shannon Knightsmith invited you to stay and I'll tell him I agreed on his behalf because he was so busy. It's not a big deal anyway. Does he know about Ben?"

"No, at least I've not told him."

"I think he picked up your emotions when you played that D-minor Mozart concerto. It made me think of love and its sadness. Your papa can taste human feeling on the air."

"He's a genius."

"Just remember the golden rule of cops and lovers. Only lie if you have to but if you do, that lie is your truth. Stick to it. Never tell your papa I was in on this or anything about it."

Cressida hugged her.

"You're great, Helen. I'll never let you down."

She'd come a long way with this young woman and for sure there'd be the pains of love and struggle ahead. At least she was going to be on that life journey beside her. Suddenly she realized that maybe Cressida didn't know her papa was going to marry her.

"Did you see my ring?"

"Yes, but not on your hand. Papa asked me to help."

"What? You knew before me?"

"Not really. He wanted to involve me, not just announce I was getting a stepmother."

Helen smiled.

"He didn't know I was going to say yes."

"No, but he knew you weren't going to say no."

"The ring is so beautiful."

"He asked my advice and I told him not to hold back. I told him to get a ring filled with passion and color."

"Did he ask you not to tell me he'd spoken to you about it?"

"No, if he had, I would have lied and said I'd never seen it."

"That's good. You've passed the police integrity test. Let's go see a boy who's Lanza's latest companion.

CHAPTER THIRTY

Helen had heard of Vandervell O' Brien, the film director. He'd shot to fame with his tongue-in-cheek socialist epic "*Red Flag of the Grimethorpe Zombies*." Now, on set at the scene of the concert she watched him approach. He was an enormous bearded man wearing a mauve kaftan. He reached out a huge hand to shake.

"So, this is Lanza. Look, main thing is that he doesn't squat down for a shit, or piss on the Queen or George Clooney. Can you make sure he's fully emptied out?"

It was the day before the concert. A red carpet covered the bridge across the lake that led to the stage. She felt out of place in her police uniform. The film crew shot footage of her and Lanza running through some long grass.

"That'll be sexy slow motion with music for the trailer," boomed Vandervell.

Then they shot take after take, of Lanza walking at her side, looking up, tongue out. All day the loudspeaker systems belted out sound tests and ear-splitting audio feedback. Over lunch she encountered DCI Shannon Knightsmith.

"How's your stepson, Ben?"

"In love, as if you didn't know. I sort of gather Marco wouldn't approve."

"All boys are sex-mad predators plotting to defile his virgin angel."

"Oh, to be a virgin angel again," said Shannon with a laugh in her voice.

"I'll tell Marco that Cressida is staying again, to help with stuff."

"It won't be a lie. She's doing a piano recital for some of our

191

guests after dinner. The French royals and the Duke and Duchess of Yorkshire are already here."

"Papa will be very proud."

"He should be. She played last night for the prime minister and you could have sold tickets."

"The prime minister for God's sake?"

"Sure, my husband advises the government on world trade stuff."

Shannon seemed to shrug off such things without a care, as if it were nothing out of the ordinary. She saw Vandervell O'Brien carrying a huge steak and kidney pie to a table set with pints of beer. Already seated was a man she knew. She nodded a quick acknowledgement. Just the presence of Bastian Wolf made her feel secure.

When her day was done she was glad to escape. It seemed impossible that all this chaos could pull together to make a show. There would be an attack, she was sure of that. Maybe a clean-skin guy dressed as a technician, maybe a plane would get through to dive into the stage? Maybe a heavy truck attack with grenades and AK 47s. There could be a dreadful carnage and all the resources in the world couldn't be sure of stopping Kashi ben Quaffir. His terror machine had killed thousands and enslaved whole peoples. He was the head and heart of the snake. And he was out there, certain to pounce.

It was soothingly normal to shop for dinner. She picked up some salmon, rice, and salad. She was frying some onion when he crept in behind her. His lips came to her neck as his hand ran down her spine.

"I love you," he said.

"You love savory rice with salmon in Chinese five spice with piccolo tomatoes and salad tossed in balsamic olive oil."

"Yeah, that's what I meant, but you got in the way."

"How's the voice?"

"It's OK, but not perfect. It's an outdoor concert so I'm not looking for close up purity. These gigs are big on power, less on finesse. The studio voice still isn't there, but tomorrow I'm going large. We fixed a medley for three tenors. There's Johann Manstimme, Paolo Carambar, and little me. It's going to lay them out."

"Marco, you know, you've guessed this event could attract an attack by someone looking to shock the world while they're watching it on TV."

"Sure. I can't worry about that. You can't tell me that Kashi ben Quaffir is in London and desperate to fight back. You can't tell me that Scimitar of Holy Vengeance has killed and tortured without mercy. I'm a professional singer. You folks are professionals too. Your Queen went to Royal Ascot knowing they were out there. Regular citizens get on trains and planes or walk down the street and these creatures see them as targets."

"And Cressida?"

"Helen, I've seen your work and its risks. I respect your courage. How can I accept your life and not let Cressida live like others? A parent has to let go. I've spoken to your Bastian and he'll stay close. Anna La Salle let slip that perhaps my daughter has a young man—a strong young man of a good family. I can't stop her living to the full."

"You're a wise and wonderful man, Marco. This is your last evening before you're a cosmic megastar again. Let's just be regular girl and boyfriend in these few sane hours."

After the meal she lay on the sofa with her head in his lap. He stroked her cheeks and forehead, watching her pleasure with his kind, dark eyes. This was paradise.

The day had come. A firearms unit delivered her Baby Glock 26 and ammunition. She spread out her dress uniform and pinned on her military medals, won in Iraq for bomb detection work with dogs. At noon Kaitlyn arrived in a white Jaguar XF. Their appointment was for the final briefing at Scotland Yard. In the big conference room were both known and unknown faces. Dickon Maltravers from MI6 took the lead.

"Ladies and gentlemen. We're completely prepared for Christ knows what. Quaffir has a network of followers. He may well act alone. Although he's a big shot, he was a street murderer in his younger days. He has cunning and suicidal courage. We simply don't know where he is. There's just a hint that he's in a safe house with a clean-skin family or one that he's holding hostage. A crazy satellite TV station in Murdistan is predicting that Quaffir will boil the eyes of the unrighteous. We detained their one journalist and he's given us that story. It's possible he'll ignore the concert and hit a softer target. We're offering him the prize of the world's governments and every brand of fame from royalty to Hollywood. Listen to all your briefings and be ready. The instant he shows up, he's dead."

Helen zoned out while every specialist set out the tactics on the ground. Her job was simple and clear. She had to prowl red-carpet land, presenting Lanza to whomever, and get him to the stage to receive his medal. She would have a firearm if all else failed, but she was certain that nothing and no one would get that close. It had been decided that King Charles and Sophia of France would present the medal and also commemorate Diesel, the Belgian shepherd dog, who had died on duty in a shootout with religious terrorists in Paris in 2015. This would be the most dangerous moment. She shuddered inwardly. She'd smelled the blood and seen the horror of limbs and charred flesh. Shannon had said that our civilization couldn't live with this stuff. It had to be defeated. There was no point in living in subjection and fear.

Back at the house she said goodbye to Marco. He was going ahead with his agent and musical director. A deep blue Bentley Mulsanne had pulled up.

"I love you, my man. See you after the show."

He smiled slowly and took her in his arms. He sang softly a song from Bernstein's West Side Story:

Now it begins, now we start,
One hand, one heart;
Even death won't part us now.
Make of our lives one life

"I wanted it in the show for you. I'll sing this for you tonight."

She watched him go. He would stand in front of a world and risk it all for that high note and he would fear nothing. He was Marco Ambastilias and the simple man who last night had stroked her hair until she had slept.

Her own task was to brush Lanza and put on her uniform. Her TV studio hair was in a bun under her hat. She'd chosen a skirt so she could do a concealed-carry of her firearm. It had worked for her at Ascot and she trusted her skill. It would never come to that. Her medals clinked on her tunic as she put it on and squared her shoulders. In a world of fame and celebrity she was a nobody but she was proud of what and who she was. It was time to re-find that woman she'd been before she'd responded to that emergency call those few short weeks ago.

CHAPTER THIRTY-ONE

The arena was buzzing. Helicopters were still landing, laser rangefinder lights flashing red. Three RAF Tornadoes did a low pass and climbed away vertically, jet engine afterburners roaring out fearless aggression. The chaos she had seen the day before had transformed into a perfection of sound and color. The teen idol band Boymondo was on stage singing their own take on some big classics, mainly from musical films. Showbiz was just so magical. How she would have loved some talent. She waited in the manor house looking out across the lake to the stage. Dusk was falling as Vandervell O'Brien, now in a golden kaftan, led her and Lanza out to meet the glitterati and powerful of the planet. Her mission was simply to mingle and give everyone a chance to meet the hero. Royal after royal, actress after actress, bent or crouched to make a fuss of him. The Russian leader, Vladimir Pinupskin actually knelt to hug him.

"I am the alpha of my dogs. I hunt bare-chested like a real man with my wolves. If someone disrespect one of my pack, they die." he said, fixing her with his blue eyes and stiff-lipped cold smile.

Helen smiled back, as officials and diplomats hurried her on. The Russian leader certainly had an engaging aura. She could see how he would get along with Bastian. It was close to the scheduled start of the concert. Along the red carpet there was still a line of dignitaries and important folks hoping to touch Lanza. Because of his titanium chest plate, she had him on a soft medical collar, which helped to give him a wounded soldier look. As a working dog he would have worn a chest harness. A couple of times he'd whined and almost pulled away, licking his own nose and shooting her glances. He was a civilian now and had a hippy Labrador friend to show him sloppy human ways.

"Lanza, stay," she ordered.

He whined and sat down uneasily. He wasn't happy. He butted her hand with his nose.

"Lanza!"

He sat down again and quietly yelped to himself. The situation was overwhelming. She just had to get through to the interval, get him to the stage and their work was done. She heard the orchestra start and an enormous roar from the crowd as Marco launched into "*E lucevan le Stelle*" from *Tosca*. He had them in his hand as the stars came out and the light show played on the face of the manor house. She closed her eyes as he climbed the steps of the music towards the peak of the aria. Yes, yes, he hit it with pure power as if it were a day in the office. In other worlds, it was a home run, a knock-out punch, a double flip on the high trapeze. The crowd went wild, bellowing out their own joy.

Lanza was butting her hand, pulling away, being really naughty. She felt a surge of anger. He caught her eyes and barked, really barked. He was angry too. To her right she saw quick movement. She knew that body shape. Lanza's bark had alerted Bastian. Then the stardust fell from her eyes. She'd been so stupid. He was warning her, he'd caught a trace on the air. It had to be explosives.

"Good boy—find," she whispered.

He gave her a look of joy to see they were together again. They were hunting. She believed in him. Somewhere in the massive crowd was a killer. Everyone around her was a world leader or superstar. The president of the USA was seated just a few yards away. The last thing she wanted was to alert the target. Although the concert had started many people still weren't seated. Outside the VIP area, many thousands had brought picnics and watched the show on giant screens. A red carpet ran from the parking area and late arrivals filled every inch. Bastian had come to her side. Everyone wanted to pat and cuddle Lanza. Some guy she'd seen hosting a TV quiz show demanded a selfie. For the moment they'd lost the scent. A delegation of diplomat types with obvious security, were moving through the crowd about fifty yards away. In the center of the group she caught glimpses of a small man in a business suit. Lanza's head swiveled. His gaze arrowed in

197

on this man although he could only have seen his legs. He pulled away, pushing through the crush. Bastian touched her arm, nodding at her to follow him, in drawing her firearm. Her heart pounded, Lanza was tugging as if his life depended on it. She pulled the Baby Glock and kept it low out of sight. Could she go through with this? If Lanza identified a target could she open fire? Did she have that total trust in him? The group had stopped. In front of her was a big young man wearing an official security badge, with a flag on his lapel. The country name read *Republic of Larunda*. Lanza barked and pulled towards the small older man. He was almost smiling with thin wet lips, clean shaven, maybe mid-fifties. His eyes were dead and expressionless. She'd seen his photo but he'd always worn religious robes. This was Kashi ben Quaffir in a blue business suit. Life went into slow motion. On the stage Marco was singing a duet from Carmen. Lanza was growling. Bastian was bringing up his Walther PPK double handed looking through the sights. She heard her own voice call out.

"Armed police...."

In front of her the big man began to reach into his jacket. Bastian fired, then again, then again. In two seconds, the security guys were all down. Quaffir had his hands in his pockets. There had to be a suicide bomb or grenades. Lanza was certain but if she just fired it was murder in the police book. She would have to fire one handed off balance unless she let go of the leash. She glanced at Bastian. The Walther PPK cracked out two rounds, one head, one heart. Job done. Weapon put on safety and returned to holster. Short fair hair pushed back, jacket adjusted.

"I didn't rush. I thought you might like the honor," he said, turning and moving away through the crowd.

Normal time resumed. Clocks restarted. A crowd of thousands was applauding the singing. Uniformed police were clearing the area. Agents and detectives were closing in around the casualties. Was that Quaffir? Had Bastian Wolf just murdered a diplomatic delegation from Larunda? All they'd had was Lanza's nose and courage. A bomb disposal soldier called out.

"There's grenades. All personnel out of the area."

No one needed to be told twice. Still she stared. One of the young men on the floor was moving. Agents were recovering guns. A hand was on her arm pulling her away. Lanza still wanted his

198

prize and his treat. She looked down at him. He looked into her eyes as if nothing had happened, other than he'd been a good boy.

"Good boy, good boy," she said, finding him a dog treat from her pocket.

Marco was singing *Nessun Dorma*, the big show stopper from *Turandot*.

"Helen, Helen, Helen!"

Deputy Assistant Commissioner Anna La Salle was at her side.

"Anna—what the fuck?"

"This mess will be gone in a few minutes so re-focus on the show. Do you remember what you have to do?"

"Yeah. Cross the bridge on the red carpet with all the spotlights on me. Give a few waves and big smiles. Meet some French royals and let Lanza get his medal. Miss World teeth and pout for camera and then hide away with a bottle of scotch."

"You got it. Just focus on that. We're pulling together the picture of how Quaffir got to be here. For now, fix your mind on the show, there's only two billion viewers."

"No pressure then," she said with a nervous laugh.

They waited at the end of the bridge. Vandervell O'Brien opened his arms in greeting.

"Don't be nervous. Dogs always steal the show, so you'll be invisible. All the same sex it up just in case. Glad you've got a skirt. Lovely legs, so I'll try and get some politically incorrect angles for the boys at home. If the dog shits, just kick it away from the royals and give a Princess Diana over the shoulder coy look. Walk slow and I'll make you a star. Now do it."

For some reason a massive man in a gold kaftan speaking with such direct cynicism brought her back to the moment. She pushed everything else out of her mind. She could do this. She would do this.

Marco was singing Verdi's *Celeste Aida*. He looked fabulous in his black tie and tails. Around her the great and the famous were spellbound, many wiping away tears. This was why a world was watching. This was her man, a man who loved her. The applause went on and on. Finally, he raised his hand and spoke.

"Thank you so much. Thank you for being here tonight. I wanted to end the first half of the concert with that aria, which I always think belongs to Mario Lanza. Now we have another Lanza who is the real star of the show. I was so proud when he invited me to sing."

The crowd stamped and cheered.

"This is a very special dog for me but let us remember all the working dogs and animals of the world, even the ones who work simply by giving us loyalty and love, maybe when we don't always deserve it. Your majesties, lords, ladies and gentlemen I give you Lanza, with the beautiful Helen."

The orchestra began to play the Triumphal March from Aida. Spotlights swung to the red-carpeted bridge. She stepped out, Lanza at her side, almost seeming to match her smiles. He knew he'd done good, she could see it in his eyes. She didn't walk too fast. On distant giant screens she could see the cameras closing in on Lanza and very often on her too. The roar of the crowd was like a huge breath. Every time she waved there was an extra cheer. She mounted the steps to where Charles and Sophia of France were waiting with the Sackman-Platinum world gold medal for animal gallantry on a red velvet cushion. Marco had stood back but was still on stage. This wasn't in the script. The French king spoke.

"It is a fabulous honor to be here. Tonight, we honor our hero Lanza and all animal heroes. For my own people I will mention again our comrade Diesel who died in a terrorist shootout in Paris. He will always be in our hearts. Thank you all once again for supporting the Lanza Foundation."

Helen gave Lanza the order to sit, slipped off his collar and stood back into the shadows. A hand took hers.

"I couldn't miss this," said Marco.

They watched as the king knelt and placed the medal around Lanza's neck. Spontaneously he held out his hand to shake. Lanza gave a glance back at Helen. She smiled and nodded approval. Her little boy held out his paw as countless cameras created what would have to be a world icon. He'd never been trained to do that but had watched Sam use it time and time again to get his way. The audience exploded into applause that seemed never to end. She stepped forward to reclaim the hero. Marco bowed and waved. Suddenly he pulled her to him and kissed her in front of the whole world. He went to the microphone.

"My friends, perhaps you've read our story in the papers. If

200

you walk a dog you just never know what will happen or who you might meet. See you in twenty minutes."

More applause, more laughter, more cheers. Just one man, confident that he could hold an audience of any size, of any character. They made their way to the dressing area behind the orchestra. She took a deep breath. As far as she knew Marco knew nothing of what had happened. He didn't need to be distracted. She spotted Shannon Knightsmith with her husband, the earl and owner of the estate. Marco was eased away to talk music with the conductor.

"Shannon, don't say anything to Marco. He needs to focus."

"Hey, you're on top of the wife job already. Sure, man what a triumph so far. That trick with the paw. Vandervell would have peed his pants in joy if he'd been wearing any. The whole thing's gone mega viral."

"So how did those terrorists get in here?"

"Details are a bit thin, but it's bloody. Two days ago, he got into the Larundan embassy by turning up as a delivery man. It's a small country so they don't have a lot of resource for security and they're peaceful guys in any case. He kills the ambassador, his family and his three staff. Then he replaces them with his own followers, jumps in the official car with the diplomatic plates and uses the official invitation. We don't or can't search diplomatic bags or personnel. Teams of cops are at the embassy. Looks like they put up a fight."

"So, it was Quaffir."

"Yes, confirmed. He had a Semtex vest and three fragmentation grenades. If he'd gotten lucky he would have taken out fifty world leaders. His assistants had handguns and one had a homemade TATP suicide bomb."

"People saw what happened. It has to hit the news."

"Yeah, luckily no police bullets so no fake outrage by sweet kind journalists. There's a rumor it was the Russians, a crack ex-KGB operator who escaped. The cops called out a warning and were doing it right when their hit-man stepped in. Their government must have been in on it and got him away in a chopper. Someone's putting that story around. Some are even suggesting it was Viktor Pinupskin's finger on the trigger."

"Someone like cops, or that Dickon Maltravers."

"Who cares? Scimitar of Holy Vengeance is destroyed. Your boy deserves a truckload of medals."

She needed a drink, but she was in uniform. There was still a world of celebrity who wanted to meet Lanza. The music re-started, the crowd roared, and now she could be one of them, free of the threat of death or maiming by terrorism. Quaffir had ordered the death of thousands, had ruined lives and families and still believed his cause was in the name of God. Marco had begun to sing. It was the piece from West Side Story he'd added in, to sing for her. She listened, unable to control her tears.

"Make of our hands one hand, Make of our hearts one heart...."

Cressida must have seen her distress and came over to take Lanza. Her little boy almost cried with happiness to see her, licking her hands with kisses. This girl's caring soul had saved him more than anything. A very handsome young man was with her, a young soldier. Their intense looks and smiles proclaimed they were in love. She had no clear faith, but seeing them she prayed for peace and that he would come back from Iraq. Her own young warrior was gone and yet his love of opera had planted a seed in her own heart which would always be of him. She was hearing this music now for him, with him, to feed back into that soil of time from which her future would always grow."

"Are you OK?" asked Cressida"

"I'm just happy." She wiped her eyes and looked at them. "When you have love in your heart there's nothing else, except everything. It's not worth doing anything for any other reason but love."

Fin

A MESSAGE FROM EMMA

Sheesh! Did you enjoy that?

Maybe you've got that empty feeling when a story ends? Join my VIP Reader Club, to get a little bit more. Find out what's in store for Helen, Marco, Cressida and of course, Lanza. Get a FREE exclusive copy of the ebook, *Epilogue to Guilt*.

Go to this link: http://www.smarturl.it/LeadFromGuilt
OR scan this QR code:

If that's still not enough, don't worry, you've just discovered the naughty seductive world of *Passion Patrol*. A thrill of hot cops, hot crime and hot romance.

Meet the strong and sexy women who starred in *Guilt*. Know their full stories. Discover their sexy lovers and follow their courage and adventures:

    Anna La Salle: ***Combat***
    Shannon Knightsmith: ***Dynasty***
    Sophia of France: **Crowns**
    Paula Middleton: ***Santa***
    Kaitlyn Thorne: ***Wealth***
    Cop's Kitchen Cookbook: ***Seduction of Taste***

And new for 2019, Olivia Johnstone-Denny: ***Power***

Buy each title direct from my website:
    www.emmacalin.com/emma-calin-seduction-series

…and save at least 30% on other retail platforms. Automatic delivery direct to all reading devices, including Kindle.

Save even more when you buy boxsets direct on the same link.

If you like this book, please leave a review. I cannot compete with the big guys who employ complex machines and budgets to promote their titles, but your feedback helps other readers find my work and means so much to me.

Link to Amazon Review page:
    http://www.smarturl.it/SedGuiltReview

Hoping to share your thrills.
Love
Emma x

A FREE BOOK FOR YOU...
FREE DOWNLOAD

Meet the Passion Patrol Team

Hungry For More?

**Get this Exclusive Epilogue
FREE
when you line up with
The Passion Patrol**

**...Join Emma Calin's
VIP Reader Club**

*"Emma Calin has written another
gripping romantic suspense
with plenty of both."*
P. Rees-Rohrbacker

Get My Free Download

http://smarturl.it/LeadFromGuilt

If you enjoy my books, why not keep up to date with my new releases by joining my Passion Patrol VIP Club? As a valued reader, you'll get exclusive freebies, special offers, goodies and giveaways, un-published extras and the chance to get pre-release editions of my new books before they go on general release. Join now and in return I'll send you the *Epilogue to Guilt*. I like to reach out a few times each month, but don't worry, I won't bombard you or share your details. You may of course unsubscribe at any time.

http://smarturl.it/LeadFromGuilt

OTHER TITLES BY EMMA CALIN

PASSION PATROL SERIES BOX SET 1

Grab the first three books in the series PLUS a companion cookbook in one **bargain** bundle. Titles included: *Combat, Dynasty, Seduction of Taste* and *Crowns*.

http://www.smarturl.it/webbox1

Or if you prefer to buy each ***Passion Patrol*** title individually...
 Combat
 Dynasty
Seduction of Taste
Seduction of Dynasty Plus (2-book bundle)
Crowns
Santa
Wealth

COMBAT

A Mafia plot, an undercover cop and a gorgeous world champion boxer.

Interpol cop, Anna Leyton, spirals down into a hopeless vortex of sexual and emotional passion as she fights to keep her professional cool. Who is deceiving whom in this fast-moving ride across continents? What motivates her art-loving prize bull of a lover, Freddie La Salle? The power of love and trust stands against greed and crime as conflicting forces grapple for that knockout punch.

A romance novel with a twist of suspense that will take you on a roller-coaster ride of passion, deception and love.

(Previously published as Passion Patrol 1 – Knockout))

http://www.smarturl.it/webcombat

DYNASTY

A sexy aristocrat. A wild-child inner city cop. A crime wave of passion.
(Previously published as Passion Patrol 2 - *Shannon's Law*)

http://www.smarturl.it/webdynasty

Blurb:
A steamy romance novel introducing a sassy female police officer who locks up criminals and always gets her man.

The second book in the *Seduction* series featuring hot cops, hot crime, and hot romance. Following the success of *Seduction of Combat,* the drama in this novel revolves around another feisty female cop—Shannon Aguerri.

Moved out from the city after one-too-many maverick missions, Shannon discovers there's more going on in the sleepy country village than meets the eye. The son of a local aristocrat arouses suspicion of drug crime activity... but his widower father arouses more animal instincts!

Could she really mix with the British Royal Family? Can she risk her heart and career on yet another high-risk unauthorized investigation? Can she get justice for an innocent boy? Dare a kid from the gutter dream of being a countess?

Wild child inner city cop Shannon Aguerri walks a dangerous line between her methods and justice. When the bosses lose their nerve, she is transferred to green pastures to play out the role of a routine village cop. In Fleetworth-Green she encounters signs of people and drug trafficking and homes-in on serious millionaire criminals. As a loner she has attracted men, but nothing has stuck. When she meets Spencer, the hunky and widowed Earl of Bloxington, there is an immediate rapport between them. Their social differences mean nothing to their passion and need. Already in the mix is an upper-class female rival who has long plotted her way into the earl's bed. The jealousy is an evil shade of green and the anger is a violent scarlet.

Often inhibited by a sense of duty and honor, Spencer is slow to reveal his feelings. When Shannon confronts him with the need to choose between her word and that of her rival, he does not immediately support her. All the same, when they are forced together to carry out a desperate rescue mission, their love is stronger than everything ranged against them.

Please note: This book contains joyful sex between adults in a consenting relationship. There is also strong language in high-stress police confrontations with criminals.

5 Star Reviews from *Dynasty* (when published as *Passion Patrol 2 -Shannon's Law*)

"Move over Mr. Grey there's a new earl in town! Dramatic, mesmerizing and incredibly sexy. The ultimate fairy tale." Jenny Marston, UK.

"Will draw you in from page one and hold you fast, immersed in the love and suspense until the end." Anneli Purchase, Canada.

"A fast-paced and intense story where two different social worlds collide in a vortex full of love, hatred, intrigues and passion. Emma Calin has done it again. A book hard to put down before its end." Petra Rovere, Slovenia.

SEDUCTION OF TASTE

Hot Cops. Hot Crime. Hot Romance..... Hot Food?
http://smarturl.it/webtaste

Seduction of Taste is the companion cookbook to the hot romance novel, *Dynasty*.

A total of thirty-one recipes from appetizers and main courses to suggestions for sandwich fillings at a traditional afternoon tea. Late night suppers and romantic meals for two.

Food is the music of love. It sets the tone and the pace. It provides those moments when tastes and textures shared at the table form a metaphor for the physical appetites of love and lust.

As tough girl cop Shannon Aguerri abandons herself to love with a sexy aristocrat, many meals are shared. From the finest cuisine fit for royals, to the big power passion patrol fuel served in police canteens, *Seduction of Taste* gives you the recipes. You won't want to put the novel down. With the cookbook you can tickle your taste buds as Emma Calin's full on total romance

211

tickles your mind. If it touches the lovers' lips in the story, you can experience that moment with a meal cooked for your own special lover, be they a cool cucumber or a passionate pepper.

Read the romance, feel the passion, taste the love!

Download the cookbook:
                    http://www.smarturl.it/webtaste

Or, as of November 2017 grab the bumper gourmet edition—with both the story and recipe books combined and linked –

Seduction of Dynasty Plus
http://www.smarturl.it/webdynastyplus

SANTA

An International Bad Boy Billionaire Romance in the *Passion Patrol Series*, from Emma Calin. This time with a holiday twist. I wonder what this naughty Santa has in his sack for our intrepid cop?

http://www.smarturl.it/websanta

CROWNS

Introducing street cop Sophia Castellana who gets drawn into a world of international political intrigue, crime, romance and adventure, after rescuing a young pop idol from a violent attempted kidnapping—and who demands to have Sophia as his private bodyguard and more....

http://www.smarturl.it/webcrowns

WEALTH

Wealth. Introducing traffic cop Kaitlyn Thorn who gets drawn into a world of international crime, romance and adventure, after arresting the enigmatic high-flying banker, Randolph Quinn, when he crashes his brand-new Maserati in her district.

http://www.smarturl.it/webwealth

POWER

New for 2019 - *Power*.

Meet brave rookie cop, Olivia Johnstone-Denny as she grows into her new role within the police. The passerby who helps her tackle a knife-wielding homeless guy on the streets of London, turns out to be a visiting congressman and would-be future president of the USA. From that moment their lives are linked and she is enmeshed in a dangerous political drama and a forbidden hot passionate affair.

SUB-PRIME (#1 THE LOVE IN A HOPELESS PLACE COLLECTION)

Two powerless beings are swept together in a transient struggle for survival. Could the human spirit transcend the brutality and indifference of their brief experience before they are once again swept helplessly apart? Far more than a love story—this is a story about love

Sub-Prime: a short story of our times.
http://smarturl.it/Sub-Prime

THE CHOSEN (#2 THE LOVE IN A HOPELESS PLACE COLLECTION)

A woman, a man, a van, and a plan. When the luck runs out; the lucky walk away. A short story set in the extremis of everyday.

Available as an e-book (For Kindle and Kindle Apps for iPad, Android, PC MAC etc.) at Amazon worldwide on the following link:

http://smarturl.it/ChosenThe

ESCAPE TO LOVE (#3 THE LOVE IN A HOPELESS PLACE COLLECTION)

Even in the barren wasteland of urban decay, new green life is possible. In nature and in love, that which can be, somehow finds a crack, a corner or ledge and grasps its chance of life.

A woman on the run from domestic violence with no one but her vulnerable autistic teenage child as a companion lives in isolation and fear. While her hand-to-mouth scenarios are played out in the shadow of a threatening suspense, a story of crime and love unfolds around her.

http://smarturl.it/Escapetolove

ANGELA (#4 THE LOVE IN A HOPELESS PLACE COLLECTION)

A mystery tale of a late-night taxi ride where the final passenger may not be all that she seems.

http://www.smarturl.it/shortAngela

LOVE IN A HOPELESS PLACE (#5 THE LOVE IN A HOPELESS PLACE COLLECTION)

A mature woman finds the truth of herself. She cannot go back even though physical and emotional violence erupt around her.

Dare she give in to love?

Will sexual passion and fear overwhelm her stable life?

Whom can she trust to love her for herself?

http://smarturl.it/LIAHP

THE LOVE IN A HOPELESS PLACE
COLLECTION

Emma Calin's complete set of short stories and novelettes, available in one bargain "boxed set." This edition includes *Sub-Prime*, *The Chosen, Escape To Love, Love In A Hopeless Place* and short story: *Angela*. It is available as a paperback and e-book.

http://www.smarturl/it/LIAHPCollection

CHILDREN'S BOOKS BY EMMA CALIN
The "Once Upon a NOW!" Series

The *"Once Upon a NOW!"* books form a series of illustrated, interactive children's stories, in the true fairy tale tradition with modern-day settings. Each is available in paperback, Kindle, and audio book formats. Digital versions come with clickable links to bonus video clips, photos, and drawings to color. The paperback has QR codes to scan and take you to the same bonus material to enrich the stories.

http://www.smarturl.it/webkids

ALF THE WORKSHOP DOG

How could a scruffy dog in a bus depot, and the call of crows link back to another world of power and love?

The ancient Kingdom of Zanubia and a stray dog looking for scraps in an inner-city repair garage, hold the secret. A wicked king, a beautiful girl, a young prince and the struggle between right and wrong maintain the fable tradition.

http://www.smarturl.it/Alf

ISABELLA'S PINK BICYCLE

There's something strange in the woodshed....

A poor little girl in a faraway land dreams of riding a pink bicycle. When she meets a strange animal, her dreams come true. Her happiness turns to sadness when a tragedy occurs in the town and her father doesn't come home.

Maybe her new magic friend can find him?

http://www.smarturl.it/IsabellaPink

KOOL KID KRUNCHA AND THE HIGH TRAPEZE

Charlie finds it tough when his parents divorce, but Auntie Kate helps him overcome his greatest fear.

When Charlie has to move from the country into the city, he leaves behind his home, his mates, and his beloved football team. He will need to make new friends. With his small size and red hair, some people aren't kind to him. He wonders if he can face another day at school.

A trip to the circus gives him the strength to see himself and others in a new way.

http://www.smarturl.it/Kruncha

ABOUT EMMA CALIN

Novelist, philosopher, blogger, poet, would be master chef. A woman pedaling between Peckham & Pigalle, in search of passion & enduring romance.

Emma Calin writes romance novels, gritty short stories and children's fiction about love and survival in the 21st century. She has published a number of digital, paperback, and audio books which are available from Amazon and other good bookstores worldwide.

She blogs about her dual life in St-Savinien sur Charente in Southwest France and Romsey, a market town in southern England. She feels extremely lucky to be able to experience the world and life through these two very different lenses. She spends any time she can, when not writing, on her tandem exploring the countryside.

Emma also records and produces audio books and plays the trombone (although not at the same time).

FIND EMMA CALIN ON THE INTERNET

Website: **http://www.emmacalin.com**
Blog: **http://emmacalinblog.com/**
Twitter: **http://twitter.com/EmmaCalin**
Facebook: **http://www.facebook.com/emma.calin**
Facebook Fan Page:
http://www.facebook.com/EmmaCalinAuthor
Goodreads:
http://www.goodreads.com/author/show/4915751.Emma_Calin
Amazon Author Page:
http://smarturl.it/EmmaAmazonWorldwide

Bookbub: **https://www.bookbub.com/profile/emma-calin**

PUBLISHER

This book was published by Gallo-Romano Media. For details of other books and authors or if you would like to submit your book for publishing:

Email: contact@gallo-romano.co.uk
Web: http://www.gallo-romano.com

www.ingramcontent.com/pod-product-compliance
Lightning Source LLC
Chambersburg PA
CBHW030300200626
46816CB00002BA/715